What others are saying:

"*I'm Your Angel* is a true depiction of friendship...the characters in this book are memorable, without a doubt."

—Ernestine Driver

"*I'm Your Angel* is a story about true love and romance that every person wants in their life. I love this story!"

—Gail Herring

"*I'm Your Angel* is an encouraging book that teaches you about patience and how in due time when God knows you are ready, He will bless you in ways you would never ask or even imagine."

—Jeannette Hester

"*I'm Your Angel* made me a true believer in love, faith and hope. This story depicted true love, rather than empty words that we may hear everyday. We need more excellent books like this story."

—Myishia Harvin

"Veronica allows you to walk in the footsteps of her characters... you can believe in love again. [Veronica] is the missing ingredient from other books on the market."

—Theresa Williams

"I'm Your Angel"

Veronica A. Grayson

Tate Publishing, LLC

"I'm Your Angel" by Veronica A. Grayson

Photo credit for photo on front cover and page 8 to Ernest Neely of E and W Photo.

Published in the United States of America
by Tate Publishing, LLC
127 East Trade Center Terrace
Mustang, OK 73064
(888) 361–9473

ISBN: 1-5988622-3-5

Acknowledgments

I give all praises to God for making this possible and I believe whole heartily He will do many more with my gift in writing. "Thank You Jesus!" I thank my mom who is also my best friend, Agnes Grayson, for her belief in me, her faith, and prayers that were answered that my dream will become a reality. My dad James L. Grayson, there is light at the end of the tunnel and thanks for everything. My grandma Annie Mae Davis, I feel the results of your prayers everyday and I love you so very much. My grandma Elise Harvin, you are a wonderful woman who brought great joy to the family and you are appreciated. I can't forget my first manuscript readers Kathryn Street, Nancy Kline, Angela Pearmon, and Donna Harvin. You all will always be in my heart. Alicia Terry, my Sunday School Teacher back in the day, advisor, and most of all, my friend. Thank you so much for being there for me and also believing in my dream. And, special thanks to my relatives and my friends. Especially Apostle Prince Davis, thanks for your encouraging words that this day would come and your dreams concerning my writing that encouraged me to continue to move forward. Lundan McKoy and Makala Perry, you girls look absolutely beautiful on the cover of the book. Many, many thanks to you and your family.

To my new readers, I want to thank you in advance for taking a chance on a new author such as myself and I hope you fall in love with the characters who seems so real to me.

This book is dedicated to my late grandfather and grandmother Sarah Ann Harvin and Moses Harvin, and my sweet Aunt the late Luvenia Harvin who arc resting peacefully in God's arms.

Foreword

"I'm Your Angel" is an enchanting and enlightening story that will make you feel that anything is possible. The story circles around two little girls who instantly became best friends in elementary school. One of the little girls was raised by her father and the other schoolgirl was brought up by her mother. The girls wish to one day to experience the reality of the missing parent's love. The masterpiece of the story are the parents who experience devastated lost in their lives therefore they were able to be each other confidant and later became the best of friends as well.

This isn't a rush read story like our lives can be at times. The story will court you, it will serenade you, and you will clearly envision what you are reading. The book will keep your interest as you wonder what's going to happen next. When you think you have figured the story out it takes a turn and it appears that love won't conquer all or will it? Every time I pick up the book to read, I feel I'm sitting on a lounge chair absorbing the life of the characters. This is a must read book.

Mary Young

Chapter One

Kianna loved to spell words or sing to her father, Philip, in the mornings on the ride to school in Tinley Park, Illinois. Once Kianna's father parked the car on the school's premises, she unbuckled her seatbelt and then opened the car door. Her father walked over to the passenger side of the car to help his daughter out. As her father opened the back door to get her book bag, she would stand there in her burgundy, gray, and white striped uniform, white ankle socks, and burgundy shoes. Even though it was the fourth week of September, it felt like summer months were just beginning. The assistant principal would always greet the parents and students as they entered the building. Kianna and her father would walk into the school smiling hand-in-hand. Once they reached the classroom, Kianna would look for her best friend Sabrina Kennedy.

This particular morning Sabrina was at her desk looking through her book bag for something. Kianna let go of her father's hand and ran over to greet her friend.

"Kianna, where's my hug?" Philip smiled.

"Sorry, daddy," Kianna said, as she smiled. She turned around and ran over to her father. "I love you," she said, as she hugged him.

"I love you too, precious," Philip said with meaning, as he smiled at Kianna. Sabrina ran over to them. "Hello, Sabrina, how are you?"

"Fine," Sabrina giggled.

"Good," Philip said.

"Come on, Kianna. I've something to show you," Sabrina

said, as she took Kianna's hand and they started to run over to Sabrina's desk.

"You two stop running and walk," Philip said.

"Yes, daddy," Kianna said while looking back at her father.

"Have a good day," he said. The girls waved good bye to him.

Then the girls eased back to the desk tiptoeing and giggling. Kianna stood anxiously at Sabrina's desk to see what her friend wanted to show her.

"My mommy told me not to take it out during class," Sabrina said, as she showed Kianna a small pink vinyl heart-shaped bag. Inside of it was a cologne splash bottle and body lotion. Sabrina smiled as she took the cologne out of her bag and opened it. "Smell it."

Kianna smelled it as she took it from Sabrina's hand.

"I like it. It smells like flowers. Can I put some on?"

"Sure," Sabrina answered, as Kianna smiled. "When we wash our hands, we can put on some lotion. It makes your hands feels silky smooth." Kianna put some of the cologne behind both ears and her wrists.

"You smell good, Kianna," a little boy said, as he walked past them.

The girls looked at each other and grinned.

Everyday the girls would tell their parents about their day that they had together in school. The girls were seven years old and they were born on the same day, May 23rd, three hours apart. Kianna was the oldest. Kianna was a pretty brown round-faced child, with brown eyes, and long thick dark brown hair that hung down to the middle of her back. Sabrina was also a pretty brown child as well but a little smaller than Kianna. Her eyebrows were slightly thicker than Kianna's. She had brown eyes and soft black hair that hung to her shoulders.

The school had their first Parent and Teacher Association meeting and the girls' parents got a chance to meet for the first time. They chatted for a while, mingled with the other parents, teachers, and later their parents chatted again with one another. Kianna and Sabrina were always excellent students in their studies.

It was a late Saturday afternoon where Sabrina and her mother Courtney were walking through the long corridor of the Water Tower Mall. Sabrina's mother brought her something that all seven-year-old girls wanted, and she carried it proudly in the white plastic bag with the store's red and white logo on it through the mall. As they turned a corner, Sabrina looked down the hall and saw someone she knew then her smile spread across her face.

"Mommy, look," Sabrina said pointing. "Kianna!" she shouted, as her voice echoed for a couple seconds.

"Sabrina," Courtney said surprised, as Kianna and Philip looked around.

"Daddy, it's Sabrina," Kianna said happy to see her friend. "Hi, Kianna!" she waved. It seemed like she shouted louder than Sabrina.

Kianna and Sabrina began to run toward each other.

"Walk!" Philip and Courtney said, at the same time to their daughter.

Kianna walked fast to Sabrina. "Sabrina, guess what I got? A Kelly-T doll!"

"I do too! Here is mine," Sabrina said, taking the plastic carton out of the bag. "Where is yours?" Philip and Courtney smiled at each other as they approached the girls.

"Right here," Kianna said, turning around to her father while taking the bag out of his hand.

"Hi, Mr. Franklin," Sabrina said.

"Hi, Sabrina," Philip said.

They had the same kind of doll. "We're twins!" the girls said collectively, as they put the plastic cartons side by side. Their parents smiled.

"Courtney, how are you?" Philip asked.

"I'm good, Philip," Courtney said smiling. "I don't have to guess what you came here for," she smiled even more as he nodded his head smiling as well.

"Hi, Ms. Kennedy," Kianna said, walking over to Courtney and then she hugged her small frame body then she went back over to Sabrina talking about their dolls.

"It was enough working long hours today and Kianna calling me every hour reminding me how important it is to get this doll." He said. Then he lowered his voice. "A doll that doesn't even do anything." Courtney laughed. "I must have stood in line for 40-minutes while Kianna was playing on a toy. The store was unbelievably crowded."

"I guess you would have to be a little girl to understand the reason for this Kelly-T doll. By looking at her, you've made her day." Courtney said, smiling at his daughter.

"You're right," he said, smiling looking at his daughter as well.

"We were at that store three hours ago and we were in and out in 15-minutes," Courtney said, as Philip looked at the seven different shopping bags sitting on the floor next to her.

"I see," Philip said smiling. "Kianna and I are going up to the food court. Would you and your daughter like to join us?"

"Oh, no, thank you. We'll get something later," Courtney replied.

"Mommy," Sabrina whined, "I'm hungry now."

Courtney thought for a few seconds of things she had to do, but as she looked at her daughter's facial expression, who was wanting to spend time with her friend, she changed her mind.

"All right," Courtney agreed, as the girls smiled.

The girls walked in front of their parents, who were talking while heading towards the escalators.

Philip held Kianna's hand going up the escalator and the other hand filled with six of Courtney's shopping bags. Kianna looked back at Sabrina and smiled. "Kianna, turn around and pay attention to where you are going. Remember what I told you about being careful riding on the escalators," Philip said.

Sabrina was holding her mother's hand on the escalator then she looked up at her and they both smiled at each other. Once they found a table, Philip put Courtney's bags on the side of them by the wall.

"What does everyone want to eat?" Philip asked.

"McDonald's!" the girls said, at the same time then they giggled.

"Philip, go ahead and get something for you and Kianna. I'll get Sabrina's when you get back," Courtney said.

"No. I got it. Tell me what you want," he said, looking at the different eatery places. "Do you want pizza, steak and cheese, a salad, oriental chicken or Chinese food? Whatever you want."

"I can have a plain burger and an orange drink from McDonald's," Courtney said smiling. Philip gave her a disbelieving look. "Really that's all I want."

"Mommy, why don't you get a happy meal then I can have your surprise," Sabrina suggested, as she put her head on her mother's arm smiling up at her.

"Daddy, you can get a happy meal too," Kianna hinted.

As Philip walked away to get something to eat, the girls took out the plastic cartons with their dolls inside of it. Sabrina had her mother to help with her doll. Kianna could have taken her doll out herself but she wanted Courtney to do it for her. Kianna sat there looking at her best friend with her mother wishing she had a mother like Courtney and her other friends.

"Kianna, do you want me to help you open your carton?" Courtney asked. Kianna nodded her head then she brought it over to Courtney. As Courtney opened the carton, Kianna stood close to her and watched her pretty brown caramel face closely. Then she put her hand on Courtney's shoulder not caring that Courtney's silky curls danced on her hand as Courtney moved. Courtney smiled at Kianna as she gave her the doll.

Minutes later, Philip came to the table with the food. After the girls finished eating they played with their dolls while Philip and Courtney talked about work.

"Well," Courtney said, as she looked at her daughter, "we better get going." Then she looked at Philip, "Thanks for dinner."

"You're welcome," he said, as the girls looked across the table sadly.

"Mommy, we aren't finished playing," Sabrina said.

"I'm sorry, baby. We have another stop to make before we go home," Courtney said.

Philip threw away the trash and they all went downstairs to the second level of the mall. "Thanks, Philip." She reached out her hands for the bags.

"I don't mind walking you to the car to help with your shopping bags," he said to Courtney.

"That's okay. I got it," Courtney said, taking the bags from Philip. "Bye, Kianna. I'll see you on Monday morning, okay?"

"Bye, Ms. Kennedy. Good bye, Sabrina," Kianna said sadly.

Sabrina waved slowly to her friend and Philip.

"See you later," Philip said, as he took his daughter's hand.

Philip and his daughter went the opposite direction from Courtney and Sabrina. As Philip and his daughter took their time strolling, he turned around and looked back at Courtney and her daughter then smiled to himself as he turned back around then they turned a corner.

Courtney saw how unhappy Sabrina looked.

"Sabrina, I know I'm not Kianna or any of your friends that you play with but if you like when we get home, we can play with your new doll," Courtney said.

"I love playing with you, mommy." She smiled.

One evening Courtney had to work late. After she got home, she helped Sabrina with her homework and then had a difficult time preparing dinner. They were sitting at the dinner table.

"Sabrina, how is your turkey dinner?" Courtney asked. "I left the first one in the microwave for fifteen minutes like the instructions stated. I don't know what happened."

"I can eat this one, mommy. Thank you. Mommy," she said.

"Yes, Sabrina," Courtney answered.

"Could Kianna come over to our house and spend the weekend with us?"

"Sure honey, but we will have to see what her father says about it," Courtney replied.

"Kianna asked Mr. Franklin last night and he told her yes if it's okay with you," she smiled.

"Well, I guess it's fine," Courtney said.

"Yea! When can Kianna come over?" Sabrina asked anxiously.

"I'll have to speak to her father first," Courtney replied, looking discouraged with the over-cooked macaroni and cheese microwave dinner. Then she smiled at Sabrina and winked.

All the second graders were scheduled to go on a field trip to downtown Chicago to the Museum of Science and Industry for The Anatomical Exhibition of Human Body. Philip and Courtney were two of the ten parents as chaperones. All the children were very excited as they lined up quietly in their classes ready to get on the school busses. Courtney was walking out of one of the class rooms behind the last child to make sure they were all staying together and boarding the bus. Kianna and Sabrina were sitting together on one of the buses. They tapped on the window of the bus and waved at Courtney. She waved back, smiling and also waving at the other children. Philip and three other fathers were making sure no children were standing outside of the buses. As the busses pulled off, the children became more excited about going on their field trip. Some of the children turned around in their seats and some of the children sat on their knees turned backwards talking to each other.

STOP

There were a few students getting up walking over to talk to their friends. The chaperones were able to get them to sit down and enjoy the ride.

Once the children arrived at the museum they went from one exhibition to another. Philip looked over at Courtney who was bent down tying the same child's shoes for the third time. When she stood up watching the child walk away, she looked around at the other children to see were they okay. She saw Philip waving at her as she smiled waving back.

An hour later, the same child found Courtney to tie his shoes again. She smiled at the little boy as Philip walked over to her.

"It looks like someone has a crush on you." Philip said.

"You think," Courtney said humorously while smiling, as she was about to bend down again.

"Let me do this," Philip said. He read the child's name tag, "Hey, Melvin. Why do your shoes strings keep coming a loose?" He bent down to Melvin reaching for his shoe string.

Melvin moved his feet back. "I know how to tie my shoes," he boldly uttered, as he bent down on one knee and tied one shoe at a time perfectly. Then he looked at Courtney smiling and then gave Philip a mean look while walking away.

Philip and Courtney laughed.

"That young man shouldn't bother you again," Philip said comically.

"Well thanks for rescuing me." She laughed. "I would have never guessed he was deliberately loosening his shoes strings."

"I didn't know you were one of the volunteers."

"I found out late yesterday at work that a meeting was cancelled for today. So, when I talked to Sabrina's teacher yesterday, she stated they still need more chaperones. I thought this would be a good time to do it just in case I am unable to participate on the next field trip. So, how is it going?"

"Good!" he said looking around at the children. "How was your business trip to London last week?"

"How did you know about that?" Courtney asked, as she thought about it. "Don't answer that. It was Sabrina."

"Yes. She told Kianna and so on and so on. I hope you don't mind me asking?"

"Oh, no," she said in a lighthearted tone. "Not at all. Sometimes I failed to realize how close Sabrina and Kianna are. Anyway, the trip was good. I hated being away from my baby," she said, as she looked over at Sabrina who was showing one of her classmates how to properly use a magnifying glass.

"I know what you mean," Philip said. "After today, I'll be going out of town myself for a couple of days. I hate to leave Kianna even though she's either with my mother or my sister. I feel like I'm abandoning her in a sense. But, I have to do this for our future. I have dream to pursue."

Courtney was very impressed as she nodded her head in agreement with Philip in what he was saying to her and how he expressed his feelings as a man about his responsibility and love for his daughter. It was like a needle in a haystack for her to hear of a single father seeing his child like a true mother does.

Chapter Two

For several weeks Kianna begged her father to get in touch with Courtney so they could decide when she could spend the weekend with Sabrina. Philip left an envelope for Courtney at the school in order for her to get in touch with him but it was impossible for them to speak. They would miss one another's calls at work and at home. One morning, Philip and Courtney brought the girls to school at the same time.

"Hi, Philip," Courtney said.

"Good morning, Courtney. Hi, Sabrina. How are you two doing?" Philip asked.

"Fine, thank you," Courtney replied, as she helped Sabrina with her sweater. "Hi, Kianna."

"I'm running late, I really have to go," Philip said, as he handed Kianna her book bag.

"I know what you mean," Courtney said. Then she looked at Sabrina, "Come on give mommy a kiss, sweetheart. I have to leave," she said quickly.

"Daddy, aren't you forgetting something?" Kianna asked.

"I'm sorry, baby," Philip said and kissed Kianna's forehead.

"Not that daddy!" Kianna exclaimed. "You and Ms. Kennedy are supposed to discuss when I can spend the weekend at their house."

"Come on, mommy. Please!" Sabrina begged.

"It will only take a couple of seconds," Kianna said, as she looked at her father and Courtney.

"Okay," Courtney said, looking at her watch. "How about this weekend?"

"Are you sure?" Philip asked Courtney. "Don't let Kianna pressure you. Sometimes she can be a little demanding."

"No, she's fine," Courtney said, as she smiled. "We have been promising the girls for a while about them spending some time together. I have to work late tomorrow night." While thinking to herself she uttered, "Which means, I'll have to pay a late fee at the school day care." Then she looked at Philip, "I should be by your place tomorrow night no later than seven."

"Kianna, you will be coming over to my house tomorrow night," Sabrina said, excited.

"I can't wait!" Kianna said, with a joyous smile while jumping up and down.

"Why don't you two go to your classroom. I'll see you this evening, Kianna," Philip said. The girls walked away to their classroom vivaciously, their excitement was apparent about their weekend together. Then he and Courtney walked out of the school. "Courtney, I can take Sabrina home with me tomorrow when I pick up Kianna. When you get off from work, you can come by my place to pick up the girls. Then you won't have to concern yourself about the late fee of picking up your daughter after school hours. So you don't have to worry about the late fee," he suggested, as he walked her to her car.

"You don't have to do that," Courtney said.

"Really it won't be a problem. We're helping one another."

"Okay," Courtney smiled. "I'll accept. Thanks. I don't have time right now but this evening I'll sign a form that will allow you to get Sabrina tomorrow."

"That's fine. I'll see you tomorrow morning," he said, as he opened Courtney's car door for her. "Have a good day."

"Thank you. You do the same," she said. He shut her door and walked to his car.

When Courtney got off from work Friday evening she

went over to Philip's house to pick up the girls.

"Hi! Come on in, Courtney," Philip said smiling making her feel welcome.

"Thank you," she said, as she walked into the foyer.

"The girls are upstairs playing. Have you eaten?" he asked, as he closed the door.

"No," Courtney replied. "I probably will stop somewhere and get us a pizza."

"The girls already ate," Philip said.

"That's really kind of you. Well, since the girls have eaten, I guess I'll have some noodles when I get home."

"I saved you a plate," Philip said.

"Oh, really!" she said surprised.

"Let me take your jacket." As she unbuttoned her jacket, he helped her take it off. "Why don't you freshen up and come into the dinning room, which is around the corner here. The bathroom is down the hall, first door to your right. I also have a wash cloth and a towel out if you need it."

While Courtney washed her hands in the bathroom sink, she looked in the oval mirror at her week old lose curls hanging at shoulder length.

"It's time for a hair cut," she said softly, while turning off the water.

As she walked past the living room, she noticed brown leather furniture that complemented the elegant oil portrait of Philip and his daughter over the mantle piece of the fireplace. Then she walked into the dinning area on hardwood floors. The walls were light beige with white trimmings around the upper and lower boarders. A medium size solid brown wood dinner table was sitting on a beautiful wool rug with detailed designs of geometric lines and stylized foliage of little colors of red, gold, olive, and ecru. A dark brown steel chandelier hang from the high ceiling had six shades of lights. Philip walked into the dinning room with her dinner and utensil wrapped in cloth napkin. The aroma from the plate scented the room making her appetite came more alive.

"Courtney, please have a seat," Philip said, pulling out a chair with his other hand.

"Thanks," Courtney said, sitting down. Then he sat the plate in front of her. It was Cornish hen, brown rice, mixed greens, and corn bread. "It really looks good. This is really nice of you."

"It's not a problem. I hope you like it. Would you like a glass of wine?" He got a coaster from one of the drawers of the sideboard and put it on the table.

"No, thanks. A glass of water would be fine."

"Are you sure? I have club soda, ginger ale. I can make you ice tea."

"Water is fine," Courtney smiled.

"Water it is," he said, walking to the kitchen. Courtney sat the napkin on her lap and prayed over her food. Then she picked up her folk and knife and cut a little piece of the tender Cornish hen. She smiled impressed as she chewed it. Philip brought out a glass of water and sat it on the table. "Are you okay? Do you need anything?"

"No. This is delicious." She smiled.

"Thanks. I'll let the girls know that you are here," he said, walking away again.

Then she looked straight ahead admiring his antique wood glass china cabinet with brown and eggshell color dishes.

A minute later Courtney heard running feet in the house.

"Mommy!" Sabrina shouted, as she and Kianna stood beside Courtney smiling.

After Courtney finished eating vanilla ice cream for dessert, she and Philip talked a little at the dinning table while the girls continued to play upstairs. Later the girls came downstairs wanting Philip and Courtney to play old maid cards with them. It seemed that Philip was losing most of the games because he kept getting stuck with the old maid card.

Saturday morning Courtney took the girls out for breakfast then she dropped them off at a girlfriend's house while she jogged near by. Later on that day she took the girls swimming, shopping, to the movies, out to dinner, and finally Courtney read them a bedtime story. The girls stayed up playing until Sabrina became upset with Kianna because she called one of her favorite dolls ugly. Sabrina sat on her twin bed pouting with her back to Kianna with her arms folded, and Kianna on the other bed lying back on the headboard looking over at the back of Sabrina's head rolling her eyes. Ten minutes later they made-up and by then it was time to go to bed. Sunday morning they all got up and went to church. Kianna wasn't use to going to church and sitting for a length of time. Since Kianna and Sabrina kept talking during service, Courtney had Kianna sit on the other side of her. Later, Kianna took Courtney by her hand and held it on her lap then she leaned her head on Courtney's arm. Courtney put her arm around Kianna who promptly fell asleep. After church they went over to Courtney's mother's house for dinner. When Courtney and the girls got home she attempted to call Philip to let him know that she was home but he wasn't there. She contacted him through his pager. Courtney sat on the floor while the girls sat on the couch doing her hair pretending that they were beauticians. An hour later the doorbell rang.

"I'll get it," Sabrina said, running to the door. "Who is it?" she asked, trying to sound like an adult.

"It's Philip."

"Mommy, it's Mr. Franklin," Sabrina shouted.

"Let him in, sweetie," Courtney said.

Philip and Sabrina walked into the living room where Courtney and Kianna were.

"Hi. I see you are getting a new hairstyle," Philip said, smiling.

"Hello. Yes I am," Courtney said, smiling as she handed Kianna a bobby pin.

"Hi, daddy!" Kianna said, excited to see her father. She walked over to him and hugged him around the waist. Philip smiled as he stooped down and kissed her forehead. Then she went back over to Courtney playing with her hair.

"How did it go?" Philip asked Courtney.

"Great. After Kianna talked to you on Saturday morning, she became more comfortable around us," Courtney said.

"Daddy," Kianna said quickly with excitement in her voice, "we went swimming, shopping, to the movies and," she said, as she slowed down concentrating on how to pin a section of Courtney's hair up, "and church!"

"Church?" Philip asked, startled.

"Yes, church," Courtney said, wondering why he sounded astounded.

"That's good," Philip said, not knowing what to say.

"I'm sorry, Philip, please have a seat. Can I get you something?" Courtney asked.

"No, I'm fine," Philip replied. "Are you ready Kianna?"

"No," Kianna answered, as she continued to put more bobby pins in Courtney's hair.

"Honey, we have to go," Philip said.

"Sabrina, go with Kianna upstairs to get her suitcase off the bed," Courtney said, as she turned around taking the comb from Kianna's hand smiling. The girls looked sad as they walked slowly up the stairs. "Philip, I hope you didn't mind me taking Kianna to church." She sat up on the couch.

"Oh no, not at all. I was just surprised. I feel ashamed," Philip said, while sitting down on the chair, "when I say I don't go to church unless it's a wedding or funeral. I can tell Kianna had a nice time with you and your daughter. Thank you."

"It was our pleasure. Kianna is a nice young lady to be around."

"Courtney, I like your place," he said, as he looked around at her burgundy and gray colors and a host of family pictures sitting around.

Kianna came down the stairs teary-eyed. She left her suitcase by the staircase then she walked over to her father as he stood up. She hugged him around the waist looking up at him as he looked down at her.

"Daddy, could we stay here at Ms. Kennedy's place?" Kianna asked.

"No," Philip replied. He looked embarrassed. "Courtney, I'm sorry about this." He rubbed his daughter's back. "Kianna has never acted this way before."

"It's okay. Kianna, come here," Courtney said. Kianna walked over to her as tears came down her face. Courtney hugged her then looked into her eyes. "Oh, it's okay." Then she wiped her eyes with her fingertips. "Your daddy needs you at home just like I need Sabrina here with me. You know what? Whenever you want to come over just have your daddy call me. You are always welcome here."

After Kianna calmed down then Sabrina started to cry, not wanting her friend to leave.

The girls started spending every other Saturday and every Sunday together. Kianna liked going to church on Sundays. Philip would sometimes bring his daughter to church and pick her up after the service.

One day, Philip suggested that Sabrina spend a weekend with him and Kianna. Courtney was kind of uncomfortable with that idea because the only three people she really trusted were her mother, her sister and Sabrina's godmother. It took Courtney some time to agree to it. The night Philip picked up Sabrina, Courtney gave him a list of do's and don'ts. The list consisted of Sabrina's allergies, blood type, the doctor's telephone number, and her mother's telephone number just in case an emergency comes up and he couldn't get in touch with her. Sabrina was only gone from home two hours when Courtney called Philip to see how her daughter was doing. He pulled Sabrina away from her play to talk to Courtney.

"Hi, mommy," Sabrina said, while smiling at Kianna making a funny facial expression. "Fine," she said quickly. "Yes, I'm having fun. Mommy, you don't have to worry about me," she said frankly. Then without thinking, "Mommy, Mr. Franklin is not molesting me, and I know how to . . ." she whispered, "dial 9–1-1. I love you. I have to go, mommy." She handed the phone to Philip and ran up the stairs with Kianna.

"Philip, I'm sorry how that came out," Courtney said embarrassed. "I didn't teach her that because she was spending the weekend with you and Kianna. That's with anyone."

"It's okay," Philip said, as he grinned. "I understand. I taught the same thing to my daughter. You can never be too careful these days. Sabrina is fine," he said reassuring Courtney. "You can call here as many times as you wish. So you know, we're leaving early tomorrow morning to go to the amusement park."

"That should be fun for the girls. Tomorrow is going to be another warm day. I'm use to cold weather this time of year."

"I know. We'll get it soon enough."

After the girls ate their dinner they watched a video. Then they took their baths and put on their pajamas. Now they were ready for their bedtime story but before Philip began to read he had Sabrina call her mother.

Kianna loved to sit on her father's lap or sit close to him as he reads so she could follow the words of the story. Sabrina sat on the bed watching Kianna with her father. Kianna told Sabrina she could sit on her father's other knee. At first Sabrina sat straight up then she laid her head on his chest. Philip would say words incorrectly to see if the girls were paying attention. At one point Kianna had her eyes closed imaging she was one of the characters in the story that her father read with delight. Sabrina smiled then she rubbed Kianna's hand. Kianna smiled while opening her eyes as she snuggled closer to her father. Then the girls fell asleep sitting on Philip's lap while he was reading to them.

The next day they were at the amusement park when it opened. The girls rode on all the kiddy rides and Philip played most of the games. Philip took turns carrying the girls on his back when they got tired of walking. They all had a lot of fun.

Sunday morning the girls were fully dressed knocking on Philip's bedroom door telling him it was time to go to church. He looked at them as if they were speaking a foreign language.

Courtney was sitting in church listening to the choir sing when she heard little girls' voices saying excuse them. She looked up and saw Kianna, Sabrina and Lord behold, Philip. Courtney couldn't believe it as she moved down on the pew. After church they shook the pastor's hand as they walked outside.

"Mommy, since Monday is a holiday, can I stay over Mr. Franklin's house until tomorrow evening? I want to go fishing with him and Kianna," Sabrina said.

"Honey, I have plans for us tomorrow," Courtney said.

"Can't it wait until next weekend?" Sabrina asked.

"I don't mind," Philip said, as he smiled. "If you want you can come along with us. Tomorrow suppose to be a really nice day."

"Mommy, why don't you come along with us?" Sabrina asked smiling.

"No thank you. If it's okay with Mr. Franklin then it's fine with me," Courtney said.

"It would be nice if you would come over to our home for dinner. I'm going to have barbecue spare ribs," Philip teased.

"No, thanks. I need to catch up on some reading," Courtney said.

"I would really enjoy the company," Philip said with sincerity.

Courtney finally agreed to go over to Philip's place for dinner after the girls pleaded with their adorable faces of blissful smiles.

As they all sat at the dinner table, Philip asked Courtney to say grace. Kianna looked at her father a little stunned at first then she smiled. Actually everyone was a little surprised. After dinner, Philip and Courtney washed and dried the dishes since the dishwasher was broken.

"Philip, you cook like a chef. Dinner was delicious. Thank you for the invitation," Courtney said.

"You're welcome. I'm glad you enjoyed it. Do you cook?"

"I thought I did until Sabrina suggested I stick with microwave foods and noodles," Courtney replied.

"I don't believe that," Philip said, laughing.

"I'm serious," Courtney said, as she smiled. "We go over to my mother's on Sundays for home cooked meals. My mother went out of town this weekend. Believe me, you saved us."

"Would you like to go out back to get some air?"

"Sure," Courtney replied, as she put the dishtowel away.

"How long have you been cooking like that?" Courtney asked, as they stepped outside.

"For a while, but I was never serious about it until Kianna started eating table food," Philip replied.

"My mother would call me into the kitchen when I was a teenager to teach me how to cook but I always managed to get out of it. She would say I would regret it one day," Courtney said. "I told my mother, I'll marry a prince that will be very rich and we will have a maid to do everything." Then the tone of her voice changed as she continued to smile. "Well, I sort of missed not learning how to cook."

"It's not too late," Philip said, reassuring Courtney.

"True enough, but cooking doesn't interest me. I know that this sounds terrible but between my mother and my sister, Sabrina still has home cooked meals," Courtney said, as she sat down on the step.

"Kianna watched her grandmother and me in the kitchen then she would want to try to do it herself," Philip said.

"Well that's good. Maybe she could give Sabrina some pointers. Does Kianna take after you more or her mother in wanting to learn how to cook?" Courtney asked, as Philip sat down as well.

"Me," Philip replied in a mellow tone. "I was married to

Kianna's mother for three years. I thought we had the perfect marriage and she believed that too until she became pregnant. Before we got married, I thought she wanted the same thing as I did. I would have the ideal profession, home, cars, healthy bank accounts, and a retirement plan for our future. You know the whole nine yards. The only thing I wanted from her was to have my babies. I love children," he said passionately, as he looked straight ahead. "She was five months pregnant when she had her annual exam. She continued to have her menstrual cycle until her seventh month. She wanted to have an abortion. I couldn't believe it. I had to beg my wife, not a girlfriend, but my wife, not to abort our child or have an accident to lose our baby. It seemed like she was adjusting to the idea of becoming a mother but it was a put on. She kept complaining every minute about her pregnancy. I didn't have time to enjoy her pregnancy like rubbing on her stomach and talking to the baby in her womb. Because of her constant grumbling of her pregnancy, my attitude towards her was 'come on nine months.' To celebrate her gift to me of our baby, I told her that I had a surprise for her. Due to her complaining about pregnancy, I brought her a new BMW in her eighth month.

She didn't even want to take the time to choose a name for the miracle that was growing inside of her. I chose Kianna's name proudly myself," he said, as he smiled and looked at Courtney. Then he continued as he looked away from her, thinking about the hardship he experienced at that time, "After she had been home with Kianna for a week, she told me that this wasn't going to work for her and she wanted a divorce. She felt it was best to come out with the truth at that time then to hurt me later on in life. I didn't take her seriously. I though she was going through the post dramatic depression."

"You mean postpartum depression," Courtney said.

"Yes," he replied, smiling again. "That's it. The next day, I was getting on the elevator at work going to an appointment and a man got off the elevator asking the receptionist for Philip

Franklin. I said, that's me, while holding the elevator doors opened. The man got on the elevator and asked me, you are Philip Franklin? I stated yes. He handed me an envelope. I asked him what this was about. He said nothing as he looked straight ahead. When I got into my car, I opened the envelope; it was divorce papers.

Later that day when I got home, she had her things packed in her new car. She said she would be staying at her mother's place. I asked her what about our daughter; she told me that Kianna was all mine alone since I wanted to be a father.

I went to Kianna's mother time after time before the divorce became final asking her not to do this to me, but most of all to Kianna. I was willing to let her do whatever she wanted to do. I didn't want to get a divorce and most importantly, I didn't want Kianna to be without her mother.

My father became ill. He had a prostate operation and it looked as if he was getting better. The doctor was going to discharge him a couple of days later. The day before the divorce my father and I talked for hours in the hospital. My father was my best friend," he said, smiling. "I could talk to him about any and everything. I even talked to him about my first encounter with a woman. We would meet every Saturday morning faithfully for breakfast. The next day, I was divorced from Kianna's mother. The following day after that my father died hours before he was discharged. He died from natural causes."

"Philip, I'm so sorry," Courtney said with genuine compassion.

"My father was fully dressed at the hospital waiting for my mother to pick him up," Philip said, as he shook his head. He still couldn't believe that his father was gone. "My mother helped me out with Kianna. Kianna came into my life at the right time.

During the first four years of Kianna's life her mother would disappear and reappear in our lives. Courtney, I was truly in love with this woman and at that time if she wanted to get married again, I probably would have, even though at that time I knew it wouldn't work. I knew I would regret taking that chance. My mother told me some things that hurt my feelings, which was at that time the truth. She told me if it was only me that wanted to be made out of a fool that was my business, but she doesn't need to make one out of Kianna's life by giving her false hope to something that will never be.

The last time Kianna spent some time with her mother was three years ago. Kianna was grabbing hold to her clothes because she didn't want her to leave again. Her mother tried to tell her she would be back soon but Kianna couldn't understand that. She didn't even know what Kianna wanted. I can still remember it as if it were yesterday how Kianna's little fist was pulling on her mother's dress. When her mother got her to let go of her, she slammed the door in her face. I wanted to run after her to tell her off, but Kianna was screaming and she didn't want anyone to touch her except for me. As I held her crying, I promised myself I'd never allow Kianna to go through that pain again. I kept a picture of Kianna's mother in her room so she wouldn't forget her. One day I came into Kianna's room and found the picture frame of her mother turned down in a drawer. I'm sorry; I told you almost our life story."

"No, it's okay. I'm deeply sorry that happened to the both of you. You did an excellent job with Kianna. She's a beautiful girl and well mannered," Courtney said.

"It's really my mother who deserves the praise," he said.

"Well, she deserves some praise, but you deserve a pat on the back because you took the responsibly as the other parent to carry on and not to put all of the responsibility on your mother or someone else."

"Thank you," he said, smiling.

"After my third date with Sabrina's father, I knew in the back of my mind that it wasn't going to work," Courtney said. "After several months of dating him, I didn't want to start over, which was a cop-out. Sabrina's father told me things that I wanted to hear which was marriage and children. Months later he met my mother. Thirty seconds after my mother met him, she asked me to help her with something in the other room. She told me he wouldn't be good for me or any other woman. Good old mom," she said, as she smiled. "Since we always talked about marriage, I had new hope we were meant to be, which was a trap I was setting up for myself believing things that he told me. He asked me to move in with him, and I said 'why not since we know we're meant for each other.' That's what I used to justify my morals. Moving in with a man taking the responsibility of a wife, which includes my bad cooking," she said, as she smiled again. "I thought it couldn't get any better than this because I had a man that truly loved me. My dad and especially my mother were very disappointed in me, but they still showed me love.

Later I became pregnant, I wasn't worried because I knew this joker was going to marry me. During my whole pregnancy, I was upset. I'm surprised Sabrina doesn't have a nervous condition. He would stay out all times of the night and sometimes he wouldn't come home at all. When I would ask him where he had been, he would say it was none of my business, he's a grown man, and there are no legal papers between us just bed sheets. He would start arguments just to have an excuse to leave the apartment.

As for Lamaze classes, he didn't even attempt to come to them. After the second time he stood me up at the Lamaze class, my sister became my coach. Towards the beginning of my ninth month of pregnancy, I came home one evening after work and the apartment was cleared out. Nothing was even left in the refrigerator but an old jar of mustard. He left a note saying here are your bed sheets you brought, I'm getting new ones. I didn't tell my father at the time what happened because I knew my father would kill him. Several days later, after Sabrina's father moved out, one of my brothers paid him a visit and gave him black eyes."

"Don't you mean a black eye?" Philip asked.

"No," Courtney answered. "The next day Sabrina's father decided to go after my brother, so they fought again and my brother gave him another black eye. A year later Sabrina's father married someone else and they had children. The last that I heard, he has affairs all over the city.

On special holidays Sabrina's father would send cards with money and she would take the envelope and put it in a drawer. She never spent a dollar he sent her."

"I'm sorry that you went through that terrible trauma," Philip said, as his heart went out to her and Sabrina.

"I never thought of it that way, but that's a perfect description of it," Courtney said, as if she was in a daze.

"It's a shame that Sabrina's father is missing out on precious times like this that he could never get back. Are you over him?" Philip asked, as Courtney looked at him.

"Yes, I'm over him," Courtney replied. Then she looked straight ahead. "When the first labor pain started and he wasn't around for me in the delivery room, I got over him quickly. I guess it was for the best," she began to say jokingly, "because Sabrina would have really cried if she would have seen black circles around his eyes."

Then she became serious again and said, "You know, I didn't even cry when he left me. I had this attitude that I didn't need him because I could take care of me and my baby. I was fortunate to bring my baby to a new home that I purchased. At least we had a roof over our heads to call home, food, and our family who never left our side.

One day I was at the mall and I saw these parents that were so proud of their baby. This man was so happy pushing the baby carriage and holding his wife's hand. I smiled casually thinking to myself that's cute. That night while I was feeding Sabrina looking into her brown eyes, I remembered the couple I saw at the mall and I began to cry. I became angry at myself because I wanted my little girl to have a wonderful family life like I had with my mom and dad," she said. Then she cleared her voice. "Philip, thanks for dinner again, I'm going to get ready to leave." They both stood up from the step.

"Courtney, are you okay?" Philip asked, concerned.

"Yes," Courtney replied smiling. "How about you?"

"I'm fine. I never talk like this with anyone except my mother. I enjoyed your visit," Philip said.

"Thank you. I feel the same way," she said.

The girls came outside.

"Mommy, what are you doing out here?" Sabrina asked.

"Nothing, sweetheart. I'm getting ready to leave," Courtney replied smiling.

"You can't leave now, Ms. Kennedy. We have a surprise for you," Kianna said.

"A surprise?" Courtney asked.

"Come inside but first you have to close your eyes and we will lead you to it," Kianna said.

"No way. You two won't have me walking into walls," Courtney said, smiling. Philip laughed.

"Mommy, trust us," Sabrina said smiling from ear to ear.

"Yea, trust them," Philip said. "I'll help them guide you."

"You know about this surprise, Philip?" Courtney asked, suspiciously.

"I guess you could say that," Philip replied, smiling.

Courtney closed her eyes as the girls led her to the couch. When they told her to open her eyes there was a big stuffed teddy bear with a red bow around the neck.

"Thank you, I love it! This is huge!" Courtney said.

"Daddy won stuffed animals at the amusement park for all of us," Kianna said.

"We wanted to give you the biggest one, mommy," Sabrina said.

Courtney hugged and kissed the girls and shook Philip's hand.

"I don't know if I can get it into the car," Courtney said.

"We can take it over to your house now if you like," Philip

offered.

"You don't have to do that. You can bring it tomorrow when you bring Sabrina home," Courtney said.

"Mommy, you should take it home with you now. Then you won't be alone tonight. He's a nice teddy," Sabrina said, rubbing on it.

"I see. Philip, if you can get it in the car, I'm sure I can get it in the house," Courtney said.

Philip helped Courtney put the teddy bear into her car. He also had her call him once she got home.

The next day Philip and the girls had their hooks in the water while they were lying back with their legs crossed waiting for a fish to bite. The girls became bored. They started whispering something in each other's ears and laughing softly. Philip told fish stories and later a fish bit on Sabrina's hook. Philip called Sabrina over to show her how to reel it in. She was scared, excited and jumping up and down while the fish was wiggling on the hook. It seems fish were coming from everywhere. Hours later they went past a fish market to have the fish cleaned. Then Philip went home and cooked some of them. Philip paged Courtney to see when he could bring Sabrina home but since Courtney was already out she picked up Sabrina.

"Mommy," Sabrina said, as she hugged Courtney. "We had fun fishing!"

"You did! I'm glad, sweetheart," Courtney said.

"We caught," Sabrina said thinking to herself of how many fish they caught that day then she stopped for a second, and looked at Philip, "how many fish, Mr. Franklin?"

"Maybe 40," Philip replied, as the girls smiled at each other knowingly his statement wasn't true.

"40? Really?" Courtney asked in disbelief.

"Approximately," Philip replied smiling at Courtney seeing her skeptical look. "Have you eaten?"

"No not yet," Courtney replied.

"We have fried, bake, grilled, and barbecue fish," Philip

said.

"Barbecue fish?" Courtney asked with an unsettled look.

"I like to experiment. It's not that good. Maybe you like roast fish," Philip said humorously.

They both laughed.

"You will like it, Ms. Kennedy," Kianna said.

Later after dinner Courtney said, "Sabrina, it's getting late for us. Go get your overnight bag."

"Mommy," Sabrina said sadly while shaking her head no, "I'm not ready to go."

Courtney and Philip looked at each other.

"Ms. Kennedy, can't she stay here another night then my daddy can take both of us to school tomorrow?" Kianna asked.

"Kianna, you will see Sabrina bright and early tomorrow morning," Philip said.

"I'm sorry, sweetie but I'm afraid not. Like your dad said, you will see Sabrina early tomorrow. Sabrina, go ahead and get your bag. Go on," Courtney demanded.

Tears started rolling down Sabrina's face as she and Kianna went up the stairs.

"It looks like my daughter had a good time with you and Kianna," Courtney said.

"We enjoyed her company," Philip said.

"I'm glad," Courtney said, as she smiled.

"I would like for you to take some fish home with you," he said.

"That's okay. I don't think I can cook it like you did," she said.

"Yes you can. You and Sabrina seem to like baked fish. I've some already seasoned. You can give some to your mother."

"Now that's a thought. What is taking them so long?" Courtney asked, as she looked in the direction of the staircase.

"Let's go upstairs and see," Philip said.

As they approached Kianna's room they over heard them talking. They stood outside of the room.

"I wish I didn't have to leave," Sabrina said sadly to Kianna.

"Me too. I like your mommy. She's really nice and pretty too," Kianna said.

"I like your daddy. He's strong and very generous. Too bad we can't exchange parents for a while."

"Maybe we can, Sabrina," Kianna said with assurance.

"What do you mean, Kianna? How can we?" Sabrina asked, puzzled.

"Remember the story my daddy read to us about a little orphan boy who prayed to God every night for a mother and father that would love and take care of his brother, sister, and him?" Kianna asked. "The angel came down from heaven and guided them to a loving mother and father. They never wanted for anything else again. Maybe if we pray an angel will come down from heaven and let us exchange parents for a couple of days," she said. Then her eyes lit up, "or they could get married!"

"That would be even better!" Sabrina said. "Then you and I would always be together."

Courtney and Philip looked at each other in amazement at what the girls were saying about them. Courtney cleared her throat as she tapped on the door.

"Sabrina, I thought your clothes were packed," Courtney said seeing some of her clothes unfolded on the bed.

"They were," Philip said, as he looked at Kianna.

"Daddy, you didn't do it right," Kianna said, smiling.

Philip and Courtney looked at each other knowing that the girls deliberately took some of the clothes out of the bag to make them stay a little longer.

"Kianna, I like your room," Courtney said looking around.

"Thank you, Ms. Kennedy," Kianna said.

"Are you ready, Sabrina?" Courtney asked, as Sabrina put the last piece of clothing in the bag.

"Yes, mommy," Sabrina replied softly, as she zipped her bag closed.

They all went downstairs to the front door entry.

"Bye, Sabrina," Kianna said. "See you tomorrow at school. Thanks Ms. Kennedy for letting Sabrina come over."

"You're welcome. Sabrina, why don't you give Kianna a hug," Courtney said.

After Sabrina hugged Kianna she went over and hugged Philip.

"Thank you for a nice time, Mr. Franklin," Sabrina said.

"Sabrina, you are always welcome here. I have something for you," Philip said, as he got something out of the closet. Then he walked back to her and bent down, "You can have this."

"This is mine?" Sabrina asked thrilled.

"Yes, it's yours. Next time when we go fishing, you will have your own fishing rod," Philip said.

Sabrina hugged Philip again, but this time even tighter.

"Oh, thank you, Mr. Franklin," Sabrina said very pleased.

"Philip, that's very kind of you. Thank you," Courtney said.

Chapter Three

As time went on the girls spent time at one another's homes, but most of the time was spent at Courtney's place. The girls got a chance to meet one another's grandparents, aunts, uncles, and cousins.

One night Kianna was staying at Courtney's place, and she was having a bad dream. She woke up sweating and calling for her daddy. Sabrina got out of her bed asking Kianna what was wrong. Courtney came to Sabrina's room.

"Sweetheart, let me sit here," Courtney said to Sabrina, as she sat on the edge of the bed.

"What's wrong, Kianna? What did you dream about?" Courtney asked, as she reached for a Kleenex from the night-stand. Then she gently wiped Kianna's eyes.

"I want my daddy," Kianna cried disheartened.

"Sabrina, go back to bed. I'm going to change Kianna's clothes," Courtney said, as she walked Kianna out of the room.

"You will be all right, Kianna," Sabrina said, as she walked to her bed, saddened for her friend.

After Kianna's clothes were changed, Courtney took her downstairs for some warm milk.

"I want my daddy," Kianna said, sniffing and then she sipped on her milk.

"Kianna, it's 3:00 in the morning," Courtney said, as she pulled out a chair to sit down next to her. "You want me to wake your father up?"

"Yes," Kianna replied anxiously. "I want to see my daddy. I want to go home," she said, as tears flowed down her cheeks.

"Okay. How about you drink your milk first and if you still feel the same way after you are finished, we will call your father to pick you up," Courtney said, as she ran her index finger across her cheeks. "Is that all right?"

"Yes."

"Kianna, do you want to talk about your dream? You might feel better," Courtney said.

Kianna said nothing for a few seconds as she looked at Courtney not sure whether she should talk to her about her dream.

"Sometimes," Kianna said softly as her face frowned, "I dream about my daddy leaving me or I can't find him. It's like I died and I'll never see him again."

"Honey, what do you mean, it's like you died?" Courtney asked.

"In my dream, I would call for my daddy and he would walk past me or through me like I was invisible. Then sometimes in my dreams, I'm somewhere in a crowd of people where I can't find my daddy anywhere and I get scared," Kianna said, as more tears developed in her eyes.

"Have you told your father about your dreams?" Courtney asked, as more tears came down Kianna's face.

"Yes," Kianna replied. "My daddy tells me he is not going anywhere and he loves me."

"Do you believe your daddy?" Courtney asked.

"Yes," Kianna replied.

"How long have you been having these kinds of dreams?" Courtney asked.

"It comes and goes at times."

"Come here," Courtney said, reaching out for her hand. Kianna sat on her lap. "You know what?" she asked, as Kianna looked up at her. "Those dreams will go away eventually for good because you believe what your daddy tells you. I know that your father loves you so very much, and he will never desert you in any way. Anytime you get a feeling that something bad is going to happen to you or your daddy, I want you to say to yourself my daddy is not going to leave me because he loves me," she said, as she hugged her. Kianna began to feel better as she listened to Courtney's voice that sound soothing and the words made her believed she would be fine. "Kianna, I know I'm not your mother but I see you like my daughter. When something is on your mind, you can call me no matter what time of day or night it is. It can be here at home because this is your home too or you can call me at work. I'm here for you, Kianna. Never forget that."

"Thanks, Ms. Kennedy," Kianna said, as she put her arm around Courtney's waist as she rested her head on her chest.

"I want you to call me Courtney, okay," she said, as she gently rubbed Kianna's back.

"Yes," Kianna replied. "I'm sorry I woke you up."

"Honey," Courtney said, as she took Kianna's other hand, "don't apologize. You didn't do anything wrong. Do you still want me to call your daddy?"

"No," Kianna said, as she shook her head.

Courtney held Kianna in her arms not saying a word until she fell asleep. Courtney put Kianna to bed but she woke up within minutes. Courtney allowed her to sleep in her bed. When Courtney woke up later that morning, both of the girls were asleep in her bed.

One day Philip called Courtney to see if it would be okay to come by her place to discuss a matter. They both were in the living room talking then Philip went into what was on his mind.

"Courtney, I need to ask you something since Kianna seems to be really close to you," Philip said.

"Okay, shoot," Courtney said.

"You know, I've been dating Stephanie for awhile now and she keeps saying she wants to meet Kianna. What do you think? Do you feel Kianna is ready for that?" Philip asked.

"Let me ask you this question then I'll be able to determine an answer or an opinion. How do you feel about Stephanie?" Courtney asked.

"What do you mean?" Philip asked.

"Are you serious about this woman who wants to meet your daughter?"

"We have been dating for the last four months."

"And what? What is that suppose to mean to me?" She asked.

"And," he said, speechless.

"Philip, I'm not going to say yes or no. Only you can make that decision but I'll say this, first of all, if I bring a man into my home to meet Sabrina, I would know whether I'm serious about him without hesitation. It would be a commitment on both our parts.

Secondly, I wouldn't want him to meet Sabrina because we have been dating for several months, but he would have some kind of special qualities about himself that I would want in a person. In other words, he would have to make a tremendous change in my life that I would want him to be part of the other circles in my life like family, friends and when it comes to my heart, my daughter. He wouldn't have to ask when he is going to meet her; I would be the one to ask him first. If I don't ask him then I'm the one who isn't ready."

"Thanks, so you're saying no," Philip said. Then they laughed.

"I didn't say that. Just think about the reason why Stephanie should meet Kianna. Kianna loves you, Philip. Whatever makes you happy makes her happy. She has expressed that to me many times."

Just then the doorbell rang. Courtney excused herself to answer the door and then she walked into the room with someone.

"Philip, this is my sister Ashley. Ashley this is Philip, Kianna's father," Courtney said.

"Oh, so this is Kianna's father," Ashley said smiling, as

she and Philip shook hands. "Nice to meet you. Your daughter is a lovely young lady."

"Thank you. It's nice to finally meet you," Philip said smiling at Ashley. "Your niece talks about you all the time. Well, I should be going. Thanks, Courtney."

"Sure. I'll talk to you later," Courtney said, as she and Philip walked to the door. Then she walked back to the living room.

"Wow! He's tall, medium built, brown skin, flawless face, sexy smile and he's nice. You failed to tell me how handsome he is," Ashley said impressed, as she smiled at Courtney. "Why don't you talk to him?"

"We do talk all the time," Courtney replied, carefree.

"Courtney, you know what I mean," Ashley said, becoming serious.

"Ashley, please. We're friends and the reason for that is because of the girls."

"Have you ever thought about making it a little more than that?" Ashley asked teasingly.

"No," Courtney said, firmly. "I'm not ready for a relationship. I have too much on my plate already. I'm thinking about taking more college courses."

"For what, Courtney? You have seven years of college under your belt. More education can't take the place of a man. If God would send the man to you right now, you would tell God you're not ready. What are you afraid of? Before you know it, Sabrina will be grown and on her own and you will be alone. No one to share the rest of your life with."

"Well, I have eleven years or more to go!" Courtney said sarcastically while picking up her purse and keys. "Are you ready to leave?"

Courtney took off from work for a few days. The third day when she dropped Sabrina off at school, she noticed Kianna had her head down on her desk.

"Kianna, hi," Courtney said, smiling.

"Hello, Courtney," Kianna said, as she raised her head from the desk not looking well in her eyes.

"What's wrong?" Courtney asked, while bending down to her.

"I don't feel good," Kianna replied slowly. Then she vomited on the desk.

Courtney got in touch with Philip right away. Since they both had each other down on record at the school to get one another's girls, Courtney was able to take Kianna to the doctor's office where Philip met them. Kianna had the flu. Courtney watched Kianna at Philip's place while he went back to work. After work Philip picked Sabrina up from school and brought her over to his place where Courtney was.

A few weeks later, Ashley and her husband Preston had a dinner party on a yacht at the Navy Pier one Saturday night. They invited over 200 people. The band was playing good music.

"Courtney, have you seen Philip?" Ashley asked, as she looked around for him.

"No, Ashley," she replied.

"Did he tell you whether he was coming?"

"He told me the same thing that he told you, he would try to make it," Courtney replied impassively.

"I hope he doesn't bring a date," she said despondently.

"Why not?"

"Because you two need to get to know each other a little better without Sabrina and Kianna around," Ashley replied.

"Here we go again. Philip and I are friends. I only came here to have fun. You know I came to see friends I haven't seen in a while and to see some of Preston's new creations from his practice. I'm not—" Courtney started to say.

"I know what you are about to say, Courtney. You are not ready for a relationship."

"Hey, Ashley!" A guest said laughing at what someone was saying to them. "Excuse me, would you please come over here for a second." Then the guest continued laughing.

"Good, one of your guests is calling you," Courtney said smiling with relief.

"We will continue this conversation later," Ashley said. Then she walked away.

Courtney stayed up on the upper deck chatting with some friends. Later she became hungry. She came down the back stairs of the boat to the lower level.

"There you are," Ashley said, grabbing Courtney's hand. "I've been looking all over for you. Look there he is, Philip." she said excited, as she looked away from Courtney to Philip. "Doesn't he look great! About time he got to the bottom step, women were on him like white on rice. Obviously, he came alone," she said pleased.

Philip waved at them while dancing with a lady.

"I'm glad he made it, maybe you can stop breaking your neck every time you see someone coming down those steps. See you later," Courtney said, as she began to walk away.

"Wait a minute. Courtney, where are you going?"

"To get something to eat," Courtney replied.

"I don't think Philip had anything to eat yet," Ashley said. "Maybe you two can eat together at one of these secluded tables."

"I keep telling you, I'm not interested in him like that or any man. Got it, Ashley," Courtney said, getting irritated.

"Why don't you open up?" Ashley asked firmly.

"On second thought, I'm tired," Courtney said angry. "I'm going to leave. I'll talk to you tomorrow." Then she turned around to leave.

"I'm sorry," Ashley said, as she grabbed Courtney's arm. "I'll back off for now," she promised.

Then Philip walked over to them. Ashley and Courtney smiled.

"Hi, Courtney. Where have you been?" Philip asked.

"I was on the upper deck. It's really nice up there," Courtney said, as she smiled.

"Excuse me. I'll talk to you two later," Ashley said, walking away seeing someone she wanted to speak to.

"Would you like to dance?" Philip asked Courtney.

"No, I don't dance. I don't know how. Really no," Courtney murmured.

"What?" he asked not hearing what she said because of the intensity of the music.

"I'm not a good dancer at all but thanks anyway for asking," Courtney said.

"Come on, just follow my lead," Philip said.

"Hello, Courtney," a woman said walking to them. "Philip, come on let's dance to this one. This used to be my song back in the day!" she said, as she snapped her fingers to the music.

"Go ahead, Philip," Courtney said. "I really don't want to."

Courtney went back to the upper deck to eat her snack and to look out on the waters. She really wanted to enjoy the scenery and look up at the billions of stars in the sky, as a light cool breeze blew through her hair. One of the singers sang, 'Express Yourself.' Courtney looked around and saw no one near by. Everyone was downstairs dancing their hearts away. She stood up from the lounge chair and started dancing like Madonna on one of her videos. At the end of the song she posed then she heard someone clapping. She quickly turned around to see who it was.

"Philip, you startled me," Courtney said stunned. "How long have you been standing there?"

"Long enough to see that you can dance," Philip said, as slow mellow music played. "Come on dance with me out here to this song."

"I really can't slow dance at all," Courtney replied in a discouraging tone.

"I'll teach you," he said, as he took her soft hands and pulled her gently to him. "Like I said earlier, follow my lead," he said, as he looked into her eyes. Then he pulled her even closer to him as they began to dance.

Philip and Courtney were dancing partners all night. Courtney noticed it was getting late as she looked at her watch. The girlfriend she came with wasn't ready to leave so Philip offered to take her home. They talked about the party while riding to Courtney's place.

"Courtney, I think you were pulling my leg. You are a good dancer," Philip said while driving.

"I wasn't pulling your leg. When I was a teenager, I would dance in front of the mirror but not in public. It was like I had two left feet. You are a smooth one."

"A smooth one? What does that mean?"

"You were determined to get me out on the dance floor," Courtney said, as she smiled.

"I normally get what I want," he said teasingly with a proud look. "I'm persistent in everything I do. However, I'll take that remark as a compliment." He smiled.

The week of Thanksgiving turned brutally cold. Light sweaters and jackets season were over; it was the holiday season once again. Courtney's mother's home wasn't big enough to accommodate everyone in the family and friends for Thanksgiving. Every year everyone celebrated Thanksgiving at Ashley's home. Their mother came over to the house a day before Thanksgiving to start cooking some of the food. On that special day, the in-laws and some of the cousins helped finish cooking dinner. The tradition was to say grace over the food at 3:00 p.m. Before dinner, Courtney's father, who was divorced from her mother, would come over for a couple of hours to spend with the family. Then he would go to his own home and spend the remaining day with his wife and children.

Philip and his sister helped their mother cook dinner. They would have about 15 guests over his mother's home for Thanksgiving. Everyone would do their own thing like watching television mostly the football games, playing cards, and the children running around the house playing hide and seek. Philip and his sister prepared a dish of the same food to see who could cook it the best. That year it was homemade butter rolls.

Before the blink of an eye, Christmas was only a few days away. The week of Christmas the school had a play where Kianna played as Mary, Jesus' mother, and Sabrina played as one of the angels. On Christmas Eve every year Courtney would wait until the last minute to buy a tree and two of her neighbors would help bring the tree in the house. Courtney and the girls had a great time decorating the tree, listening and singing Christmas carols. They popped three bags of popcorn to make a garland for the tree. Later that evening Philip came over to pick up Kianna. He brought in a big bag filled with gifts.

"Thanks, Philip," Courtney said, as he gave her the bag.

"You're welcome. I hope you and Sabrina like the gifts," Philip said, smiling taking off his gloves.

"I'm sure we will," Courtney said, walking over to the tree.

"Philip, would you like some eggnog?" Sabrina asked, as she put the gifts under the tree.

"Your mom didn't make it herself, did she?" He asked, as Sabrina laughed. He rested his coat on a chair. Then he looked at Courtney, "Everyone I ran into makes their own eggnog and it tastes horrible!" he said frowning.

"No, I didn't make it, Mr. Smarty. Sabrina, he doesn't want any," Courtney said teasingly.

"Yes, I would love some. Thank you," Philip said, as he laughed.

Sabrina went to the kitchen to get Philip some eggnog.

"Kianna, if you look under the tree you will find something with your name on it," Courtney said, smiling.

"It's not there. I looked. I mean, I checked the gifts under the tree to make sure all the names were spelled correctly," Kianna said, disappointed.

"Oh, I wondered what you were doing," Courtney said, as she and Philip smiled looking at Kianna. Sabrina handed Philip his drink then she stood by Kianna "When was the last time you checked the gifts?"

"A little while ago," Kianna replied, as Sabrina smiled at her.

"Why don't you look again," Courtney said while looking under the tree. "Philip, would you mind putting this star on top of the tree. You're taller then I am and that stepladder is not working for me."

"Sure, my pleasure," Philip said, as he sat his drink on a coaster on the center piece table and walked to the tree.

"Here they are!" Kianna said, excited as she looked at the Santa Claus wrapping paper. "Daddy, you have some presents too!"

"Courtney, can we open one of our presents now?" Kianna asked, as Sabrina handed Philip who was standing on the stepladder the star adornment to put on top of the tree.

"Yea! Why don't we," Sabrina said smiling.

"No, we can wait until tomorrow. Right, Philip?" Courtney asked, as he stepped off the stepladder.

"Yes, I agree," Philip replied.

"Come on mom, we won't be together tomorrow morning to see one another's expression on our faces," Sabrina said.

"I have an idea, tomorrow when you open your gifts, you can call one another and express your excitement then," Courtney said smiling.

Sabrina and Kianna looked at one another disappointed.

"That sounds good. Are you ready, Kianna?" Philip asked.

"Yes," Kianna replied slowly.

"Kianna, come here and give me a hug," Courtney said. "Christmas day will be here before you know it then you can open your gifts. Merry Christmas, baby," she said, then she hugged and kissed Kianna.

Before Philip left he wanted to greet Sabrina and Courtney for the holiday.

"Merry Christmas, Courtney," Philip said, as he hugged

Courtney.

"Merry Christmas, Philip," Courtney said, smiling.

"Daddy, you and Courtney are standing under the mistletoe," Kianna said, smiling.

Philip and Courtney looked at each other and smiled. Philip placed a gentle kiss on her cheek.

All four of them had a nice Christmas. Sabrina received a computer game and a doll and Courtney received a music box with a tennis bracelet inside of it from Philip and Kianna. Kianna received a doll that spoke in different languages and a savings bond, and Philip received a cufflink set with a tie and a gift certificate for an in home massage from Courtney and Sabrina.

Later that day, Philip and Kianna left his mother's house after dinner and went over to Ashley's home for his daughter to spend some time with Sabrina and her family. When they went inside the house they saw Courtney and her oldest teenage niece Zakeya, Ashley's daughter, singing Christmas carols together while Preston played the piano. Sabrina's grandmother was sitting in the living room looking through a Christmas Carol book. Sabrina introduced Philip to her grandmother who had a warm smile. He gave her grandmother a pretty wrapped Christmas gift. When she opened it, it was a white silk scarf. She thanked him but he couldn't really tell whether she liked it or not because her smile never changed. Later that night, Kianna was showing her father in the kitchen where to get a bag of mixed nuts that was up in one of the coverts. Something fell out the covert while Philip was giving his daughter the nuts. She left out the kitchen as he put the item that fell out of the covert back up. Pamela, a distant cousin who came around the family once a year was trying to flirt with Philip in the kitchen. Zakeya walked into the kitchen as Pamela was talking to Philip.

"You have a lovely child. Kianna is a sweet girl and I see where she gets her good looks from," Pamela said.

"Thank you," Philip said. Then he looked at Zakeya and smiled.

"Cousin Pam," Zakeya said while putting her arm around her shoulders walking away from Philip. Then she lowered her voice. "Philip belongs to your cousin Courtney. You know the Kennedy women don't play when it comes to their men."

"Oh, well I didn't know," Pamela whispered, as they walked out the kitchen. Zakeya came back into the kitchen.

"Philip, I hope you are enjoying yourself. Thank you for coming," Zakeya said.

"Thanks for the invitation. I'm having a nice time. You have a beautiful voice," Philip said.

"Are you serious? Do you think I'm good enough to make a record deal?" Zakeya asked waiting for an answer with anticipation.

"Yes," he replied sincerely.

"You have made my day!" Zakeya said, smiling excitedly. "Philip, I want to be a singer so bad I can taste it! I don't want to be a doctor, or a lawyer, or an accountant. I want to go to a university that teaches music. Preferably, Julliard Arts. My father says being a singer isn't a real job. He wants me to get a college degree in something that will carry me through life. I told my father I want to get a degree in music, he won't hear of it. He tells me that once I get a degree in something more stable then I can do whatever I want to do.

My father hasn't really taken his time to hear me sing. I mean he listens to me but he doesn't hear my talent," Zakeya said.

"I know what you mean and I also understand your dad's point of view as well."

"I do too, Philip but I could be out there like other young ladies my age letting their talent be known today, not tomorrow. I'm taking voice lessons. Who knows," Zakeya said downhearted.

"You know what, Zakeya? Sometimes we like to run ahead of ourselves and in doing that we can mess up something that could really be successful." Philip said. "Take your time and let your mind slow down. That angel voice of yours isn't going anywhere. Keep taking voice lessons and continue to get as much education as you can, so that you can achieve at anything. Your gift will make room for you but you have to have patience."

Zakeya smiled.

Sabrina's grandmother Jackee' thanked Philip again for the scarf.

"I'm glad you like it, Ms. Kennedy," Philip said.

"I know Kianna gave you a tour around the house showing you all the Christmas decorations that Ashley did around here. I'm sure she didn't show you Preston's collection of paintings. He doesn't like the children to go into that room not even Zakeya at her age. Let's see them shall we," Jackee' said as they walked down the hall. "You have made some kind of impression on my granddaughter, Sabrina," she said in an impressive tone.

"She's a beautiful child. I'm glad that Kianna and Sabrina are best friends."

"Well, Sabrina thinks the world of you, Philip. I'm not trying to discourage you in a positive way, but I have never been known to beat around the bush. If you are not sincere about Sabrina or you feel sorry for her then you don't need to be around her. Sometimes, we as adults tend to change like the weather when it comes to someone else's feelings, especially a child. A child's feelings should always be first. Being selfish shouldn't be an option in anyone's life, but especially a child. I've always said to people, question your intentions because sometimes it could be for selfish reasons. Courtney and Sabrina need friends who are going to be there for them. I've told Courtney the same thing concerning Kianna whom I see as my granddaughter as well. Do we understand one another, Philip?" Jackee' asked.

"Yes, ma'am," Philip replied attentively. "I understand."

The girls spent the night at Ashley's place. Philip followed Courtney home because it was late when they left Ashley's.

"Thank you for making sure I got home safe," Courtney said, as Philip walked her to front door.

"You're welcome. Not only are you a dancer but a singer too," Philip said.

"I can carry a tune here and there," she said smiling.

"Zakeya told me you could have been a professional singer."

"I never took it to heart," Courtney said. "What else did you and my niece talk about? You two talked for a while. I didn't know what you were saying to her but you put some kind of smile on her face."

"She is a very intelligent person for her age."

"She is indeed. My mother says she's an old lady that has been here before and sometimes she acts like it in a 14-year-old body."

"Speaking of your mother did she say anything about me?" he asked curiously.

"Anything about you? Like what?" Courtney asked. Then she smiled.

"Whether or not she believes I'm a bad person."

"I see where this is going," Courtney said, laughing. "My mom thinks you are a nice man who brought her a lovely scarf for Christmas. I saw when you and my mother disappeared. Where did you go and what did you talk about?"

"It was a general conversation," He replied. "We were getting to know each other. Your mother showed me Preston's impressive painting collection."

"Mmm. I see." Courtney thought that Philip was trying to change the subject.

"I'm going into the office tomorrow, so I better get going," Philip said.

"Why? It's Saturday?"

"I know. I have some things I need to do. When it comes to the world of business, it's never a holiday. Go ahead in the house and make sure you lock the door," Philip said.

"Goodnight," Courtney said.

On New Years Eve, Courtney was home alone sick with

a cold. Everyone she knew was either celebrating New Years at church, going to parties, or at home like she was watching Dick Clark's New Year Eve special on television waiting for the New Year to come in. She wasn't upset that she was home sick but she was glad to be alive and overall healthy.

Chapter Four

One weekend, Philip and Courtney took the girls to the Ice Capades. After leaving the Ice Capades, Philip remembered he needed to drop something off at his mother's home. He asked Courtney if she would like to come into the house. She declined since he was only going to be a few minutes. While the girls went in with Philip, Courtney rested her head on the back seat with her eyes closed enjoying the pre-spring breeze coming through the windows. Five minutes later, Philip came to the passenger side of the car.

"My mother wants to meet you," Philip said.

"Me?" Courtney asked.

"Is there anyone else in here?" he asked, as he opened and closed the back door.

"Philip, I'm not dressed properly to meet your mother."

"You look fine. Come on," he said. Then he opened the door and helped Courtney out the car. She looked uncomfortable as she got out the car. "She's not going to bite you. However, she's going to have you sit at a table with bright lights shining in your face to make you sweat a little while she asks questions," he said humorously. They both laughed. "My mother wants to meet the woman that my daughter fell in love with. Oh, by the way, my mother wants us to stay for dinner. Do you mind?"

"No. I'm sure I'll be hungry after the interrogation with the hot lights beaming on me," Courtney said, as they both smiled.

When they walked in the house, Philip's mother was coming down the long staircase.

"Mother, this is Courtney. Courtney," he said, while putting his hand on Courtney's back "this is the number one lady in my life, my mother."

"Hi, Ms. Franklin. It's nice to meet you," Courtney said, as she gracefully smiled.

"Please call me Beverly, and it's nice to finally to meet you, Courtney. Can I get you something before dinner?" Beverly asked.

"No, ma'am," Courtney replied.

"Please, come this way," Beverly said.

They walked to the living room where Philip's sister Lauren and their cousin Eve were sitting. Everyone was talking, laughing and having a nice time. Courtney sat there wondering to herself why she was so nervous. As Beverly stood up saying something to Philip, he got up hugging his mother telling her he wasn't going to let her go. Everyone laughed as his mother tried to pull away from him.

"I know, you don't want Courtney to see you get a spanking," Beverly said to Philip, as she tapped him on his hand.

"Courtney, I want you to come into the kitchen to taste my homemade chili," Beverly said.

"Sure," Courtney said, as she stood up from the couch.

"Courtney, whatever mother asks you tell her you don't recall," Lauren said laughing.

"You are another one who needs a spanking," Beverly said to her daughter, as Courtney walked over to her. "Courtney, Philip tells me you don't cook."

"He told you that?" Courtney asked looking embarrassed. Then she turned around and gave Philip an evil eye.

"Mother!" Philip said in shock.

"See, I told you I was going to give you a spanking," Beverly said smiling.

Beverly and Courtney walked into the spacious kitchen.

"Do you like spicy chili?" Beverly asked.

"Yes ma'am, with plenty of cold water," Courtney replied.

"I'll make sure our housekeeper, Jennifer, keeps your glass

filled with cold water."

"Thank you."

"However, you will have your choice of plain or spicy chili. Lauren is allergic to spicy foods," Beverly said, smiling as she stirred one of the pots of chili. "Sabrina is a well brought up child. Courtney, I'm very good with people's characters. When my son told me about your relationship with Kianna, I was skeptical. Kianna has told me some very impressive things about you. I want you to answer a question for me, and I don't want to hear that you don't recall," she said, smiling again. Then she became serious, "Why did you take interest in my granddaughter?"

"Kianna took me by surprise," Courtney replied. "I would see her in the mornings when I would take Sabrina to school and she would come over to speak to me. I would hug her and ask her how her morning was going. We would have little conversations sometimes. By her being my daughter's best friend, I thought maybe once in a while she would come over to spend the night and that would be it. I took a special interest in Kianna because we connected so well like my daughter and I. She has a lot of love to share and she wants to share it with me. Kianna is a very special child that I have the joy of knowing. I feel like she's my own child."

"I like that honest answer from you. I want to say thank you for being so kind to my granddaughter," Beverly said, as she smiled.

"It's my pleasure," Courtney said smiling back.

"Are you ready to try my homemade chili?"

"Yes," Courtney replied.

After dinner they relaxed in another room in front of the fireplace. The girls were on the floor coloring and watching an animated tape. Philip came over to Courtney with a photograph album showing her the family pictures. Everyone except the girls stopped and looked at them and smiled. He showed Courtney pictures of his father. He and his father were spitting image of one another. When Philip left the room his sister came over to Courtney.

"Courtney," Lauren said, "the reason why we looked at you and my brother earlier, when he brought over the photo album, is because Philip wouldn't go near the photos of our father. I mean if he did it was probably when no one was around. Courtney, just between you and me, is something going on between you and my brother?" she asked suspiciously.

"No," Courtney replied. "We're turning out to be good friends."

"Well that's even better," Lauren said.

Later Courtney went to see where Philip was. She found him sitting out front on the step.

"What are you doing out here?" Courtney asked, sitting next to him.

"Are you ready to go?" Philip asked, as he looked at her.

"No, not really. Are you okay?" she asked, as he looked away from her.

"Yes," he replied, as he smiled. Then he looked back at her again. "I'm great."

He stared at her for a few seconds then she looked away from him.

"I love your mother's house," Courtney said with delight.

"My sister and I were literally born and raised in this house," Philip said.

"Wow! That's great!" Courtney exclaimed.

"It seems like every three years my mother is having something remodel in the house."

"Courtney," Lauren said, walking over to them.

"Yes, Lauren," Courtney answered, as she turned her head looking up at her.

"Would you like to come to my wedding?" Lauren asked. Then she looked at Philip.

"Sure," Courtney replied. Philip gave Lauren a senseless stare as he shook his head to his sister. As Courtney turned around to look at Philip, he smiled.

"Good. I'll have my wedding consultant put an invitation in the mail for you this week. I'll get your address from Philip. Philip, mother wants to know if you are going to take your dessert home with you?" Lauren asked.

"No. I'll eat it tomorrow when I come over," Philip replied.

"See you two later," Lauren said. "I'm getting ready to leave. I enjoyed your company, Courtney. Hopefully, we can do it again soon. Goodnight."

"I had a good time, thank you. Goodnight," Courtney said. Lauren walked away. "Philip, why did you look at Lauren like that? You don't want me to come to your sister's wedding?"

"No that's not it. See, I already have a date. Michelle, a friend of the family, asked me months ago to be her escort."

"What does that have to do with me, Philip? We're friends. It's okay," Courtney said.

"I know that but it will seem kind of awkward since we hang out a lot with the girls."

As Philip was driving Courtney home from his mother's, he looked over at her and smiled.

"Are the girls asleep?" Philip asked.

"Yes. I don't think they are going to want to get up for church tomorrow morning."

"Kianna will. She's been telling me everyday this week how it's her turn to collect the children's Sunday school offering," Philip said.

"That's right, I forgot about that. She probably will wake me up early to make sure we get to church on time," Courtney said.

"My mom likes you," he said, smiling.

"I like her too. She's a beautiful woman."

"That she is. My father used to always say by her being so beautiful almost messed it up with him."

"Why is that?"

"He felt beautiful women were conceited." Philip said.

"My mother has a friend that she is seeing who wants to marry her, but she not ready."

"Do you and your sister like him?"

"I hate to admit it but he's a good man. In the back of my mind, I don't think she will ever marry again. My mother tells my sister and me that she is not interested in what we think when it comes to her happiness," he said smiling.

"That's right, mom! That's telling them," Courtney said laughing.

Sunday morning when Kianna got up to announce the children's Sunday school offering, she waved to her grandmother and Philip who were sitting in church.

Time flew so fast that before Courtney knew it, Sabrina was helping her wrap Lauren's wedding gift the day before the wedding. The next day at the church the wedding started 20 minutes late. Someone sang until the wedding party was ready to march in. Philip looked very handsome walking down the aisle with one of the bridesmaid. Sabrina got Philip's attention as he approached the row where they were standing. He winked at Sabrina while passing their row. Kianna looked so pretty walking down the aisle as the flower girl.

The minister asked the guests to stand. The lights dimmed as the music started to play. Then they heard Lauren's voice all over the church. She began saying words blending it into the music. All of the guests, the groom Vincent and some of the people in the wedding party started looking around wondering where her voice was coming from. The doors opened then she walked down the aisle singing to the groom. She looked so beautiful in her slim pearl dress with an cathedral length train.

Vincent made eye contact with the engineer to turn his microphone on as he surprisingly sang along with her. People were smiling, crying and cheering them on as they hit a high note of the song. They sang the way they really felt about one another.

"Mommy," Sabrina said looking up at her mother.

"Yes, Sabrina," Courtney answered as she bent down to her daughter.

"Where are Lauren and Vincent's microphones?"

"It's a small microphone pinned to her gown and to the groom's tuxedo, honey," Courtney replied.

When Courtney and Sabrina arrived at the ballroom of the hotel, one of the hosts escorted them to their table. A waitress came over to see what they would like to drink.

"Yes, I would like to have a Sprite, please and my daughter will have—" Courtney began to say.

"Mommy, I want to order for myself," Sabrina said. "I would like to have a glass of milk on the rocks, please."

"Sure," the waitress said, smiling then she looked at Courtney. Courtney nodded her head.

"I'll be back with your drinks ladies."

"On the rocks, Sabrina? Where did that come from?" Courtney asked.

"I just heard one of the waiters say it to that man, here is your scotch on the rocks," she said.

Later the MC came to the microphone calling everyone's name as the wedding party entered. Then the lights dimmed as the two skylights shined on the bride and groom. The saxophone played while they walked to the head table.

Everyone was served dinner at the same time while the pianist played. Later people were mingling, approaching the bride and groom table. The MC called the special couple up for the first dance. Everyone in the wedding party made a big circle around them. As the bride and groom danced the wedding party blew bubbles around them. Then the wedding party danced with their partners. People thought it was so cute how Kianna was dancing with the ring bearer and they were not smiling at all. They didn't even want to touch each other, much less dance together.

Later Lauren and Vincent walked around talking and thanking people for coming. One of the bridesmaids was helping

Lauren with her train. Then Lauren walked over to Courtney's table.

"Courtney, thank you for coming," Lauren said, as they hugged.

"You're welcome. Thank you for inviting Sabrina and I to share in your special day. You look so beautiful! The wedding was absolutely fabulous," Courtney said.

"Thanks. I see Kianna came over to get Sabrina. Kianna called me last night asking me if Sabrina sit at our table. I was already on pins and needles. I told her sure, why not. She really loves Sabrina."

"We love her too," Courtney said.

Then Philip came over to the table.

"Doesn't he look handsome, Courtney?" Lauren asked, as Philip hugged her.

"He does," Courtney said, smiling.

"Are you having a good time?" Philip asked Courtney, as his sister walked away talking to someone else.

"Yes," Courtney said, gracefully.

"Come with me. There are some people I want you to meet," Philip said, as he took Courtney by the hand.

Philip introduced Courtney to his family, friends, and his date Michelle. While Courtney was speaking to someone, Philip and his cousin Jack were standing around talking.

"So, that's Courtney. She's a beautiful woman. Is she dating anyone?" Jack asked, as he watched Courtney.

"You wouldn't be interested in a woman like her," Philip replied in a discouraging tone.

"Why because you are?" Jack asked smiling.

"I was kind of interested at first but she's not ready to get involved with anyone right now. We're good friends."

"Come on, man. If that's true, you can put in a good word for me. She is in luck that a handsome single man such as myself is available," Jack said boldly. "I'm sure I can—"

"Before you go any further," Philip said, as he interrupted

Jack, "you are not ready for a woman like her. There are two types of women. You have the ones you can sleep with and if you have to make false promises to keep them around until someone else comes along or you get tired of them, you do that. Then you have those that don't take any foolishness. They won't settle for anything less. Courtney is the marrying type if you know what I mean. She not the putting out kind."

"Philip, she has a lot going for herself. I could change but the way you are going on and on, I won't bother her because I can tell you really like her," Jack said spoofing, as he pat Philip on his back.

"That's not true. We're good friends, and I'm not going to let her get hurt," Philip said in a protective tone.

"Just friends, huh," Jack said in disbelief, as he looked at Philip smiling. "Tell me anything that doesn't mean I'm going to believe it. Courtney is worth the wait in more ways than one. Look at her, she looks like a million dollars outside as well as inside. A heart of gold," he said, as if he already knew her. "Well, let me mingle with the other single woman. You better be glad you are my cousin for me not to lay on my charm to Courtney. Who knows between me and her it could probably be another engagement in the family." Philip looked at Jack, speechless. "Talk to you later."

As Philip danced with Michelle, he kept watching Courtney dancing with Sabrina and Kianna. Jack came over to Philip.

"Hey man," Jack said, as he put his hand on Philip's shoulder, "let me dance with Michelle." Then he whispered in Philip's ear, "Philip, go ahead, I know you want to dance with Courtney." Then he got Michelle's hand and turned her around on the dance floor. "Excuse us," he said to Philip.

"See you later, Philip," Michelle said, as she smiled at Jack.

Philip walked around a little on the floor then he walked up to Courtney and the girls.

"Excuse me, ladies, can I dance with Courtney?" Philip

asked.

"Hi, it seems the music changed," Courtney said, as the girls walked away.

Then she turned around to walk off the dance floor. Philip reached for her hand.

"Do you remember how I taught you to slow dance?" Philip asked, as he looked into her eyes. He took her into his arms and they began to dance. "Why were you turning down men who wanted to dance with you?"

"I didn't turn all of them down and anyway I was enjoying dancing with the kids," Courtney said. "I loved dancing with your little cousin Eric, he would tell me when to turn around at the same time he did. He doesn't act like he's five years old. You know you are not so bad yourself," she said teasingly, as they smiled at one another.

"Let's say I'm a big kid at heart," Philip said, chuckling.

Jack was doing okay with Michelle but once every few beats, he would step on her toes. After a third time she had enough. She saw Philip enjoying himself dancing with Courtney and she became jealous as she took off her shoe to rub on her toes.

Later, it was time for Lauren to toss her bouquet. All the single women got into a group.

"Okay, are you ladies ready to be the next one to get married? Here we go!" the MC said loudly over the microphone.

Lauren turned around and tossed her bouquet backwards. Courtney caught it. People clapped.

"All right," the MC said, "a beautiful Ms. Courtney Kennedy caught the bouquet. Now here comes the special chair for Mrs. Markerson to have a seat. Now, Mr. Markerson will remove his bride's garter belt."

Men were clapping and chanting Vincent's name while he was removing Lauren's garter belt. Then he turned his back and threw the garter belt to the single men. Philip caught it.

The MC made the announcement of Philip catching the

garter belt. Philip and Courtney took pictures together with the bouquet and the garter belt. Afterwards Michelle walked up to Philip.

"Philip, whose thigh are you going to put that on?" Michelle asked, seductively smiling.

Courtney smiled at them as she walked over to Philip's mother.

"Ms. Franklin, I caught this for you," Courtney said.

"No, you caught it, you should keep it. It will bring you luck," Ms. Franklin said.

"I saw when you got up to join us to catch the bouquet but then you changed your mind."

"Those women looked like they wanted to fight one another to catch that bouquet," Ms. Franklin said, as they laughed.

"I know. I was a good catcher when I played baseball in school. Beverly, please accept this," Courtney said, sincerely.

"Okay, since you insist. Thank you, I'll accept," Beverly said proudly, as she took the bouquet.

After Vincent and Lauren left for their honeymoon, Philip was sitting down in one of the chairs holding Sabrina and Courtney was holding Kianna.

"I'm getting ready to leave. It's late and I have to get up in the morning while other people are sleeping in," Courtney said.

"Daddy, can I go over to Courtney's house then you don't have to—" Kianna began to ask.

"Yes, Kianna," Philip said smiling interrupting her sentence. "Why don't you two go over to grandmother to let her know you are leaving." The girls leaped off Philip and Courtney's laps walking over to his mother.

"You are amazing, Courtney," Philip said.

"What do you mean?" Courtney asked.

"That was really nice of you to give my mother your bouquet."

"No problem," she said, as she took her car key out her purse.

"I'll walk you ladies to the car," Philip said. "Ready?"

Chapter Five

One Friday night the school had a special program for the children. The parents brought food for approximately 150 people. Philip and Courtney took off from work to bake homemade brownies and cakes. After everything was successful over at the school they headed back to Philip's house where Courtney had left her car. She remembered as they walked into Philip's house that she left her cellular phone and pager on the kitchen counter. As she checked her phone and pager, she noticed repeatedly Ashley's number.

Ashley left messages on Courtney's voice mail of the cellular phone asking Courtney to call her as soon as possible. While Courtney was calling Ashley on Philip's phone the girls ran upstairs.

"Sabrina, don't get lost up there. We're getting ready to leave," Courtney said. Then her sister answered her phone. "Oh, hi, Ashley. I'm sorry I didn't—what?" she asked in shock. "Oh, no! I'll be right there."

"Courtney, what's wrong?" Philip asked, as he helped her hang up the telephone.

Courtney looked up at Philip then she grabbed her purse.

"Can Sabrina stay the night here?" Courtney asked, as her voice cracked.

"Sure. What happened?" Philip asked.

"My mother is at the University of Chicago Hospitals. She had a heart attack. How could something like this happen to my mother?" Courtney asked, as she tried to come up with an explanation in her mind that would elucidate her mother's tragedy.

"She's smaller than I am. She is a health nut. I don't understand. I need to get to the hospital!"

"I'll call my sister to come over to watch the girls. It will take her no time to get here then I'll drive you to the hospital," he said.

"No, thanks. I don't want to wait. I'll be fine. Please don't tell Sabrina what's going on. I don't want her to worry."

"I won't."

Courtney walked out the kitchen to the staircase.

"Sabrina, honey would you come here for a second," Courtney yelled, as she cleared her throat.

"Mommy, can I spend the night, and I double promise I'll come home tomorrow?" Sabrina asked standing on the top of the staircase.

"Yes, that's fine," Courtney replied, as she opened her purse looking in it as if she was trying to find something while fighting back the tears and her worse fear of losing her mother. Sabrina could tell by her mother's response that something wasn't right.

"Mommy, what's wrong?" Sabrina asked while walking down the steps.

"Honey," she said looking up smiling, "I'm getting ready to leave. I want you to be a good girl for Philip. I have to go. You two come here and give me a hug."

Philip walked Courtney outside to her car.

"Call me," Philip said.

"I will. Thank you for everything, Philip, Goodnight," Courtney said softly.

Philip watched her drive away.

Courtney walked into the ICU unit of the hospital where Ashley, Preston, her two brothers Carlton and Maxwell and their wives were standing around looking at their mother, hoping for the best. The nurse came in the room and told them only one visitor at a time. Courtney remained in the room with her mother as everyone else left out. Her hands began to shake as she touched her mother's hand.

"Mom, I love you. I'll be here when you wake up," Courtney whispered nervously, as she tried to smile.

Later on that night, Courtney sat in the waiting area with her family, still hopeful, waiting for the positive news about their mother. Courtney wanted to stay in her mother's room but the doctor wanted her mother to continue to rest. It seemed Ashley's children were calling her cellular phone every thirty minutes to see if there were any changes in their grandmother's condition. An hour later, Courtney finally sat down after pacing the floor for what seemed like an eternity. She rested her head against the wall and closed her eyes, constantly praying that her mother would be all right. Around 1:00 a.m., she felt a tap on her shoulder.

"Hi, Philip," Courtney said, sitting up.

"The girls are fine. My sister is at the house with them," Philip said.

"That's fine. I'm not worried, I trust you. Thanks for coming."

"Since you didn't call I was sitting at home wondering what's going on. How is your mother?" Philip asked.

"About the same, no change."

"Can I get you something?" he asked.

"No, I'm okay. Thanks. I just want her to wake up," she said worried.

Ashley and her husband walked over to them.

"Philip, thank you for coming," Ashley said, as Philip stood up from his seat.

"No problem, Ashley." Philip said. Then he looked at her husband and acknowledged him, "Preston."

"Philip, we appreciate you being here," Preston said, as they shook hands.

"This waiting is driving me crazy," Ashley said, looking at the nurses station. "You would think they would have said something by now." She sat next to Courtney and held her hand. "It's going to be okay." Courtney just stared straight ahead.

While everyone was sitting around talking, Courtney paced the floor then she went into her mother's room.

"Mom, please open your eyes," Courtney begged, as tears rolled down her face while she held her mother's hand. "You have always been there for me no matter what. Now, I want to be there for you, I want to take care of you. I'll take cooking lessons so you won't get sick when I prepare your meals." She smiled and then she became sad again. "Mom, please don't leave Sabrina and me. We need you. I need you most of all." Her mother opened her eyes and looked at Courtney for a couple of seconds trying to squeeze her hand. Courtney held her mother's hand a little tighter smiling as she kissed her mother's hand then her mother closed her eyes. Courtney pushed a button on a remote that was on the side of her bed. The doctor and a nurse came in right away.

"Ms. Kennedy, you shouldn't be in here," the doctor said.

"I know and I'm sorry. My mother just opened her eyes!" Courtney said anxiously.

"That's impossible!" the doctor said. "According to her vital signs there is no change in her condition since we stabilized her," he said, while reading something off a machine.

"What's going on, Courtney?" Ashley asked, as she came into their mother's room.

"Ashley, mom opened her eyes. They don't believe me but she did!" Courtney said getting upset.

"I'm sorry but all of you have to leave the room now," the doctor said firmly, as the nurse checked the liquid going through the I.V. in their mother's arm. "Your mother needs rest."

"I believe you, Courtney. Come on. Let's go so the doctor can check mom," Ashley said.

"What's wrong?" Philip asked, as he and the others stood up from their seats walking over to Courtney and Ashley.

"Philip, mom opened her eyes. She's going to be okay," Courtney said, looking hopeful. "No one believes me but I know what I saw." Then she looked around at her family.

"Courtney, I told you, I believe you," Ashley said, trying to reassure Courtney.

"I believe you too. It's okay," Philip said, putting his arm around Courtney's shoulder as everyone walked back to the waiting area.

Hours later they were all still sitting in the waiting area. No one wanted to leave the hospital. All of a sudden Courtney felt a strange chill run through her body then she sat straight up in her seat. She looked at her watch; it was 4:35 in the morning.

"Are you okay?" Philip asked.

"Yes, I'm fine. I wonder how mom is doing," Courtney said softly.

Ten minutes later the doctor came over to them and everyone stood up.

"I'm sorry," the doctor said, sorrowfully. "Ms. Kennedy didn't make it. She passed away 15 minutes ago. We tried to save her but we couldn't revive her again."

Ashley grabbed hold of her husband, and her sister-in-laws hugged her brothers as they broke down in tears. Courtney ran past the doctor into her mother's room. It seems Courtney's heart stopped beating for a few seconds as she looked at her mother's lifeless body. She laid her head on her mother's chest and stomped her foot crying out. Philip was standing behind Courtney and as she rose up then she lost her balance. He caught her around the waist. When she turned around Philip hugged her as she continued to cry. She hugged onto him for dear life. Philip closed his eyes remembering how he felt when he lost his father. Ashley rushed in the room. She hugged Courtney telling her it was going to be okay. Ashley asked the doctor and the nurse to leave for a minute so they could spend a few moments alone with their mother. Carlton and Maxwell's wives walked over to their mother-in-law and kissed her and went outside the room.

"Ashley, I don't have anyone to lean on anymore. What," Courtney said choking up. "What I'm I going to do?" She cried out. “Oh, my God, why?” She screamed, as her brothers came over to her. They all hugged one another.

“We’re going to be okay. Look at her, Courtney. She’s at peace. Mom always believed God in everything she did. You know what she would always say, God brought her too far to leave her now. Well, God didn’t stop there he took her home,” Ashley said.

“What am I going to do?” Courtney asked in a daze, as she looked at her mother.

“You told me that mom opened her eyes, right?” Ashley asked, as tears rolled down her face.

“Yes,” Courtney replied softly, as she continued to look at her mother.

“Look at me, Courtney. Come on look at me!” Ashley demanded. Courtney looked at her as tears ran down her face, “Mom did that to let you know that everything is all right even though none of us knew why this happened and we didn’t know what the outcome was going to be. There is nothing else we can do. Let’s go home,” Ashley said with composure.

“No. She just died and you want to leave! No. I can’t leave her,” Courtney said, raising her voice.

“Courtney, what Ashley is trying to say is, we have been here since mom arrived,” Carlton said. “Now, she is gone to a better place. She not here. You need to get some rest.”

“Courtney, I’ll drive you to wherever you want to go,” Philip said.

“Thanks, Philip but I’m taking Courtney home with me,” Ashley said. “We will send someone over to your home to get Sabrina later or you can bring her to the house.”

“No, Ashley. I’m going home. I can drive myself. For now, I’m going to stay here with my mother,” Courtney said, as she walked back over to her mother. Then she moved her fingers through her mother’s silver gray hair while staring at the most beautiful face she ever saw, knowing that she would never see her mom alive again.

"I'll wait for you however long it takes, Courtney. You are not in any shape to drive," Philip said.

Courtney didn't hear what Philip was telling her.

"Courtney," Ashley said, as she wiped her eyes with a kleenex.

"What?" Courtney said softly.

"You shouldn't drive," Ashley said.

"Right now, I don't care about driving, going home, or anything else. Nothing matters now. If you all are ready to leave go. I'm fine," Courtney said not looking away from her mother. Ashley walked over to her sister and rubbed her back.

"Philip, Preston, give us a minute. Wait in the hall." Ashley said looking back at them. Her husband hugged her then he and Philip left the room. Ashley walked on the other side of the bed and grabbed her mother's other hand. "Her hand is getting cold. Mom, we love you. Thank you for being there for all of us," she said. Then their brothers came over and kissed their mother's face and then they left out of the room. "We will see you in heaven." Then she looked at Courtney, "She looks like she's asleep doesn't she?" An hour later, Ashley walked over to Courtney and put her arm around her. "Are you ready, Courtney?"

"No, but I know I have to leave," Courtney said in sorrow.

As they walked to the door Courtney turned around for the last time and looked at her mother as Ashley grabbed her hand then they walked out the room hand-in-hand to the waiting area.

"I'll have someone pick up your car and bring it to your house," Ashley said to Courtney, as everyone walked over to them. "Let Philip take you home. Why don't you and Sabrina come over later and stay over my house."

"No. I want to be alone, but I'll probably bring Sabrina over later. Right now I can't think," Courtney said feeling tired.

Philip drove Courtney to his home. The girls were up early

waiting on Lauren to make strawberry and banana hot cakes.

"Mommy, you still have on the same clothes from yesterday," Sabrina said.

"Yes, sweetie," Courtney said, as she bend down and kissed Sabrina's forehead.

"Mommy, your eyes are puffy," Sabrina said looking at her mother's glassy eyes. "Someone made you sad?"

"I have something very important to tell you, sweetheart," Courtney said.

"Lauren and Kianna, let's go to the other room. They need their privacy," Philip said.

"It's okay," Courtney said to Philip, Lauren, and Kianna. "You are just like family to Sabrina and I." Then she looked back at her daughter as she took her hand, "Sabrina, grandmother died early this morning in the hospital."

"Grandma, died?" Sabrina asked puzzled. "Why?"

"Something was wrong with her heart," Courtney said, as she kissed her daughter's hand. "I'm sorry."

"She left without saying goodbye," Sabrina said. Then she hugged her mother tightly.

Courtney took a deep breath as her daughter hugged her. It took all the strength that Courtney had not to burst out in tears. Kianna came over to them and put her arms around Sabrina.

"Your grandmother is gone to heaven like my grandfather," Kianna said.

"That's right, Kianna," Courtney said, smiling. "Grandma is gone to heaven. She loved both of you," she said to Sabrina and Kianna. "Sabrina, I have some things to do. You can stay here or go over to Aunt Ashley's house."

"Mom, I want to be with you," Sabrina said.

"You will but I have grown-up things to do first, and I don't want you to be bored," Courtney said.

"I want to stay here, mommy," Sabrina said.

"Okay," Courtney said. Then she kissed the girls.

Philip drove Courtney home. As soon as she got in, she

packed Sabrina's clothes for the weekend. Courtney assured Philip she was fine. After he left, she looked around her living room where pictures of her mother were displayed then she started crying. Later, she took a bath and sat in a corner of her room in complete darkness and rocked herself until she couldn't go forward or backward anymore. She couldn't eat, sleep or do anything. When the telephone rang, she wouldn't answer it unless she saw on the caller I.D. Ashley, her brothers, or Philip's number. Sabrina called her mother that night to see how she was doing. Courtney had to fake over the telephone that everything was fine so Sabrina wouldn't worry but Philip knew better.

Even though it was hours later, it seems like time was creeping along like a movement of an ant as Courtney sat emotionless in the corner of her room preoccupied by memories of her mother and a heart of hollowness. She got dressed and went over to her mother's place. As she entered and shut the front door, she was greeted by memories of how she used to call out for her mother when she would come inside. She walked through the first level of the house recalling in her mind important things that happened in every room like their long talks in the living room while drinking tea and nibbling on scones, countless dinners in the dining area, and her mother's study room, which was called the prayer room. Then she walked up the stairs to her mother's room and at that moment she felt her heart breaking again into thousands of pieces. She sobbed as she lay down on the side of the bed where her mother used to sleep.

"God, why? I won't be able to handle this!" she cried out, as she took short breaths due to her emotion of pain. She fell asleep unexpectedly for a short time with one of her mother's robes clutched in her arms. When she got herself together she went home.

The next morning, Courtney ran several miles, took a shower and sat in the same corner again. Ashley called.

"How are you holding up?" Ashley asked.

"Not good. How about you?" Courtney asked.

"About the same. Junior and Zakeya took it the worst out of all the children. Junior was always over mom's house for one reason or another."

"I know. Last night I saw Junior's sweater laying on the back of a chair in one of the rooms."

"You went over to mom's place alone?" Ashley asked.

"Yes. I thought I would feel better."

"You should have called me; I could have been there for you. Do you want some company?"

"No, I'm fine," Courtney said softly.

"Have you talked to Sabrina?"

"I talked to her last night and this morning. Thank God Philip said he would take her to school tomorrow. He's coming later to get her clothes."

"Courtney, you should see Sabrina. Matter of fact, she needs to be with you," Ashley said.

"I'm going to see her. She is coming with Philip to pick up some things. Sabrina, is fine where she is."

"You know Sabrina can stay here," Ashley said.

"Of course," Courtney said. "I asked her what she wanted to do. She wants to stay with Kianna and she said she wants to go to school tomorrow instead of staying home."

"We're meeting tomorrow afternoon at one o' clock at my house to discuss funeral arrangements. Is that a good time for you?" Ashley asked.

"I can't," Courtney said, as tears rolled down her face. "It's still difficult for me to accept our mother's death even though I saw it with my own eyes. I really have to go."

"Courtney, it's not easy for any of us. We're going to have to survive off each other's strength. We need you, Courtney."

"Bye, Ashley," Courtney said. Then she hung up the telephone.

Later on that evening Philip came to Courtney's home.

"Courtney, are you okay?" Philip asked, as they walked into the living room.

"Yes. Where is Sabrina?"

"My sister took the girls on a picnic and they haven't returned. I talked to her while driving over here and they are about to leave. I'm sorry they lost track of time."

"It's probably for the best. How is Sabrina holding up?" Courtney asked.

"Well after we left my place yesterday morning, Lauren told me Sabrina lost her appetite. When I came home she was upstairs in Kianna's room lying on the bed crying."

"I was so busy thinking only of myself, I didn't think that she would have taken the news that way. I thought since she was around Kianna she would be okay. You should have called me right away. She could have come home," Courtney said.

"I talked to her. Lauren and Kianna went out for a while. Sabrina and I went to the park and talked about her grandmother. I got her to smile then we went to lunch. She's fine. Ashley has been calling the house checking on her."

"You are just too good to us. Thank you," Courtney said gratefully. "I don't want her to see me like this."

"It's okay for our children to see we have feelings like they do. You shouldn't be here alone. Why don't you go over to Ashley's? I can drive you over to her place."

"No, Philip. I handle things better alone. Ashley wants to discuss mother's funeral arrangements tomorrow. I don't think. I mean, I don't want to do it. I'm frightened. I don't feel that I can make it," Courtney said, as she began to cry. "I'm sorry, Philip. I don't mean to be a crybaby. I am supposed to be strong, right?" she asked, feeling empty and lost. She sat on the couch.

"You're talking nonsense. You are talking about your mother. It's okay to be frightened not sure how to handle a lost that no one can replace and how to go on with life without your love ones. But you have to be strong. It was hard for me when my father died. I didn't want to do a thing but I was the only man in the family, so I had to be everyone's backbone. Courtney, you can do it. It's not going to be easy. I know you want your mother to look nice. You want to say you had something to do with the preparations. Your family needs you more then ever before."

"You're right," she said in despair.

Philip walked over to Courtney and sat next to her while putting his arm around her. She laid her head on his chest and cried. He comforted her with encouraging words. Later she stopped crying. She got up from the couch and walked over to a table, picking up a framed picture of her mother.

"Have you eaten?" Philip asked.

She shook her head.

"I got your shirt wet," Courtney said. "I'm sorry."

"It's not that bad. You look better. Let me fix you something to eat."

"No, Philip. I'm not hungry but I'll eat something later. I know you need to get home; you have work and two little ladies to take to school tomorrow. I'll be fine. Thanks for being here."

"Are you sure you're okay?" Philip asked.

"Yes. I'll pick Sabrina up from school tomorrow," Courtney said.

"I can pick her up tomorrow and bring her home or over to Ashley's place," Philip offered.

"I don't want to impose on you anymore then what I already have."

"You're not. How about this, I'll call you tomorrow and we will discuss it then," he said.

After Philip left the telephone rang.

"Mommy!" Sabrina said happy to hear her mother's voice.

"Sabrina, sweetheart, I miss you," Courtney said, as she smiled.

"I miss you too," Sabrina said.

"Did you enjoy the picnic?" Courtney asked.

"Yes. Mommy, you have been on my mind and Kianna said you have been on her mind too," Sabrina said. "What Kianna? Kianna says she loves you, mommy."

"Tell her I love her too and thank you," Courtney said, as she smiled.

"Lauren already gave us our bath and we're getting ready for bed. Mommy, I want to come home," Sabrina said sadly.

"You will tomorrow but if you want to come home now I'll come and get you. Philip left here with your uniform for tomorrow. Can you wait until tomorrow to come home?" she asked.

"Yes. I love you, mommy. Goodnight," Sabrina said.

Courtney's father received word about their mother while he was away on vacation with his family. They cut the vacation short and flew back to town. Her father talked to Ashley on the plane. Once the plane landed, he went over to Courtney's house.

"Daddy, mom died alone. I never understood what really happened between you and her. She was a good woman," Courtney said.

"Courtney, there are some things that a child would never understand when it comes their parents' divorce," her father said. "Your mother and I became good friends. Actually, she was my best friend. I could talk to her about anything, years after our divorce. We even talked about my marriage with Tiffany. She gave me good pointers that kept me married to my wife today.

Your mother chose not to remarry. That was her choice not yours, not your sister's, or your brothers' or mine. She didn't die alone, honey and I'm not saying that because she had God in her life which is a big plus, but she was happy being Jackeé."

"Daddy, I'm not blaming you for mom being a single woman," Courtney said. "I wondered how you two got along so well after the divorce. I guess you're right, there are some things that a child or in this case an adult won't understand when it comes to parents divorcing."

"Know this, Courtney, your mother and I love all of you very much. I spent quality time with all of you and put everyone through college. I'll continue to support you in anything you do because you will always be apart of me," her father said.

After Courtney's father left, she drank a cup of hot tea and looked through photos of her family. She looked through a host of pictures she took with her mother from the time she was a newborn baby until two weeks ago when she took some pictures at her mom's house. Before she knew it, it was three in the morning. She went to bed with the covers over her head.

She woke up late the next morning when the president called from the newspaper she worked for to express his condolences. Hours later the office sent her flowers and a fruit basket.

After Philip picked up the girls from school, he went over Ashley's house where Courtney was. Courtney felt so much better having Sabrina back at home. Tuesday morning Courtney dropped Sabrina off at school and went to her sister's place for a couple hours and then they went to the funeral home. Thursday came too fast. She woke up thinking, 'Today we will bury my mother.'

Maxwell picked Courtney and Sabrina up from the house and drove them to their mother's home where everyone met. The hearse and the families' cars came to get the immediate family. The pastor from her mother's church prayed at the house then everyone left for the church. The ride that normally took 20 minutes to get to their mother's church seemed like time with no end for the family. Once they arrived at the church they sat in their cars for another ten minutes because the coffin had to be taken inside the church. Ashley and Courtney walked hand-in-hand to the sterling silver coffin with gold handles. They stopped and looked at their mother. They touched her hair, face, and felt her hands for the very last time. Two ladies from the church helped Ashley and Courtney to their seats and they made sure that the family was okay. Before the service started people were already crying, giving their condolences, and saying some encouraging words to different family members about their mother. Courtney was pleased to see the reverend from her church, Reverend Mitchell Solomon, his wife, and even some of her church family during the viewing session. When Philip and Kianna came around, Courtney had her head down for a few moments. As the service began the undertakers closed the coffin. Courtney leaned her head on Maxwell's shoulder and closed her eyes. It seemed the church was spinning around and her hands began to shake a little. Maxwell put his arm around her and whispered over and over again in her ear to breathe. Ashley reached over and touched Courtney's hands wiping her nose. Sabrina got up from where she was sitting with one of her cousins and stood in front of Courtney.

"Mommy," Sabrina cried.

Courtney opened her eyes as tears flowed down her face then she sat Sabrina on her lap and held her close to her. Later Maxwell held Sabrina. The funeral seemed like a Sunday morning service. The service was wonderful. You would have never thought it was a funeral. People were singing and praising God for another soldier going home to be with the Lord. There were a group of men singing her mother's favorite song called 'On My Way Home.' Ashley stood up and started clapping her hands then the rest of the family stood up as well.

People gave three-minute remarks. The pastor asked if anyone else had anything they would like to share. Courtney found herself standing to her feet, pardoning herself to get past her siblings. As she walked to the microphone, she looked down at the coffin again with her mother's initials, JKK, standing for Jackee' Kathryn Kennedy.

"Mom," Courtney said in a sigh, "that is the most beautiful word known to man and comforting to a child of any age. My mom was a saint but I know her best as my mother. I can't speak for my sister or my brothers because I can't feel what they are feeling right now. I know that they loved her and of course we all had personal interactions with her. Whenever my sister or bothers shared anything with our mother it wasn't spread to our ears. Even if we had an insinuation something was going on with one of us she wouldn't say a word.

Whatever I had done wrong in life she never told me, I can't believe you did that, or I told you so, or even if I'm about to make the same mistake again, she wouldn't say, remember when. She was never at a loss for words, she gave sound advice then she was finished with it. She was my best friend. Mom, I miss you some kind of bad," Courtney said, as she looked down on her mother's coffin again. "Carlton, Ashley, Maxwell and I love you so very much. I have one question for you," She said as she smiled. "who is going to feed my Sabrina and me on Sunday afternoons? You know I don't cook. Love you!"

People laughed as they clapped. Ashley and her brothers stood up and hugged Courtney. After the eulogy the family began to walk out of the church behind the body to go to the family cars to proceed to the cemetery.

As Courtney and Sabrina past by where Philip and Kianna were sitting, Kianna got past her father and some other people to get to Sabrina. Philip tried to catch her but she moved a little too fast for him. Courtney looked at Philip and nodded her head and smiled to let him know it was okay. Kianna hugged Courtney around her waist. As they got into the cars, Philip walked up to them telling Kianna to come with him. Courtney told Philip they had enough room in the family car for her. After they left the gravesite everyone went back to the church for the repast. Courtney wasn't hungry, but she made sure the children ate. Philip walked up behind her.

"Courtney," Philip said, as she turned around to him.

"Philip," Courtney said, as she hugged him. "Thanks for coming."

"Sure. Do you need anything?" He asked, as he looked at her.

"Yes. I would like a ride home, please," Courtney replied.

"Have you eaten?" he asked.

"No. I don't want anything," Courtney replied. "I don't feel like talking or putting on a fake smile."

"Let me know when you are ready to leave," he said.

Courtney told her brothers and sister that she was leaving. Ashley asked Philip to stay with Courtney for a little while. The kids were playing in the back seat of the car on their way to Courtney's place. Courtney was in a daze not paying any attention to what was going on around her as she thought about her mother. Philip touched her hand and asked her if she was all right. She squeezed his hand and stated she was fine. Once they got to her house the girls ran upstairs.

"Can I get you anything?" Courtney asked in a daze, as she sat on the couch feeling exhausted.

"No, I can get it myself. You don't mind, do you?" Philip asked.

"Please, help yourself."

Minutes later he brought her a cup of tea.

"What are you thinking about?" He asked.

"About my mom being buried under all that dirt and rocks," Courtney said. "I guess you would say that's crazy."

"No, I wouldn't. I thought the same thing about my father. Is Sabrina going to school tomorrow?" Philip asked.

"I haven't even thought about it. It would be good if she does. I still don't want her to see me like this," Courtney said. "I'm not functioning well at all."

"Sabrina, is not totally functioning as the cheerful child that I know. She may have Kianna around at times to distract her attention regarding the lost of her grandmother, but she's still dealing with the grief. You and your family are getting through this fine. Just like anything in life there are steps. There is grief, laughter of fond memories, sometimes the heart feels content, and grief starts again. But there will be a time when grief no longer reigns in the capacity that it did initially. Then you start taking it one day at a time," he said, as Courtney listened to him and thought about her mother. "If Sabrina wants to go to school tomorrow, I can pick her up in the morning," he said.

"Thanks," Courtney said.

When Philip got ready to leave Sabrina asked Courtney if

Kianna could spend the night with her. Philip spoke up and told them no. Then Kianna asked if Sabrina could spend the night at their house. Courtney agreed since Sabrina wanted to go to school the next day.

The next morning before Sabrina left for school she called her mother but there was no answer. She became concerned. Philip promised Sabrina that he would get in touch with her mother after he dropped her and Kianna off at school. When Philip got to Courtney's house, he saw that her car was gone. He waited an hour then he went past the park where she ran sometimes, but he saw no sign of her. He called Ashley who became concerned herself wondering where her sister was since she didn't mention anything last night about going anywhere. Philip assured Ashley he would find her and not to worry. Philip drove past one place where she would probably be and there she was sitting down at her mother's gravesite. She turned around as he parked his car. He sat on the grass next to her.

"How did you know I would be here?" Courtney asked, as she stared at her mother's grave.

"I'm a good listener and I know you just a little bit," Philip replied, as she looked at him with a smile.

"You're not going to work?" she asked, as she looked at her mother's gravesite again.

"No. I figured a friend would need me to be around today. How long have you been here?"

"Since 5:30 this morning. My intention was to run, but I found myself parked at the front gate of the cemetery. The ground keeper was nice enough to let me in early," Courtney said.

"Courtney, your mother isn't here. Her spirit is in heaven. You do have a daughter that is here alive with you and she needs you. Sabrina called you this morning and she was worried about you."

"Your right, Philip," Courtney said, as she looked down. "Philip?"

"Yes, Courtney."

"When your father died when did the pain stop?" she asked, as tears rolled down her face.

"It took time. People say, as the days go by it gets better. That's not true. I would say as months and years go by. Some days were worse than others. For months, I would become depressed on Fridays because my father died on a Friday afternoon. Then I would think about his death from Friday through Tuesday because we had his funeral on a Tuesday. Now I feel that my father took a long trip and he's not coming back. Courtney, anytime you need to talk about anything, it doesn't matter what time of the day or night it is, call me."

"Thank you."

They sat around for a few minutes then Philip said, "Come on let's go." He helped her up and then she stumbled.

"I lost my balance for a moment there," she said impassively.

"I see," he said concerned. "When was the last time you ate?" Then she turned away from him walking to the car. He got in front of her. "Courtney, when? And I want you to be honest with me!"

"Last Friday night at the school," she said, as she looked up at him. "I'm okay," She said boldly. Then she walked around him.

"That's what you keep saying," he said, as he grabbed her arm. "Are you trying to kill yourself?"

"No, Philip, I'm not trying to kill myself!" she replied, getting irritable.

"You are going to eat something whether you are hungry or not," he said firmly.

Philip followed Courtney home and prepared her something to eat.

Once in a while, he would see tears in her eyes as she tried to blink them away. Later she went upstairs to her bedroom and slept for about six hours. Ashley was at the house when Sabrina got home from school. When Courtney woke up, she looked better and she was surrounded by family and friends.

Courtney found herself agreeing with Philip, as time goes on when losing someone close to you like a mother, it takes months before the pain even begins to ease.

Chapter Six

Philip and Courtney were on the telephone discussing something about the girls.

"Okay. That is even better. I'll pick Sabrina up Saturday morning then I'll take her and Kianna to The Children's Palace of Toys to see Barney. Courtney, do you like the orchestra?" Philip asked.

"It's okay, why?" Courtney asked.

"A good friend of mine sent me tickets as a special guest to one of their performances that will be in town. I don't think Kianna would appreciate it."

"Mmm-mmm. Your right, she wouldn't," Courtney said smiling.

"Why are you making this difficult?" He asked, as he grinned.

"I don't know what you mean, Philip." She continued to beam.

"Would you like to go with me next Sunday evening to The National Symphony Orchestra concert?"

"Yes, I would likc that," she replied.

Courtney didn't find anything she liked in her wardrobe that she wanted to wear to the concert, and she didn't have the time to go shopping due to work schedule. Days later she was at Ashley's house trying on gown after gown that made her look like she was going to a ball, but then her sister found the perfect dress that was hanging in the back of her closet that never been worn.

The night of the performance Philip and Courtney walked

through the long concert halls where people were standing around talking before the concert began. Some people began to stare at Courtney so much that it made her feel a little uncomfortable.

"Philip, do you think I'm underdressed or overdressed for this concert?" She whispered.

"I told you when I picked you up that you looked beautiful. Some people wear clothes that make them, but you make that dress. You're fine," he said, proudly.

During the concert Philip would look over at Courtney from time to time to see the expression on her face. Her eyes were glued to the stage. Once in a while she would smile, pat her hand on her lap, and move her head a little to the music. One piece played for about thirty minutes but seemed like half the time. Towards the ending of a selection Philip asked her if she was okay, she told him never better. He was impressed because the women he had brought to something like that before became bored and couldn't wait to leave.

There was a man that came out on stage to sing who was a special surprise guest. The audience stood up immediately and clapped their hands cheering this man's name before he began to sing. He stood tall and proud as he smiled graciously. Since Courtney knew how to speak Italian, she didn't have difficulty understanding the songs. The man sang so wonderfully that there was something inside Courtney that changed. It was something about the man's voice that moved anyone's soul. His voice was angelic and it made you forget the care of your life at that time then afterward you are encourage that life cares aren't all that bad. After every song the man sang people were standing up, clapping again and again. Courtney felt as though if someone were to say 'find me someone you feel that sings like God'; Courtney could say this man doesn't come any better than what her ears had the pleasure of hearing.

After the concert they went back stage to meet some of Philip's friends that played in the orchestra. Philip's friends asked him and Courtney if they would like to join them for dinner. Once they all arrived to the restaurant they were seated at an exclusive section of the edifice. Then the man that sung at the concert came in. One of Philip's friend introduced him to them. Someone asked the man if he would like to sit at an area of the table but he refused, stating he wanted to sit next to the pretty lady Courtney. Courtney related to Philip's friends so well it was like they knew one another all their lives. When Philip brought her home she told him how she really enjoyed herself. The next day Courtney couldn't wait to pick up Sabrina from school and to go to the record store to buy some CD's of classical, opera and other music that interested her.

Philip and Courtney decided to have a surprise birthday party for the girls at a place called The Children's Castle Dome. They sent invitations to family and friends. The girls' birthday fell on a Thursday. After work Philip and Courtney took them out for dinner and had an ice cream cake designed for them. Friday night the girls went over to Ashley's house believing they were going to be there for the weekend. Saturday afternoon a hundred guests were at the birthday party waiting for the girls to arrive. Ashley was running late. When they arrived at The Children's Castle Dome, Sabrina was about to run to one of the rides.

"Sabrina, come here. I want you and Kianna to sit here," Ashley said, as she wiped one of her children's noses.

"But Aunt Ashley I want to—" Sabrina began to say.

"Sabrina, I want you and Kianna to have a seat," Ashley said firmly. "Come on. I'll be back and then you can get on any ride you want."

Both of the girls obeyed. Ashley took her children to where everyone else was gathered.

"Aunt Ashley has been acting strange," Kianna said sadly because she wanted to get up and play one of the games.

"I know. She won't let us have any fun," Sabrina said disappointed, as she put one foot down on the floor leaning over to the side of the seat trying to look around the corner to see what was going on with everyone else inside the restaurant. One lady smiled at Sabrina from where she was sitting as she saw Sabrina's pretty white socks with the cuff turned down to the ankle trimmed with white lace of roses in her black patent leather shoes. When Sabrina saw Ashley coming she turned around quickly and sat straight up in the seat. "Here she comes." she said, while looking at Kianna

"Okay girls let's go. Take my hands," Ashley said, as she reached out her hands to the girls.

They walked a couple of feet and then everyone screamed surprise! The girls were surprised and ecstatic about their party. Philip and Courtney were chatting with each other's family and friends. Kids were running around, playing games, riding on rides, and some were crying. Then it was time to sing happy birthday.

After everyone sang the birthday song, Courtney said, "Honey, make a wish." She put her arms around their shoulders.

The girls grabbed each other's hand.

"We already made it months ago," Kianna said, smiling to Sabrina who was nodding her head agreeing with Kianna.

They blew out the candles and opened their presents. An hour later everyone in their party was gone. Courtney and Philip were tired. They were glad that they didn't have to clean up after anyone and wait around for parents to pick up their children.

"Come on, Kianna. Where is Sabrina?" Courtney asked, as she looked around. "There she is. Sabrina, we're leaving," She said to her daughter. Sabrina smiled as she stopped what she was doing and walked over to them. "Kianna, your dad is waiting outside for you. Did you girls have a good time?" She asked while taking the girls by their hand walking to the entrance of the restaurant.

"Yes, mommy," Sabrina said while looking around at Kianna grinning suspiciously. When they got outside Philip was standing by the door.

"We have something to ask you and my daddy," Kianna said to Courtney then she looked at her father.

"Let's go, Kianna. You two can talk to us later," Philip said.

"No, we want to talk now! How about over there on the bench. Please, this is our special day, right?" Sabrina asked, as she and Kianna looked at their parents.

"Okay," Philip said. "Come on Courtney let's have a seat or they will not let us rest tonight." He and Courtney sat on the bench. The girls stood in front of them smiling.

"You have our undivided attention," Courtney said, as her and Philip listened.

"We want to tell you our wish," Kianna said.

"Honey, you're not supposed to tell your wish because it may not come true," Courtney said.

"You don't understand," Sabrina said. "You two can make it come true. Philip, is it okay if I call you daddy?"

"Sabrina!" Courtney said flabbergasted. "You know better to—"

"Courtney," Kianna said interrupting Courtney's statement to her daughter, "I want to call you mommy," Kianna said. "Sometimes it wants to slip out but I don't know how you would take it."

"Kianna, I don't believe you!" Philip said surprised.

"We have discussed this among ourselves for a while," Sabrina said.

Philip and Courtney looked at each other then they smiled.

"Kianna, I'm flattered you want to call me your mother. I see you like my own daughter. It would be okay by me if it's all right with your dad," Courtney said.

"Daddy, is it okay?" Kianna asked waiting patiently for the right answer.

"Well," Philip said hesitating, "only if it's okay with Courtney," he said. Then he smiled, "if I can call Sabrina my daughter."

Sabrina looked at Courtney smiling.

"It's okay, Sabrina," Courtney said to her.

"We're sisters!" Kianna and Sabrina shouted as they hugged one another then they hugged Philip and Courtney.

"Do I have to give you an allowance too, Sabrina?" Philip asked, as he picked her up in his arms.

"Yes, I expect an allowance, daddy," Sabrina said, as she hugged him around his neck.

They all laughed.

Chapter Seven

During the summer months of school being out the girls spent their summer together at a local daily camp. They had lots of fun during different activities during the day but they hated homework every other weekend learning about nature. The girl's family took them on vacation a week before school started. However, they couldn't wait to see each other at school to begin third grade together. A couple days before school started, Philip had to go out of town on business. Courtney suggested to Philip to let his daughter stay with her. When Kianna came into Courtney's house, she hugged her and went into the living room and sat down on the edge of the sofa. Philip walked in and kneeled in front of her.

"Honey, I'm sorry about this. I promise I'll go with you to school when I get back. I got to take this trip," Philip said.

"Okay," Kianna said, softly fighting back the tears. Her father hugged her then he stood up.

"Courtney, where is Sabrina?" Philip asked.

"She's upstairs asleep. I can wake her. She's been asleep for over an hour," Courtney said.

"No. That's okay. Tell her that I said hi and I'll call her later," Philip said. Then he looked at his daughter who was looking down at her hands. He kissed her forehead. "See you later, Kianna. I love you. Thanks, Courtney."

Courtney walked him to the door. "Philip, don't worry about Kianna. She's going to be fine." She shut the door behind him.

As he started the car, Courtney opened the door walking

out with Kianna. Kianna came down the steps as her father got out the car.

"I love you, daddy. Please come back." she said. Her father hugged her.

"I'll. I'll call you as soon as I get to the hotel in Phoenix. I've to get to the airport now." Philip said. Then he saw Sabrina walking down the steps. He hugged and kissed her as well then got into the car and backed out the driveway, seeing the girls holding hands waving bye to him.

The girls went up stairs and played for a little while. Then Kianna came downstairs to the living room where Courtney was reading a book. She sat on the couch as Courtney put her arms around her.

"You miss your father?" Courtney asked, as she kissed her head.

"Yes," Kianna said, as she snuggled up to Courtney resting her head on her chest. "You remember those dreams I told you about my daddy leaving me?" She looked up at Courtney. Courtney nodded her head. "I had the dream again a couple days ago when daddy told me about his trip. I remember what you told me how to believe my daddy loves me and he wouldn't leave me."

"That's right. He'll be back the day after tomorrow. Whether your daddy is here or away on business, I'm always here for you, Kianna. I love you. Never forget that."

Kianna closed her eyes as she nodded her head.

Both of the girls first day of third grade was great. Kianna was very happy to see her father a day later but as ususal she didn't want to go home.

For six months, Courtney and Philip were very busy with work. When the holidays came they spent some time with family but most of the time was used to rest because the next day was back to the drawing board. No matter how busy or what was going on they would make sure to spend some time with the girls.

It was a dreary, raining Thursday morning in March that already felt like a long day. Courtney already had a meeting with the staff writers and given them assignments. Then she had another meeting with her manager, as well as a briefing with other editors that she managed. Courtney felt a little chilly sitting in her office while listening to the heavy raindrops constantly hitting the windows. She keyed some information into the computer and then she got herself a cup of hot tea. When she got back to her office, she smiled seeing that the rain stopped and the sun was coming through the clouds. She sat at her desk and began to review some articles that needed to be printed in the newspapers for the next morning edition. She received a call.

"Good morning, this is Ms. Kennedy speaking," Courtney answered.

"Hello, Ms. Kennedy. This is Mr. Franklin. How are you doing today?" Philip asked, sounding very professional.

"I'm fine, Philip and you?" Courtney asked, as she looked up from the column wondering what was going on for him to call her sounding so upbeat.

"Good. I'm calling you on this beautiful sunny morning to see if you would like to take a two hour lunch with me?"

"Two hour lunch? What's wrong with an hour? What's going on?" Courtney asked curiously.

"I can only answer one question at a time. However, I would like to answer them in person. How about I pick you up at noon?" Philip asked.

"That's fine. I'll see you then," she replied, wondering to herself again what was really going on.

Philip arrived at Courtney's office early. Since Courtney was out of her office, he picked up a newspaper that was sitting on her desk and began to read it. As Courtney entered her office, she noticed his posture was somehow different than any other time with his leg crossed over his knee with luxuriousness of gratification. He looked at her with a smile as she spoke to him walking around to her desk.

"Good afternoon," he said, putting the paper away. "I'm sorry, I'm a little early."

"It's okay. Well, Philip, look at you! You are definitely happy about something. What's going on?" Courtney asked suspiciously.

"I've been hungry since ten-thirty this morning!" he said, smiling.

Philip was all smiles on their way to the restaurant. The *maître d* showed them to their table. As the *maître d* attempt to pull Courtney's chair, Philip told the gentleman he would get her seat. Courtney smiled at the *maître d* as she sat down. While Philip was sitting down in his seat smiling at Courtney a waiter came over to take their drink orders.

"Philip, what have you so excited?" Courtney asked.

"I got a promotion, Courtney! Actually it's better then a promotion. I guess the words that comes to mind is chief. Leader," he said, as she tried to figure out what he was trying to say. "I knew," he said, as he laughed, "one day I would get there but never this early in my career."

"That's great! What is it?" she asked, as Philip clapped his hands with excitement as he looked at her. He laughed again as his facial expression filled with enthusiasm. "Are you going to make me pull it out of you?"

"No. Starting next month," he spoke slowly, as he folded his hands. "I'll no longer be a senior executive but I'll be the new CEO and President of Telecommunications at TELCOM of America."

"That's terrific!" she squeaked, as she got up from the table and hugged him.

"I'm so proud of you, Philip! I'm surprised but not as I never thought this could happen, unless you were close to retirement age. But because of your early achievement in your career with hard work and determination paid off more then what you expected. I should be buying you lunch."

"No, you have helped me out in so many ways with

Kianna. I have been working a lot of hours and going on business trips. You have been a blessing to my daughter by being a mother figure to her. When I worked long hours in the past or extensive traveling, my mother or my sister would have Kianna then I had to jump over hoops because Kianna would be upset with me. Courtney, even though we're best of friends," he said, as he reached for her hand, "somehow I feel we did this together. You are appreciated."

"Thank you. I'm so happy for you. I want to make a toast," Courtney said, as she lifted her glass. "To a man who has been a blessing obviously to TELCOM of America, to his family, and my family as well is now being rewarded for the good deeds he has done."

"Thank you," Philip said, as he was about to clink his glass to Courtney's thinking she was finished.

"Wait a minute!" she said, as she pulled her glass away from his. "I'm not done," she said, as he smiled at her, "To a man who is an example of the words responsibility, courage, stability, and honor. Congratulations again, Mr. Franklin the new president and CEO of TELCOM. Now, I'm finished."

"Thank you, Courtney," he said, as they clinked their glasses. Then he took a few swallows of his drink. "Now I'll have a car and a driver at my beckon call instead of during office hours which I probably won't use unless really I have too."

"I know," Courtney said, as she smiled. "You don't like to be handicapped. However, I feel you'll get use to the amenities."

"Maybe or maybe not. Courtney, people in the business world will see me in a different light. This is definitely new to me, being the head of a successful business in science and technology that I am passionate about."

Courtney smiled as she listened to his cheerful voice as he talked about the company and where he wanted it to go. But, at the same time she noticed how down to earth he was; not letting his success own him, rather he owned his success.

"I have to find a new house. I'm thinking a place in the suburban areas. You know to entertain my family, friends and at times have business parties. I have plenty of time for that. Courtney, I want you to help me find a home."

"That sounds like fun," she said, as the waiter brought over their meals.

Later on that evening at Ashley's house Courtney was telling her sister about Philip's wonderful news.

"House hunting? Wow! It's a shame you don't see what I see," Ashley said teasingly.

"See what, Ashley?" Courtney asked.

"Why is it you are so observant of other people's lives but when it comes to your own, you are clueless? Philip could have called a real estate agency that could find him something in minutes," Ashley said, as she snapped her fingers, "but he wants you to help him find something for him, his daughters and you, the future Mrs. Franklin," she said, trying to keep a straight face.

"What?" Courtney asked in shocked. "I don't know why I even bother to tell you anything, Ashley. You always have to read in something that isn't there," she said, frustrated.

"You know opposite attracts. I read into everything and you always act like this," Ashley said.

There were some nights Philip would work more hours then ever before. Courtney didn't mind letting Kianna spend some nights at her place during the week and taking her to school along with Sabrina. Actually Kianna was some help to Courtney by putting the bowls on the table, filling them with cereal and putting milk, toast and orange juice on the table as well.

Courtney asked Philip if he would like to hangout one Saturday evening with her. He accepted and wanted to know what they were going to do. She wasn't too sure. The morning of their getting together, he called to cancel because something came up at work. She was disappointed because she bought tickets to a symphony orchestra. She went alone. Philip called her the next day to apologize.

"What did you do yesterday?" Philip asked.

"I had tickets to the symphony orchestra at the Pavilion Hall. I went and it was really nice," she said cheerful.

Philip was quiet for a couple of seconds.

"You had tickets to a symphony concert? Why didn't you say anything?" he asked, in a dispirited tone of voice.

"No, you had to work and I understand that," Courtney said sincere.

"Did you go alone?" Philip asked wondering whom she could have gone with. "Why?" she asked, teasingly.

"I was just asking," he said trying to sound like it didn't matter to him. "I wish I was there. I'll make it up to you," He said with assurance.

"Please. You don't have to make up anything to me. I wasn't the one who missed out on anything. It was you," she said, as she smiled.

"Courtney," he said distinctly, "you may not have missed the concert but you missed my company and I missed yours. It seems since I accepted this new and challenging position, which I'm not complaining, I'm gone more then ever but it will slow down once I have everything under my belt. Being the head of a prodigious company is different then being a senior executive even though the previous president had me doing most of his work for years."

Philip's picture was on front of the business section of the newspapers and months later on every business magazine everywhere concerning his successful career at TELCOM which was the third largest telecommunication company in the world.

Since a long holiday was coming up, Ashley and Preston rented a house in the mountains in Wisconsin. Courtney and the girls went along. They were having an okay time resting. Preston enjoyed his rest from the city. A man who owned a house a half a mile walked up to them as they were sitting on the front porch.

"Hello," the stranger said.

"How are you doing? How can I help you?" Preston asked, as he stood up from his seat and walked to the edge of the step.

"I'm sorry to bother you folks, but I'm having car problems. I need a jump," the stranger said.

"Sure man. Give me a second," Preston said wanting to help.

"My name is Justin Miles. I own the house down the road."

"My name is Preston. This is my wife Ashley and my sister Courtney. I'll be back out," He said. Then he went into the house.

"Mr. Miles, is your family here with you?" Ashley asked.

"You can call me, Justin, please. No, I'm not married and I don't have any children. I needed a break from my surroundings," he said.

As soon as Justin said those wonderful words 'I'm not married,' Ashley eyes gotten wider and she became more interested in his life.

"Please, Justin, have a seat while you are waiting on my husband," Ashley said. Justin thanked Ashley as he walked up on the porch and took a seat. "Can I pour you a glass of lemonade?"

"Yes, please. It's really hot out here," Justin said, as Ashley passed him a glass of lemonade.

"Thank you. I'm really sorry to bother you," Justin said.

"You're not bothering us at all. Right, Courtney?" Ashley asked, as Courtney candidly looked at her.

"I should have bought a battery earlier before I came here but I kept putting it off," Justin said, as Preston walked outside. "Once I get a jump I'll go into town to purchase one."

"I'm going into town myself," Preston said. "If you like you can ride in town with me, we can pick up a battery. Oh, let me get the car keys—that will help."

"Thank you, I would appreciate that," Justin said, as Preston went back inside the house to get the car keys.

"What do you do for a living, Justin?" Ashley asked.

"Come on, Ashley, the man needs a jump. He's not here for an interrogation," Courtney said, faking a smile.

"It's okay," Justin said, smiling. "I'm the CEO of Commercial Banks Inc. in Texas."

"I see," Ashley said, smiling at Courtney. "Justin, do you like southern cooking?"

"Yes, whenever I can get it," Justin replied.

"Would you like to have dinner with our family this evening? We have plenty," Ashley said, as Courtney looked shocked at her.

"That's very kind of you," Justin said.

"Is that a yes, Justin?" Ashley asked, as she smiled.

"Yes," he replied, as Courtney gave her sister the eye.

"Good! Dinner will be at 6:00 this evening," Ashley said. She was pleased that he accepted the invitation. She wouldn't look at her sister again.

Justin looked over at Courtney and smiled at her, then she smiled at him. Preston came out the house.

"Okay, I'm ready," Preston said. "Baby, I'll be back. Do any of you need anything?" He asked, as he looked at his wife and Courtney.

"No, we're fine," Ashley said. "Honey, Justin will be having dinner with us this evening."

"Okay," Preston said, looking surprised.

Preston and Justin left. Courtney looked at Ashley who acted as if she was reading her book.

"I don't believe you, Ashley!"

Ashley put the book down.

"What?" Ashley asked, as she looked mystified. "Oh, about Justin? People out here are friendly like that. We never know when we may be in need ourselves."

"In need, Ashley? He's not in need for food, just a jump," Courtney exclaimed.

"Come on, Courtney, don't you think he's cute? He's successful, single, which is a plus and he loves southern cooking. I did all I can for you with this one," Ashley said, as if she was doing her a favor. "The ball is in your court."

"What?" Courtney asked confused.

"I have to start dinner. Why don't you help so I can say you did most of the cooking," Ashley said. Then she walked into the house. Courtney sat back in her seat, upset with her arms folded.

After the children were fed dinner they were sent downstairs to the basement to watch television and play games. Ashley had Zakeya and her son Junior to make sure that the kids were under control, for a price of course. When Justin arrived at the house, he brought Ashley and Courtney beautiful flowers. Justin and Preston went to another room to talk and watch television until dinner was ready. They weren't through dinner before the children became bored and wanted to come upstairs. After dinner the men went downstairs to play pool. Ashley and Courtney were putting the dishes into the dishwasher.

"Courtney, why don't you go downstairs and see what the guys are doing. No, never mind. On second thought, go downstairs and tell Preston I need him for something. I can finish up here. Go ahead!" Ashley demanded, while wiping the kitchen counter.

"No, Ashley," Courtney said getting angry. "And I want you to stop trying to force something that isn't meant to be."

"How do you know it's not meant to be?" Ashley asked feeling frustrated, as she stopped what she was doing and looked at her sister. "You hardly said anything to the man during dinner. I mean, you talked, but you didn't show any interest. What is your problem? You don't want a terrific man like Philip in your life. You keep saying you don't want more than a friendship with him. As for Justin, he seems to be really nice, he is a successful business man and he would make a woman very happy.

"If you think I'm going to jump through hoops over Justin, you can forget it! And as for Philip, you can leave him out of this. I'm going to bed before I say something I'll regret. Just stay out of my personal life, Ashley. And I mean it!"

"Courtney," Ashley said, in a soft tone. "I want you to find happiness like my husband and I. I want you to get married and have children like you always dreamed," Ashley said.

"I'm happy!" She said, as her voice screeched. "You act as if being single at a certain age is a handicap. Just because I'm not married doesn't mean I'm incomplete or incompetent that I can't function through life because I'm a Ms. and not a Mrs. I'm going to bed. Goodnight!" She turned around to the kitchen door and nudged it leaving out. Ashley took the dish cloth and threw it on the counter top shaking her head to herself as the door swung forcefully a few times.

Courtney went outside and sat on the steps to enjoy God's fresh air. Twenty minutes later Justin walked to the inside of door.

"Hi, Courtney," Justin said, through the screen door. Then he walked outside.

"Justin, hello," Courtney said as she turned around to look at him.

"Is it okay if I join you?"

"Sure," Courtney replied, as he sat on the step next to her. "I love this kind of night air. It looks like we won't need the air-conditioners on tonight."

Then it was silence between the two as they looked straight ahead into the night. It seemed that the crickets' shrills and chirping were getting louder and louder. Once in a while they would see a lightening bug light up different areas of the grounds.

"Dinner was great. You have a nice family," Justin said trying to make conversation.

"Thank you. I'm glad you're enjoying yourself," Courtney said, smiling as she looked at him. Then she looked straight ahead again.

"I know your sister was trying to fix us up," he said.

"I'm sorry about that. She can be a little aggressive at

times," Courtney said, feeling embarrassed.

"Really!" Justin said, as Courtney smiled. "I would have never known that," he said jokingly, as she laughed. "I didn't mind. It's not everyday when I meet a pretty lady such as you with brains and not pushing herself on a handsome man like myself." He laughed.

"You really believe in patting yourself on the back don't you?" She smiled.

"If I don't who will," he said, as they both smiled.

As they talked, she became comfortable around him. She found him to be a deep person that had concerns about the world as a whole. Ashley brought something out for them to drink. Later Kianna and Sabrina came out with Ashley.

"Mommy, we want to say goodnight," Kianna said.

"Come here let me give you two a kiss. Are you going to say goodnight to Mr. Miles?" Courtney asked, as Ashley walked past the opened door and noticed her sister and Justin were still sitting outside.

"You beautiful young ladies sleep well. Goodnight," Justin said.

"Mommy, can you come upstairs and tuck us in bed?" Kianna asked.

"Sure," Courtney said, as she got up.

"No!" Ashley said, opening the screen door. "I meant, you don't have to do it right now, Courtney. I'm going to read the children a bed time story."

"Okay. When I come in I'll check in on you two," Courtney said seating back down.

"That's a good idea. Come on girls let's go in," Ashley said, fanning her hand for the girls to come back inside the house.

Justin and Courtney talked for hours about their work, traveling, and she only laughed at three jokes out of ten. The only light that was left on inside of the house was at the entrance door.

"Courtney, it's 11:00 p.m." Justin said looking at his

watch.

"Really." Then she looked at her watch. "Wow!"

"I better get ready to go," he said, as he shook her hand.

"It has really been great talking to you," Courtney said.

"This is a first for me in a very long time sitting outside enjoying good company and looking up at the stars. Are you running in the morning?" he asked.

"Yes but late morning. Maybe around 11:00 a.m. if the children let me sleep," she said.

After Justin left Courtney went into one of the children's rooms to check on the girls. She went to Sabrina to kiss her goodnight.

"Mommy," Sabrina whispered.

"Why are you not asleep young lady," Courtney asked Sabrina.

"I can't sleep. Aunt Ashley made us take a nap earlier during the day," she said.

"Close your eyes and count sheep," Courtney said. Then she went over to Kianna. "Kianna, you can't sleep either?"

"No, mommy," Kianna said.

"Aunt Courtney, can I get a kiss too?" Marcia asked.

Before Courtney knew it, she kissed everyone in the room. No one could sleep. Courtney opened the windows a little more, took out a book, sat in the middle of the floor and read to the children and acted out some of the parts. Thirty minutes later the kids started falling asleep except for Ponjona one of Ashley's children. Courtney lay on the floor like she was acting out another part of the book and fell asleep.

The next morning Courtney woke up around 8:00 a.m. and went for a run then after that she took a hot shower and went back to bed until 3:00 p.m. After Courtney got her several hours of rest she came downstairs.

"Well, you finally woke up. Are you hungry?" Ashley asked.

"No not really," Courtney said, stretching. "I'll eat a fruit."

"You missed, Justin."

"Really?" Courtney asked sarcastically.

"Yes. He's gone with Preston to take the children in town. While he was waiting on Preston, he kept looking up the stairs as if he was wishing you would come down. So, what's going on between you and Justin?" Ashley asked. Courtney gave her a wicked look. "Just kidding. I thought about what you said last night and my husband got on me about match-making too. It won't happen again."

"What was that you said?" she asked not believing what she heard.

"You have my word. I'll not match make again. I'll try my best to mind my business," Ashley said, praying she could keep her word.

"I'm going to have to give my brother a hug for that one. Finally! Someone on my side." Courtney exclaimed, relieved as she walked out the kitchen.

When the children came back from town they were fed and tired. Courtney sat at the table with Preston, Justin, and Ashley watched them playing cards.

"What plans do you and your family have tomorrow?" Justin asked Preston, as he put a card down on the table.

"Nothing important," Preston replied, looking discouraged at his hands holding bad playing cards. "Why?"

"I have some good friends about 20 miles from here that have a farm. I'm going to visit them tomorrow and ride some bulls. I'm sure they wouldn't mind me bringing your family along," Justin said.

"Hey, that sounds great! What do you think Ashley, Courtney?" Preston asked.

"I know the kids would love it," Ashley replied, as Courtney agreed.

"Good. Bring a change of clothes. Wear something to the farm that you really don't care about. It's truly a farm," Justin said.

Everyone got up early for breakfast. The children was excited to do something different like going on a farm. They took the vans and Justin's truck down to the farm and they sang songs the whole way. Once they arrived at the farm, two wonderful elderly people met them at the front entrance. They were the owners of the huge farm. They had one of the workers on the farm to give them a tour around their place. After the tour they drove to the owners' house for lunch where they learned the history of their land. Then afterwards the children rode on the back of farm trucks and they got the opportunity to ride on ponies and the adults rode on the horses. The children also got a chance to feed and pat the animals. For the main event, Justin got on a bull to see how long he could ride it without falling off. Everyone clapped and cheered him on. The first time he stayed on a bull for 3 seconds and the last time he stayed on for 8 seconds. Then Preston decided he wanted to try it. Ashley wasn't having that. She wasn't ready to be a widow.

Justin took them to a hog pin.

"Where are the pigs?" Stanley asked.

"They have already been fed. There is another reason why we're here," Justin said, grinning. "I hope Courtney has a sense of humor."

Justin picked Courtney up and dropped her in the mud. Everyone looked at him in shock. Then they looked at Courtney wondering what her reaction was going to be. Courtney immediately jumped up, almost falling down.

"What!" She shouted getting up then falling backwards.

When Courtney got her bearing, she grabbed Justin by his shirt and pulled him in the hog pen with her. She began to throw mud at him and he at her. Then Courtney threw mud at Ashley and Preston standing outside the hog pin. Before they knew it everyone was in the hog pen except for Kianna and Sabrina. They stood around pointing and laughing at one of their cousins. Brian one of Ashley's sons got out of the pigpen and picked up the girls one at a time as they screamed to let them go while kicking. He did in the mud. They started to cry. Everyone jumped on Brian for what he did to the girls. Preston held his son's hands behind his back, so everyone could throw mud at him.

After the fun was over they were hosed down with water. Then they took showers and blew dry their hair. They had a wonderful dinner. Kianna was falling asleep at the table. Everyone was tired. When they got home, no one had to be told it was bedtime. Justin came downstairs where Courtney was putting something away.

"Courtney, I've already said goodnight to Preston and Ashley. I'm sorry that this has to end for me, but I'll be leaving early tomorrow morning. I probably won't be waving to you in the morning when you go running," Justin said.

"You're leaving in the morning?" She asked.

"Yes. My plane will be here first thing. I want to be well rested on Tuesday morning before returning back to the old grind. I'll keep in touch with Preston. I might be coming your way for a visit," he said.

"Make sure you do," Courtney said.

"It's been a pleasure meeting you, Courtney," he said, as he hugged her. "You're a special lady."

"Thank you. Goodnight," she said.

Courtney got up the next morning for her run. As she approached Justin's property, she saw him walking to his plane. He looked over and saw Courtney. He waved to her and she waved back to him as she ran. As the plane took off, he looked down on her smiling.

Later on that week Courtney and Philip were talking on the telephone about Kianna.

"Kianna, told me she had a great time in the mountains. Who is Justin Miles that has taken a liking to you?" Philip asked.

"Kianna, told you that?" Courtney asked, wondering how Kianna came to that conclusion.

"No she didn't," He replied. "Kianna, told me the fun time

you guys had on someone's farm. It seems you and Justin like mud. Kianna told me about the mud fight."

"Oh, we were just having some fun. Justin, is a nice man. That's it," she said, impassively.

"That's it?" Philip asked skeptical.

"Yes," Courtney replied. "Anyway he lives in Texas and I don't want anything from anyone. Like you and me for instance, I don't feel pressure when we're around one another. We go out and have a good time. Nothing more and nothing less. That's the way I like it."

Justin and Preston kept in touch with one another. Justin asked Ashley to check with Courtney to see if it would be all right if he could call her from time to time. When Courtney agreed to allow Justin to keep in contact with her, he would either communicate by telephone or they would e-mail one another occasionally. Justin began to see Courtney like a dear friend or sister type of relationship. But he wanted a little more than friendship.

Chapter Eight

It was two weeks before Mother's Day and the students had to think of something that they would like to mail to their mothers. The children had a choice of either writing a poem, making a Mother's Day card, or the school would supply selections of cards that the children could paste their picture inside. The pictures where taken with a Polaroid camera. Kianna and Sabrina had their pictures taken then they pasted it in the cards for Courtney. They also addressed their own envelopes and placed a stamp of a red rose on it. A few days before Mother's Day, a manager from a local post office came to the school and collected the mail from each classroom. The children were very excited about mailing something to their mothers.

The day before Mother's Day, Philip took the girls shopping to buy Courtney and his mother a gift. When Mother's Day arrived, Philip, Kianna, his sister, and brother-in-law spent the entire day with his mother. Then that evening he and Kianna went over to Courtney's house for dessert where he brought over a designed Mother's Day cake.

Three weeks later it was time for the children to decide what they wanted to do for Father's Day. The children had the same choices like they had for Mother's Day. Kianna wanted to take another picture and put it in a card for her father. Sabrina wanted to write a paper on what Father's Day meant to her. One school morning, Sabrina was sitting at her desk writing her paper when Kianna and another little girl named Vanessa came over to see what Sabrina was doing.

"Sabrina," Vanessa said, as Sabrina turned over her paper not wanting them to see what she was writing, "what are you writing?"

"Something about my daddy. I'm not finished," Sabrina said smiling. "Let me see what you have done for your father?"

"I'll have to show you later. Mrs. McQue is going to help me put the glitter on my card that I made," Vanessa said, as the teacher called her name. "I guess she's ready for me. I'll be back." She walked away.

"Are you going to let me see what you are writing about your father so far? How are you going to send it to him if you don't know where he is?" Kianna asked.

"I'm not writing about my real father. I'm writing about our daddy," she said.

"Really!" Kianna said excited. "I want to read it," she said reaching for her paper. Sabrina moved the paper back so Kianna couldn't get it.

"No, I don't want you to see it. I'm still thinking of what I want to say. Promise me you won't say anything to our daddy about this," Sabrina said.

"I promise," Kianna said, quickly. "Now are you going to let me see what you wrote so far?"

"No, Kianna!" she said getting hyper. "I want you to double promise me, you won't even say to daddy, you know a secret to get him curious. I want this to be a big surprise to him."

"Okay, okay, I double promise, I won't say anything to daddy," Kianna said reassuring Sabrina. "I'll leave you alone so you can finish." Kianna walked away ten steps away from Sabrina then she eased behind Sabrina's chair to look over her shoulders. Sabrina could tell someone was standing behind her as she turned her paper over again. Then she saw it was Kianna who she gave a mean look to. Kianna smiled, walking away.

Sabrina wasn't finished with her paper before it was time to go to her next class, so her teacher allowed her to finish it at home. After dinner that evening Courtney knocked on Sabrina's room door.

"Come in, mom," she said, turning over her paper.

"Are you still doing your homework?" Courtney asked.

"Yes, ma'am. I need to finish it," Sabrina said, as she turned around to her desk.

"Would you like for me to help you with it?"

"No ma'am, I can do it by myself," Sabrina said, taping the eraser of the pencil on her paper waiting for Courtney to leave her room.

"Honey, it seems you are really deep in thought. Do you want to tell me what your subject is about?" she asked, as Sabrina turned around smiling at her.

"Mom, can I use the computer to type my paper? But, I want to do it alone," she said.

"Sure, honey, come on," Courtney said, smiling.

Courtney fell asleep on the couch waiting for Sabrina to type her paper. Forty minutes later, Sabrina came down the steps in her robe with Bugs Bunny slippers on her feet. She leaned over and kissed her mother with minty breath.

"Goodnight, mommy," Sabrina said smiling.

Courtney sat up on the couch.

"Honey, are you finished typing your paper?" Courtney asked.

"Yes, ma'am and I also printed it," she said smiling. "I already took a bath and brushed my teeth," she said proudly.

"Oh, good," Courtney said smiling, as she reached for Sabrina and hugged her. "Would you like for me to read over your paper?"

"No, ma'am. It's perfect. Can I have one of your folders to put my paper in?"

"Sure. Come on, let me put you to bed," Courtney said.

Sabrina smiled as she put her paper in a blue folder then she put it in her book bag. Courtney helped Sabrina to get in bed then she gave her daughter a big hug and kiss. As Courtney turned off the lamps, Sabrina told her mother that she loved her and her mother told her the same.

The next night Sabrina's teacher read her paper with tears in her eyes. The next day the teacher asked Sabrina if they could put her paper in the weekly newspaper for next week that would be sent to parents. That Friday before Father's Day the teacher had the kids read a copy of their cards or paper. Then it was Sabrina's turn.

"What My Daddy Means To Me On Father's Day"

I have a new daddy this year so I have a lot to celebrate. He didn't become my daddy legally or through marriage, but in my heart. We only have been father and daughter for a year, but he has been a friend for years. Before he became my new daddy, I saw him as a brilliant man with soft-spoken words that linger in my heart. He has always shown me kindness, love, understanding, and most of all he gives the best hugs in the whole wide world! He was there for me when my grandmother died. He has taken more time with me even when he had a lot going on. One day he took my sister Kianna and me fishing. We had a lot of fun, he told us fish stories and we even imagined that we were on an island that he characterized in the story. Then he really made me feel special later that day when he gave me my own fishing rod. One Saturday my mother, my sister, and I were supposed to go ice-skating but something came up and my mother couldn't take us. When daddy got off from working a long hard day, he surprised us and took us ice-skating and afterwards we went to McDonald's. In my opinion, he is an example of what a positive male role model should be in a dad. I wish that all kids who don't have their father in their lives could have one like my sister and I. For once in my life, I know what a father is. I'm proud to say that Philip Franklin is the best thing that happened to me. Daddy, thank you for making my dreams come true. Happy Father's Day, Daddy.

With lots and lots of love,
Sabrina

Everyone in class clapped as Kianna smiled from ear to ear. After class some of the kids asked Kianna could Philip be their daddy too. She told them she didn't think so because her allowance would probably be cut back.

When Courtney read the school's newspaper that evening, she smiled feeling so proud of her daughter independently done a job well.

Meanwhile, Philip was at work exhausted from another long day. He just wanted to go home and unwind, but he had to wait on an important call. While trying to wait patiently on the call, he looked in his briefcase for the newspaper and he saw the school paper. The front cover read, 'Father of the Year Is:' Then he read the article. When he saw his name he felt deeply touched as his eyes became watery.

"Sabrina," he said softly in a surprised tone. Then his secretary tapped on the door. He wiped his eyes, "Come in," he said clearing his voice.

"Philip, Mr. Robinson is on the line for you and here is the report you wanted," she said, as Philip nodded not looking at her. "Philip, are you all right?"

"Yes, I got something in my eye," he said, as he looked down at the report on his desk. As his secretary began to turn around with concern, "Lillian, read this," he said, proudly as he passed the paper to her. Then he took the call.

A couple minutes later Philip hung up the telephone.

"Philip, this is wonderful! I can see why you would have something in your eye," Lillian said, as she and Philip smiled. "You must be very proud of Sabrina. You and Kianna are blessed to have her in your lives."

Philip couldn't wait to get to Courtney's house to see the girls. When Philip got to the house, he called Sabrina downstairs. She walked down the steps as Kianna peeked around the corner smiling. When Sabrina got to the last step, he kneeled down and hugged her as his eyes became watery again.

"I read the article in the school's newspaper of your paper

and it was wonderful!" Philip said, "I never knew you thought of me like that. I'm proud to be your father," he said, as Courtney smiled. "I love you so much!"

"I love you too, daddy," she said. Then Kianna came down the steps and hugged her father as well.

When Philip received the original paper that Sabrina wrote, he had it framed and hung it in his study at home. Kianna's card sat on his desk at work.

One weekend Justin came into town to see Preston and his family but Courtney was gone on a business trip for a week covering a story. He enjoyed his visit but he kept getting lost when he drove himself around the city. He came back to town months later for a couple of days and stayed in an executive suite at Wynham Hotel. When he wanted to go somewhere he had a 24-hour limousine service parked outside the hotel. Preston took sometime off from work for him and Ashley to really show Justin around. It was impossible for Courtney to take off so they met for a late lunch. They even had dinner plans but she had to cancel because of work schedule. They made plans to go out Saturday evening.

Courtney was waiting on Philip to pick up the girls but he was running late. She went on and got dressed. When Philip arrived the girls were ready to leave but he wanted to stick around to see who Justin Miles was. Minutes later the doorbell rang.

"I'll get it, Courtney," Philip said, walking to the door. "Yes," he answered, when he opened the door.

"Hi. I'm Justin. I'm here to pick up, Courtney," he said, as the girls stood at the doorway with Philip.

"Come in. My name is Philip," he said boldly.

"Hi, Mr. Miles," Kianna said smiling.

"This is our daddy," Sabrina said.

"Nice to meet you," Justin said, shaking Philip's hand.

"Same here," Philip said, as he looked at him. "Courtney is upstairs," he said, as everyone walked to the living room. "She will be down soon. Have a seat. Can I get you anything?" He asked distinctly, as if he had the run of the whole house.

"No thank you. I'm fine." Justin said, as he sat down.

Philip and Justin looked at one another bold and tensed.

"Mr. Miles, we still have our pictures you drew of us when you visited before at my Aunt Ashley's house. We have them upstairs in our room," Sabrina said.

"You do?" Justin asked, smiling.

"Hi, Justin. Philip," Courtney said, as she entered the living room.

"Mommy, you look pretty!" Sabrina said, as her smile and eyes widen.

"Very beautiful I must say," Justin said, standing up looking at Courtney smiling.

Philip gave Justin a mean look as Justin's eyes were glued to Courtney's beauty.

"Thank you," Courtney said. "I'm sorry, I didn't introduce both of you myself."

"It's okay, we did a good job introducing ourselves," Justin said humorously, as Courtney smiled. "You may want to take a jacket or a sweater. It seems all of a sudden it became cool outside."

Justin was trying to be discrete as he watched Courtney walk away. Philip excused himself to talk to Courtney. The girls continued to talk to Justin about their pictures he drew and about school.

"Hey," Philip said, as he walked to Courtney slowly. "Are you okay?" He helped her with her jacket.

"Thank you," she said putting on the jacket. "I'm fine."

"He's really trying to impress you with a limousine parked outside. I'm surprised he didn't bring you flowers and a box of chocolates flown in from Paris," Philip said, sarcastically.

"Justin gets lost when he comes here to visit and as for flowers, he had them delivered this morning. They are upstairs in my room," Courtney said.

"I see," Philip said not impressed. "And the chocolates?"

She smiled as she began to walk away. “Courtney,” she stopped and turned around to him, “I was thinking since the girls are coming back here in the morning, I might as well watch them here until you get back.”

“That’s fine, Philip, but I don’t know what time I’ll be back. If you change your mind make sure you lock up okay,” Courtney said. Philip had an odd grin, “What’s wrong? Why are you acting strange?”

“No, I’m fine. Call me if you need a ride home,” Philip said, earnestly while walking up to her.

“Philip!” Courtney said, laughing. “You are funny. I need to go. I don’t want to be rude to Justin,” she said, as she shook her head while walking out of the room.

When Courtney and Justin got to the restaurant they talked and laughed almost non-stop.

“Courtney, if the opportunity presented itself would you relocate to another state?” Justin asked.

“For what?” Courtney asked.

“I don’t know let’s see career advancement or even love,” Justin replied.

Courtney was silent for a couple of seconds with a smile. “I don’t know. That opportunity never presented itself.”

“I’m thinking about buying a newspaper company in Texas and I was also thinking that this would be a great time for you to advance especially in the news world,” he said.

“And,” Courtney said.

“What?”

“Come on, Justin. Tell me what you really want?” she asked, concerned.

“I know we only have known one another for maybe six months and for someone I hardly spent anytime with, I want to take it to another level. I want to get to know you, Courtney. I want to give you the world. I’m not talking about money. I’m speaking of companionship, loyalty, honesty, love, commitment, even if I have to fly here every other weekend for us to start building on the things that will bring us closer together. Whatever it will take, I'll do it. So, how about it, Courtney? Would you think about it and let me know?"

"Justin, I'm really flattered," Courtney said.

"Oh, boy here it comes," he said, discouraged.

"Come on, hear me out. I had opportunities to advance my career but I chose to stay where I'm because I love being a full-time mother. There is no such thing having a successful career and being a successful parent when it comes to a high power occupation. I'm not looking for anything from anyone. Again, I'm okay for now concerning my career and my personal life. I don't want to complicate my life for something or someone, I'm not ready for."

"How would you be complicating your life by getting to know me? We would be getting to know one another to see if something beautiful could come from our being around one another," he said.

"We can still get to know one another as friends, but I don't want our present relationship to turn into anything more than that. If I force myself to do something that I'm not ready for or willing to commit to, I would be complicating my life. I hope you respect my honesty," she boldly said.

"I do. If you change your mind I'm only a telephone call or pager or e-mail away. The only thing you have to do is say the words, I want us to try, and I'll get to you in four hours flat even if I had to fly the plane here myself to get to you," he said, as Courtney smiled.

After dinner they went to a park to continue to talk and walk some of the delicious dinner off. When the limousine pulled up in front of Courtney's home, Justin was hoping she would invite him in. After the driver opened the door and helped her out of the car, Justin walked Courtney to the door. Then she turned around and smiled. He could tell from her body language that he wasn't invited in. He thanked her for a pleasant evening and walked away. When he got to the car, he turned around and looked back at Courtney who waved bye. When she walked into the house; Philip was watching television. He looked at his watch thinking it was getting late but in reality it was still early. He continued to watch the boring television program. Courtney walked in the room as he smiled at her.

"So how did it go?" Philip asked concerned.

"It was great!" she said, taking off her shoes.

"I see. Do you like him?"

"Yes," she replied, as she took the remote out of his hand while sitting down. "What are you watching?" She asked, as Philip took the remote out of her hand and turned off the television. "Philip, what's wrong?"

"He's not for you, Courtney," Philip said sincerely.

"I know and I've already told him that," she said, looking at Philip strangely.

"You are something else," he said, relieved as he smiled. "You said you like him."

"And I do," Courtney said. "You didn't define the word like. That's what I like about our friendship. It doesn't matter how long we have known one another or if we have the same interest in some things, we don't expect anything from one another. You might as well say, I like going out with men that I'm not attracted to then," she started talking slow, "there is no pressure." When she realized how it sounded, she started trying to justify it. "I'm sorry, Philip. I didn't mean it that way. I meant there is nothing romantic going on between us because we're friends. Maybe I should quit while I'm ahead."

"You don't need to apologize," Philip said firmly, as he stood up handing her the remote. Believe me, I understand more than you think. It's getting late." He took his car keys off the centerpiece table. "Goodnight," he said not waiting for Courtney to response. As he walked to his car; he thought about what she said as his jaws tightened.

Philip really liked Courtney but at that moment he decided to let what he hoped could never be go. He was willing to accept what she was willing to give him, which was friendship.

Chapter Nine

Courtney was at Ashley's place talking and laughing. Then they started talking about their mother's funeral.

"It was like mom knew she was going to die," Ashley said.

"As I think about it now, Ashley, you're right. Everything was literally in order," Courtney said, as she thought back about the most sorrowful time in her life.

"You and mom always had a special bond when we were children," Ashley said, as she looked down at her hands sadly.

"Of course, being the baby of the family," Courtney said humorously. "Maxwell, who is next to me is seven years older then I am and if I'm not mistaken that makes you ten years older than me," she said, teasingly.

"Never mind that. You know, I used to be jealous of your relationship with mom. She would act like you were going to break. It was as if the rest of us didn't exist in your presence," Ashley said candidly.

"That's not true, Ashley. Mom thought I was a problem child," Courtney said, as she laughed to herself.

"No, you were mom's picked," Ashley said firmly.

Courtney could hear the resentment in her voice and she watched her closely wondering if Ashley could be kidding. It only took a few seconds for Courtney to realize Ashley was really serious. Actually she was more serious than Courtney had ever seen her sister before.

"When you used to go over grandmother's house for the

weekend, mom and I really connected as mother and daughter. But once you came home, it was like you were the only child in the family. I couldn't wait to go away to college and I hated to come home for the holidays because you were the center of attention."

"I disagree," Courtney said wholeheartedly.

"How would you know? You were too busy being spoiled. For me, being away at college for so many years was a break from you. When I did come home for the summer break, I was going into my senior year in college then that's when I met Preston. We were married that following year. After all that I found myself wanting to be even closer to our mother.

When you moved in with Sabrina's father and later you became pregnant that was the best news I had heard in my life at that time. Mom's perfect child made a costly mistake. Then I felt badly about how I thought about you for so many years."

"I can't believe you are saying this to me, Ashley," Courtney said feeling hurt. "Do you hate me for how you thought mom was treating—" She began to ask, as Ashley interrupted her.

"No, Courtney, I don't hate you. I could never hate you. You're my sister," she said, in all sincerity. "I was jealous of your relationship with mom for no reason."

"But how could you rejoice in something that I was experiencing that wasn't good for me with Sabrina's father. I was in a terrible relationship mentally that could have jeopardized my baby's future if I didn't handle it appropriately," Courtney said. She was disappointed in herself and about learning the truth of how her sister felt about her.

"Courtney, I'm not trying to start anything here between you and me. I brought this up because I felt terrible about how I had thought for all these years. I wanted to say—" Ashley said, as the telephone rang.

Ashley had to take the call in another room where she left the information concerning a business matter. Minutes later

Preston walked into the room as Courtney stood at the window with her arms folded, feeling disquieted.

"Hi, Courtney. Are you okay?" Preston asked, walking in the room.

"Hello, Preston," Courtney said, as she walked from the window. "I'm fine. When did you get in?" She looked as if she was in a daze.

"Just now. Where is Ashley?" he asked.

"She had to . . . to take a call," Courtney replied preoccupied.

"Are you sure you're all right?" he asked concerned.

"Yes. You know, I should be leaving now. Tell Ashley I'll talk to her later," Courtney said, as she walked away.

When Courtney got home, she called her brother Maxwell to ask him if he felt the same way Ashley did. He stated that he didn't. Maxwell was curious to know why Courtney was concerned about how their mother treated them compared to her. She didn't tell him the real reason. Courtney went to her room and cried. She wished she could talk to her mother. One of the girls knocked on her door to let her know Philip was at the front door. She quickly wiped her face and had the perfect smile on when she opened the door for him to come in. While the girls were in the living room watching a movie, Philip and Courtney went into the kitchen. Philip was sitting at the kitchen table talking away while eating a bowl of ice cream. Courtney had her back turned from him standing at the stove staring at the teakettle.

"Courtney!" Philip said, as he raised his voice.

"I'm sorry, Philip," Courtney said, as she turned around to him. "Yes."

"Don't you hear the steam whistle going off on the tea kettle? Do you want the water to boil?" he asked, as he walked over to her. "Your mind is on something else. Let me pour this for you. I don't want you to burn yourself," he said, as he turned off the stove. Then he looked concerned. "What's on your mind?"

"Nothing," she replied, sitting down at the table.

He poured the hot water into a teacup, steeped the tea bag a couple times in the cup, and separate and squeezed the drawstring. Then he put an ice cube in the tea.

"Be careful. It's hot," he said, as he placed the tea in front of Courtney.

"Thank you, Philip," Courtney said, as she looked down at her tea.

"Now are you going to tell me what has you upset?" Philip asked, as he sat down.

"I'm not upset," Courtney said, as she looked up at him. "My sister said something that really hurt me today. She resented me when we were kids because she felt I was mom's favorite. I couldn't believe my sister," she said disappointedly. "You're probably thinking that's stupid, right?"

"I'm not thinking anything. I'm listening. You're not giving me anytime to think on. Go on, Courtney," he said waiting for her to finish what she had to say.

"What really got to me was when I became involved with Sabrina's father and I became pregnant. Ashley was happy that I did something that hurt my parents, but most importantly how it almost ruined my life! My parents were already hurt that I was living with a man that I wasn't married to but then I had a baby by him. I did the total opposite of how my parents raised me and what they wanted for me. I can't believe my sister!" she said, upset.

"Courtney, your life wasn't ruined," Philip said calmly, as he saw the hurt on her face. "You look fine to me. You may have an unseen scar. Who doesn't?" he asked, as the telephone rang. "The scar heals by moving on with life and before you know it there isn't even a blemish." Kianna ran into the kitchen.

"Mommy, it's Aunt Ashley on the telephone," Kianna said, then she ran back out of the kitchen.

Courtney looked at Philip as he looked at her with sincerity. She got up from the table and picked up the telephone in the kitchen.

"Hello," Courtney answered softly.

"Hi," Ashley said on the telephone. "Why did you leave? I thought you were going to stay for dinner."

"I changed my mind. I knew Philip was coming to get Kianna and I didn't tell him my plans. Actually, he is here now. I should go," Courtney said.

"I know you are using that as an excuse. We didn't finish our talk," Ashley said.

"We can talk about it at a later time. I need to go. Bye," Courtney said. She hung up the telephone and walked back over to the table.

"You should have talked to your sister," Philip said concerned, as she sat down. "I could have left and went—" he began to say.

"I didn't want to talk to her right now but if you want to leave that's fine," she said, becoming defensive.

"I didn't give you any indication I wanted to leave," he said. "Courtney, you need to get a hold of yourself. I believe Ashley was sincere and she wanted to tell you how she felt at that time. I bet she wanted to apologize. Sometimes we may think something of someone that we shouldn't have and we may have to go to them to ask forgiveness. Don't they teach that in church?"

Courtney looked at Philip stunned at what he just said to her. She knew he was right but she couldn't say anything to justify how she felt.

"You are taking sides," she said.

"No, I'm not," Philip said. "Not yet but I'll say this, you are wrong in the way you are handling this matter with your sister. If I don't know anything else about your sister, I know she loves you very much. You should have heard her out first, no matter how upset you were. I know you have self-control when it comes to hearing someone out. Maybe you need to ask yourself a question. Have you forgiven yourself for what happened with Sabrina's father and the way you disappointed your parents? Because if you did it wouldn't matter what anyone said about it. It wouldn't hurt anymore," he said. Then Sabrina called Philip for something. "Excuse me. I'll be back," he said in a soft tone.

A couple of days later, Ashley called Courtney at work asking her to come to her place when she left work.

"Let's talk in here," Ashley said, as they walked into her husband's study.

"I see you've changed Preston's study again," Courtney said, as she looked around trying to make small conversation.

"I didn't mean to hurt your feelings the other day," Ashley said sincere. "I felt bad all these years knowing what you went through with Sabrina's father. What really caused me to say something about mom, you and myself was because one of the kids felt I have favorites when it comes to one of the other children. I don't have favorites with my children. It's just that I can't treat them all the same because they all have different personalities. What works for one child will not work for the other. Therefore, Preston and I treat every situation accordingly to the best of our abilities. I think that's what mom was doing with all of us. I was just plain old jealous of you and mom. I was the only girl for ten years before you came along. I felt you and I was in competition at times when it came to mom's attention. As you became older I had my own friends. My own world. Mom had to keep her eyes on her pride and joy. Someone who needed her as a child. As I think back when mom was here with us, I wasted precious time for years feeling that way about her that I can't get back. Mom has always shown me love. I just wanted most of the focus on me. I'm truly sorry for how I felt about you then and how I hurt you the other day," Ashley said, as Courtney's eyes become watery. "I'm sorry. Will you forgive me?"

"Yes," Courtney replied in tears. "I forgive you. I want you to forgive me too for the way I handled this. I'm sorry."

"Sure. I love you, Courtney," Ashley said, as they hugged.

"Since mom passed away you have been really sensitive," she said, as she rubbed Courtney on her back.

"I know. I have to stop that," Courtney cried, then she laughed as she wiped her eyes.

"Here you go," Ashley said, as she handed Courtney a kleenex off her husband's desk. "Don't forget I have a double major in psychology. Anytime you want to talk, let me know," she said teasingly, as she smiled.

"No thank you. I'm fine," Courtney assured Ashley laughing. Then they hugged one another again.

When Courtney got home, she called Philip to let him know he was right about Ashley and herself. They talked on the telephone until they literally fell asleep. Neither one of them had done that since they were teenagers.

Philip and Courtney got up early on Saturday morning with the girls to go house hunting. Kianna whined that she didn't want to move and change schools.

They saw plenty of beautiful homes. The last house they saw Courtney fell in love with. She was giving Philip some ideas on how to decorate the house. She even had Kianna liking one of the rooms that could be hers. She gave Philip an idea to have a playhouse built out back for Kianna. The following weekend it was just Philip and Courtney looking at houses with a Realtor.

"What do you think, Philip?" Courtney asked. "This is the best one we've seen today."

"I don't need a twenty-five room house for just two people," Philip said, as he shook his head.

"Good. I was thinking the same thing," Courtney said. Then Philip smiled at her, "You want something that is cozy but entertaining for your family and dinner parties perhaps. When you are home you want to feel you are in another world of peace and comfort, right?" Courtney asked as she looked at him.

"That's right," he said, as he smiled again. Then they stared at one another for a few seconds.

Courtney looked away. "Well," she said, as she looked

down at the house listings. "the perfect house for you is some where around. We have to keep looking. You know, we're not going to find something in a week or two."

"Courtney, I don't want to keep pulling you away from other things you could be doing," he said.

"You know me, if I have something to do, I'll do it. Whenever you want to go house hunting just let me know. This is fun!" Courtney said.

The following weekend Courtney and Philip were in a huge room of another new house that they had finished looking through. Philip was looking through sheets of different listings of houses with Courtney. They walked outside and stood for a couple of seconds still looking through the listings. Philip stopped and looked at Courtney's lovely skin. She felt him staring at her and she looked up at him as he smiled at her.

"You know, Philip," she said, smiling back at him then she looked down at the listings again in her hand, "we have already seen these houses, so let's mark this section out," She marked out the areas with a pencil.

"Why do you always do that, Courtney?" Philip asked.

"Do what?" she asked, puzzled as she continued to go through some papers in his hands.

"You always look away from me. I like looking at your lovely brown eyes," he said, as she acted as if she was trying to find a particular listing.

"Thanks. We haven't seen this house," she said, quickly changing the subject. "Let's go. I can drive." She reached out her hand for the car key.

On Sunday after church Kianna and Sabrina wanted to shake Reverend Solomon's hand before leaving since they didn't get a chance to last Sunday. The girls ran to the reverend and hugged him at the same time.

"Oh," Reverend Solomon exclaimed, as he laughed. "Ladies, how are you?"

"Fine!" the girls said, enthusiastically.

"Reverend Solomon, the sermon was excellent as usual," Courtney said, as she smiled.

"Thank you," Reverend Solomon said, as he hugged Courtney then he took her by her hand. "Sister Kennedy, I've been watching you on Sunday mornings and it seems you know every song whether it's in the hymn books or not. I've seen your lips move and your smile as if you are singing along with the choir. Have you thought about joining a choir?"

"No, sir. I haven't thought about it," Courtney replied.

"Why don't you pray and see what the Lord says about it."

"I don't feel I'm worthy or even ready for that matter to become part of a dedicated ministry," Courtney said, as she smiled.

"None of us are unworthy to do the Lord's work since we serve a perfect God. He has done something so incredible that we wouldn't even think about doing ourselves for when God sent His only begotten Son, Jesus, to die on the cross for all our sins so we can be worthy to do His will. You will make a fine choir member to our church. I can see you leading songs," he stated.

"Thank you, Reverend Solomon," she said, taking what he said into consideration.

"Very well. I'll see all of you and the little angels next Sunday if God permits," Reverend Solomon said, as he and Courtney walked away from one another.

Chapter Ten

It was Sunday afternoon, when Kianna walked into her house calling her father as Courtney and Sabrina came inside with her. Philip walked out to the room.

"You're home early," Philip said, as he hugged Kianna. "Courtney, hello. Hi, Sabrina," he said looking distracted. Then he looked at his daughter, "Hey, did you have a good time, Kianna?"

"Yes, I did," Kianna replied, as she looked at Sabrina smiling. Then she looked back at her father, "We went to a church picnic on Saturday, daddy. We played all kinds of ball games and hide and seek. There was also a clown, a magician and a frog contest," she said, rambling on as Courtney smiled at her.

Then an attractive brown complexion medium built woman walked in from around the living room corner. Her hair was styled in a short bob tapered around her oval face. She wore a fitted blue mini-jean dress that stopped at her bare thighs. She had on a gold tone designed belt around her flat stomach and high heel shoes that were the same material as her dress.

"Hi, Kianna!" The woman said happy to see Kianna.

Kianna's smile went away instantly.

"Bria, this is Courtney and her daughter, Sabrina," Philip said. Bria smiled at Sabrina. "Courtney, this is Kianna's mother, Bria."

"Nice to meet you," Courtney said to Bria. Bria looked away from Courtney carelessly.

"I'm so glad you're home, Kianna," Bria said.

"Well, we better get ready to leave. Goodnight," Courtney

said, as she felt she and Sabrina were intruding.

"Do you have to leave now?" Kianna asked, as she walked over to Courtney wanting them to stay longer.

"Yes, sweetie," Courtney replied, as she brushed her hand gently down her face. "Sabrina has to clean up her room sometime this evening before going to bed. I'll see you in the morning."

"Can I come back over to your house?" Kianna asked Courtney in a sad tone.

"No, Kianna," Philip replied immediately. "You will see them tomorrow. Give Courtney a hug."

"Goodnight, mommy," Kianna said, as Courtney bent down to hug her.

"Goodnight, Kianna. Sweet dreams," Courtney said smiling.

"Mommy!" Bria said baffled, as Courtney and the girls looked at her. "Philip, what is this? Is there something I should know?"

"Bria, please!" Philip said firmly to Bria. Then he looked at Courtney, "Courtney, thanks for bringing Kianna home. Bye Sabrina," he said. Then he walked over to Sabrina and hugged her. "I'll see you later, okay."

After Courtney and Sabrina left, Kianna walked around the corner then walked up the staircase.

"Kianna, don't you want to spend some time with me?" Bria asked, following Kianna to the steps. "We haven't seen one another in a while. I have some presents for you," she said, while pointing backwards with her hand to the living room where the brown paper bag was sitting on the centerpiece table.

"I had a long day. I'm going to bed," Kianna said, as she continued to go up the steps not turning around.

Bria walked back into the living room, "What's going on here, Philip?" she asked with an attitude.

"What are you talking about? You haven't seen Kianna in years then you expect for her to jump all over you like a puppy?

Well, I have a news flash for you, she's a human being that has feelings. She's not the same insecure three year old little girl anymore," he said irritated.

"Okay, okay," Bria said, as she faked a smile. "I guess you have a point but I don't understand why is Kianna calling some other woman mommy? Is that woman your girlfriend?"

"Her name is Courtney."

"Whatever! You shouldn't have allowed that, Philip," Bria said peeved.

"Courtney is the only woman besides my mother and Lauren that she would allow in her life. Courtney has really connected with Kianna," he said.

"That won't be necessary any longer. I'm back!" she said intently.

"Back for what?" Philip asked puzzled. "All the birthdays and traditional holidays, you haven't sent her a card or a small note to say you are thinking about her. I don't understand what you are expecting here."

"Philip, I'm sorry," she said trying to come across sincerely. "Like I told you before they walked in, I want my family back. I didn't know what I was doing when I gave you and Kianna up. I felt I was being tied down at the time. I have come to my senses," she said.

"I can't talk about this right now. I want to spend some time with Kianna before she goes to sleep and it's getting late for me. I need to get up in the morning to take Kianna to school and like some people, I have a job," he said sarcastically.

"A job? You are too modest. For a man who owns a billion dollar company can practically do whatever he wants. You have passed the job status in the working world when it comes to answering to someone else."

"Too bad I don't think like you. Like you nicely put it, I don't have to answer to anyone and that's not only professionally, but my personally life as well. Now, if you don't mind—"

"Can I take Kianna to school tomorrow?" Bria asked.

"No, but you can leave," he demanded.

Bria picked up her white and blue jeans purse and the bag. Then she walked over to Philip and kissed him on the cheek.

"I know you want the same thing as I do," Bria said softly, as she smiled. "I'll bring these presents back tomorrow. Goodnight."

Bria walked seductively out the door. Philip went to Kianna's room. She was sitting on her bed playing with one of her dolls.

"Kianna, your mother wanted to spend some time with you," Philip said, as he sat on her bed.

Kianna didn't say anything as she put her doll down then she moved over to her father and hugged him.

"Daddy, I want to show you what I won at the church picnic," Kianna said, not giving a second thought about what her father said to her.

The next day when Philip picked up Kianna from school they bought a pizza. Kianna had been asking for one for weeks. As they sat at the kitchen table to eat the doorbell rang.

"Kianna, go ahead and start eating. I'll be back," Philip said, getting up from the table.

"Okay, daddy," Kianna said, as she picked up a slice of pizza.

A few minutes later someone walked through the kitchen entrance.

"Hi, Kianna," Bria said, as she walked into the kitchen. "Mmm, pizza! I see you like mushrooms like I do on my pizza," she said smiling. "When your daddy and I used to get pizza, we would get half with mushrooms too. Let me taste." She sat at the table and took a slice of pizza from out of the square cardboard box. As she took a bite of the pizza she smiled, "This is delicious!" she said enjoying the pizza. Kianna got out of her seat slowly and pushed her chair under the table. She walked towards the entrance that led to the living room.

"Kianna, where are you going?" Bria asked concerned.

"I suddenly lost my appetite," Kianna said, giving Bria a mean look.

Then Kianna walked into Philip.

"Kianna, you only had a couple bites of your pizza. What's wrong, honey?" Philip asked.

"I want her to leave," Kianna said, as she hugged her father around his waste.

"Would you at least talk to your mother?" Philip asked Kianna, looking down on her while stroking her head.

"No!" Kianna replied boldly, as she buried her face in her father's stomach.

"Kianna, I'll leave but would you at least look at the presents I brought you?" Bria asked. "I hope you like them; it took me hours to pick them out for you."

"No," Kianna replied again, as she turned her head to the side. "Then our pizza would get cold," she replied with her arms around her father got even tighter.

Then Philip looked at Bria apprehensive as she contemplated to herself what she could say to get Kianna to talk to her. Philip shook his head to Bria.

"Okay," Bria said, as she faked a smile. She got up from the table and threw her pizza away. Then she wiped her hands on a napkin. "I'll leave your presents here. Would you promise me you will open them after you finish eating?"

Kianna turned her face more into her father and hugged him with all the strength she had.

"Maybe another time, Bria," Philip said firmly, as he rubbed Kianna on her back. "It's all right, Kianna."

"Sure. We can do this another time," Bria said, as she looked at Philip concerned. "Bye, Kianna," she said. Then she walked out of the kitchen.

Around nine-thirty that night, Philip's doorbell rang.

"Bria, why are you back here?" Philip asked puzzled.

"What has that witch done to my daughter?" Bria asked, walking into the house. "Kianna, won't even look at me." She walked past Philip into the living room.

"Who are you talking about!" He said confused.

"Coddy or Courtney. Whatever her name is!" Bria said frustrated.

"Courtney doesn't know you to turn Kianna against you. You should be calling yourself the witch. You are the one who happened to abandon Kianna."

"I didn't abandon my daughter!" she said, as she raised her voice.

"Bria, lower your voice," he demanded.

"I'm sorry," Bria said, shaking her head. "You're wrong. I wasn't ready to be a mother. I felt—"

"Bria, I'm not in the mood to hear excuses. You are the one who left Kianna. You abandoned your family," Philip said, as he looked at her with no remorse.

"Philip, everyday I face that terrible mistake of leaving my family. I'm so sorry," Bria said.

"Kianna and I got over it as you can see," Philip said.

"I see, Kianna opened up her gifts," she said, as she smiled. "Did she like them?"

"I opened the gifts for her. I think she liked them," he said.

"I guess, I need to give Kianna time to come around," Bria said, as she picked up one of the toys she brought and held it to her chest.

It was another Friday evening and Courtney had to work late. Philip brought Sabrina home with him and Kianna since his daughter was planning on staying with Courtney for the weekend. After dinner the girls went back upstairs to play. Kianna was on the floor coloring and Sabrina was sitting on the bed changing her doll's clothes.

"Kianna," Sabrina said, as she put on the doll's shoes.

"Yes," Kianna answered slowly as she colored something in a book.

"That lady Bria is your mother?" Sabrina asked.

"No," Kianna replied.

Sabrina looked at Kianna confused.

"Why would daddy say she's your mother?" Sabrina asked.

Kianna wouldn't respond as she colored more in her book. Sabrina put the doll down on the bed and got on the floor next to Kianna. They looked at each other and smiled.

"You want to color in my coloring book?" Kianna asked.

"Yes," she replied, as she looked at the shapes of balls. "I want to color this area. I think raspberry purple will look pretty."

"Okay," Kianna said, as she put the tin box filled with crayons between them. Then they began to color in the shapes of the balls. "Sabrina, I want to tell you something. Do you promise you won't tell anyone?"

"Yes," Sabrina replied earnestly.

"Not even daddy or mommy or even Aunt Ashley," Kianna said, as she looked over at Sabrina.

"Okay. I won't tell. What?" Sabrina asked, as she looked at her.

"It's about Bria. I don't like what she did to my daddy and me when she left us," Kianna said, as she continued to color. "She doesn't love me. She never has. I know I can't hate her because what we learned in Sunday School about God's love and how we are supposed to love everyone no matter what. But I don't trust her. I feel she's trying to come between our daddy and my relationship."

"What do you mean she's trying to come between you and daddy?"

"I over heard her telling our daddy that she wants to spend more time with him and me. She's always trying to be so helpful even when it's not necessary," Kianna said. Then she ground her teeth together and said, "Sometimes it really gets on my nerves."
Sabrina looked at Kianna sadly as her eyes became watery.
"What, Sabrina?" Kianna said, wondering why her friend's eyes

were teary.

"Do you think she will try to come between you and me too?" Sabrina asked.

Kianna shook her head right away.

"We won't let her," Kianna said.

"Let's pray that God doesn't allow her to breakup our sisterhood like she is trying to do with our daddy and you." Sabrina said. Then they both put down their crayons and folded their hands in a praying position and closed their eyes. "God, Kianna and I love each other. We love being sisters. Please don't let Ms. Bria come between us," she prayed believing God would honor their request. "Amen."

"Amen," Kianna said, as she opened her eyes and smiled. "It will be okay."

They continued to color. Then Sabrina locked her arm around Kianna's arm. Kianna rested her head on Sabrina's shoulder for a couple seconds then they continued to color. Minutes later, Philip knocked on the door.

"Come in, daddy," Sabrina said.

"Ladies," Philip said smiling, as he entered the room. "Sabrina, your mother called. She has to work a little later than what she anticipated. You can spend the night here and I'll take you both over to Courtney's tomorrow or Courtney can pick you both up tonight but it will be late," he said, as the girls sat up.

"I want to spend the night," Sabrina said, as she and Kianna smiled at each other.

"Okay. Now, would you ladies like to go with me to the movies?" he asked.

"To see what, daddy?" Kianna asked.

"The Little Mermaid," he uttered, as the girls eyes widened.

"Really!" The girls said at the same time.

"Yes, but you have to put all this stuff away, put on your shoes, sweater, and be downstairs in twenty minutes so we can catch the 6:45 p.m. show. I'll call Courtney back," Philip said.

The girls jumped up and put away their things and got ready to leave. The girls enjoyed the movie as they sat the entire time without getting restless. Once they got back to Philip's house they both called Courtney who just got home from a very long day at work. Courtney sat on the steps on the cordless phone listening to their excited voices telling her about the movie. After the girls hung up the phone, Courtney walked up the stairs and fell forward on her bed. She kicked off her shoes and in seconds she was asleep.

As weeks passed there were no change between Bria and Kianna's relationship even though Philip tried to intervene by getting Kianna to at least have a civil conversation with her mother without Kianna feeling annoyed.

One morning Bria stopped at Philip's house for a short visit since he had to go to work and Kianna had to go to school. Philip allowed Bria to drive Kianna to school. Kianna told her father she didn't want Bria to take her anywhere, but he wouldn't listen. As Bria drove Kianna to school, she asked Kianna questions about school but Kianna wouldn't respond. Bria came to a stoplight and she brushed Kianna face with her hand because she saw how uncomfortable she was with her.

"You have smooth skin like your father, Kianna," Bria said, as she smiled.

Again, Kianna kept looking down tracing letters on one of her schoolbooks until Bria pulled in front of her school.

"You don't have to walk me in. My daddy lets me out here," Kianna said in a brassy tone, as she unbuckled her seatbelt. Then Bria stopped the car. "I'm a big girl; I don't need anyone to walk me inside."

"Kianna, I would like to see the inside of your school," Bria said, as Kianna was getting out the car.

"I don't want you to see it!" Kianna said feeling angry. Then she slammed the car door. Kianna wiped her face where Bria touched her. Bria got out of the car and watched Kianna walk to the front door of the school.

"Have a nice day," Bria said to Kianna as someone opened the door for her. Kianna wouldn't look back at Bria. "Kianna," Bria said, as she thought to herself that Kianna really hated her.

Courtney was walking out of the classroom when Kianna saw her. Kianna ran to Courtney in tears.

"Sweetheart, what's wrong?" Courtney asked concerned, as she bent down taking Kianna's schoolbooks from her sitting them on the floor. "Where is your father?" she took off her sweater.

"That woman brought me to school and my daddy knew I didn't want her to," Kianna said, as she cried.

"What woman?" Courtney asked, as Kianna took the back of her little hand wiping the left side of her face while tears flow down the other side of her face.

"Bri . . . Bri . . . Bria!" she said upset.

"Oh, it's okay, sweetie," Courtney said, as she gave Kianna a hug. "Try not to be upset with your father. He was only trying to help you and your mother have a relationship. We will talk about it later. I need you to stop thinking about what happened this morning. Think about what an exciting day you are going to have in school with your teachers and your friends," she said, as Kianna's tears continued to flow down her face slowly. "Come on, Kianna I need you to stop crying. You are going to be fine, okay."

"Yes, mommy," she said, calming down.

"That's my girl," Courtney said, while taking a kleenex out of her purse. She wiped Kianna's face as she smiled telling her how pretty she looked. Then she picked up the books and took Kianna by her hand. "Let's go to class."

Courtney stayed at the school for twenty minutes to make sure Kianna was okay. When Philip picked Kianna up that evening from school she wouldn't say much to him as they were riding home.

"Kianna, I followed you and your mother to school this morning to make sure you got there okay. Did you two talk some?" he asked.

"She talked," Kianna replied.

"Baby, you're not trying at all to work with your mother," he said. Kianna didn't respond.

Courtney called Philip at home later on that night.

"Hi, Philip. It's Courtney."

"Hello. How are you?" Philip asked.

"Good," Courtney replied. "Kianna was really upset this morning because Bria brought her to school. I've been trying to stay out of the triangle concerning you, Bria, and Kianna," Courtney said.

"And I appreciate that," he said candidly.

"Now I have to say something concerning Kianna's relationship with her mother. You and Bria are pushing her too hard and too fast to get her to communicate with her mother. You two can't expect a child or any person for that matter to change over night or should I say in one month," she said boldly.

"Courtney," Philip said.

"Daddy," Kianna said, tapping Philip on his elbow, "is that my mommy, Courtney?" Courtney could hear Kianna's voice in the background.

"Philip, let me speak to Kianna," Courtney said.

"Sure," Philip said to Courtney. "Courtney, thanks for calling. I understand what you are saying."

"Philip, before you go, I would like to talk to Kianna a little about her mother if it's all right with you," Courtney said.

"Like what?" Philip asked concerned.

"How to communicate with Bria," Courtney said.

"That will be a great help," Philip said. "No, I wouldn't mind that at all. Have a goodnight, Courtney. Here you go, sweetheart," he said to Kianna, as he gave her the receiver of the phone.

Courtney talked to Kianna on the telephone about her day in school. On Saturday evening Philip brought Kianna over to Courtney's house to spend the night with her friend. While she and Courtney were waiting for Sabrina to get home from her Uncle Maxwell's house, Courtney decided that would be a good time to talk.

"Kianna, can we talk?" Courtney asked, as they sat down on the couch.

"Yes. What do you want to talk about?" Kianna asked.

"I want to talk about you and your mother Bria," She said.

"She's not my mother," Kianna said, as the tone of her voice changed.

"Kianna, sweetheart, Bria is your mother and you need to try to show her some respect. Now, I know you are thinking about what she did to you in the past and not being around when you needed her. However, it will take some time to resolve before its okay in here," Courtney said, as she put her right hand on the left side of her chest. "For now, when she speaks to you try to respond to her."

"Respond to her?" Kianna asked puzzled.

"Yes. For example, when she says hi, you should say hi back to her and when she ask how are you, tell her you are fine. You can respond to her honestly in a nice respectful way. Don't ignore her."

"Do I have to call her mommy even though you're my mommy?" Kianna asked.

"You can call her mommy because she is truly your mother. My feelings for you will not change. I love you whether you call me mommy like you do now or Courtney. You are still my baby," she said, as Kianna smiled. "Come here give me a big hug."

"I love you, mommy," Kianna said, with so much feeling as she hugged Courtney. Then she looked at her, "and I'll try to get along with *her*," she said resentfully, as Courtney looked at her with concern. Kianna looked down as put her hand on top of Courtney's hand. "I mean," she stopped, "my." She stopped again trying to say a word that she didn't feel for Bria, "mother," she said, in a better tone. Then she looked back up at Courtney.

"That's all I ask," Courtney said, as she put her head to Kianna's head smiling.

Courtney brought Kianna home after Sunday morning service.

"Kianna, it looks like your dad has company," Courtney said.

"It's not company. It's—" Kianna said then she stopped. "It's my mom," she said slowly, as if she was learning how to talk.

"Come on, sweetie; it's okay. Sabrina stay here. I'm just going to walk Kianna to the door, and I'll be right back," Courtney said. She got Kianna's luggage out of the trunk and walked to the front door as Kianna walked slowly behind her carrying a small tote bag.

Smiling, Philip opened the door.

"Come in. Courtney, let me take that from you," Philip said taking the luggage from her hand. "How are you?" Courtney smiled. Then he looked at his daughter, "Did you have a nice time, Kianna?"

"Philip, I have to go. Kianna come give me a kiss," Courtney said. Then she stooped down to her and whispered in her ear, "I love you," Then she looked up at Philip as she stood up. "See you later."

Bria walked out to the living room. She had on beige cream top that snuggled so that it revealed every curve of her upper body and a long skirt with splits going up the front and back of it which uncovered a lot of her sexy legs showing through her silk stockings, and designer high heel shoes.

"Kianna, hi," Bria said not expecting any response from Kianna.

"Hello," Kianna said, without hesitation.

Bria and Philip looked at one another stunned. Bria became excited as she smiled.

"Did you have a nice time?" Bria asked.

"Yes," Kianna replied, as her father put her luggage by a near closet.

"We're cooking dinner. You don't mind if I have dinner with you and your father, do you?" Bria asked.

"No," Kianna replied, as she looked away from Bria. Then she looked at her father, "Daddy, I'm going upstairs to put some of my things away." She carried her tote bag on her shoulder and walked out of the room.

"Fine. Come here," Philip said. He kissed her forehead and smiled.

Kianna ran upstairs.

"Philip, she spoke to me," Bria said, as she hugged him.

"I can't believe it myself," Philip said, as he smiled. Then he looked at Bria remembering how they used to smile and laughed together. He became serious and then he walked to the kitchen.

Later, Bria knocked on Kianna's bedroom door.

"Can I come in, Kianna?" Bria asked.

"Yes," Kianna replied.

"I like your room," Bria said, as she walked in looking around. "This is nice. What are you doing? Is it your homework? Do you need some help?"

"No. I'm looking over it to make sure I did it right before I turn it in tomorrow," Kianna replied.

"That's good. I see you take after your father. Your father is thorough in everything that he does," Bria said, sitting on Kianna's bed. "Kianna, I'm really glad you are talking to me. That means a lot."

"I really need to finish looking over my homework before dinner," Kianna said, as she picked up her pencil. Then she began to read out softly to herself.

"Right," Bria said, as she stood up from the bed. "I'm sorry. I'll see you downstairs."

Bria went to the kitchen trying to help Philip with dinner. She started playing with him in the kitchen. Then she stood behind him while putting her arms around his waist.

"Philip, remember when I used to help you cook from behind just like this and you would have to turn the stove off to put my fire out. You know exactly what to do to take care of all my needs." She stood really close behind him rubbing on his sweater feeling his ridged chest reminiscing of the past they once shared. "I remember the areas on your chest that are ticklish on you. Doesn't this bring back wonderful memories?" She rested her head on his strong back.

"I remember but your touch doesn't arouse me any longer," he said straightforward.

"I bet if I—" Bria began to say as Kianna walked in on them then she turned around to leave. Philip removed Bria's arms from around him.

"Kianna, I want you to set the table. We're going to eat in the kitchen. Dinner should be ready any minute," Philip said.

After Kianna set the table, she went to the living room where Bria turned on the radio. She started dancing to hip-hop music.

"Come on, Kianna," Bria said, dancing as she reached out for Kianna. "Let's dance."

"I don't dance to booty music. I'm just a little girl," Kianna replied with sass. Then she walked out of the room.

During dinner, Philip would make faces at Kianna to make her smile.

"Anyone for dessert?" Philip asked.

"Not for me. Dinner was great. Thank you for preparing it," Bria said to Philip.

"No, we did it together," Philip said.

"I'm going to get ready to leave," Bria said. Then she looked over at her daughter, "Kianna, I had a nice time with you as usual."

"Thanks," Kianna said.

Philip walked Bria to her car.

"Philip, I know you still have feelings for me," Bria said,

as she kissed her index finger and placed it on his soft lips and then she put her hand on his chest.

Philip opened the car door for her to get in.

“Goodnight. Drive home safely,” he said, not responding to her comment or gesture in any way.

After Philip put Kianna to bed he called Courtney.

“I don’t know what you said to Kianna but it worked. Thank you, Courtney,” Philip said. He was feeling hopeful for Kianna and her mother.

“Is Kianna okay?” Courtney asked.

“Yes. I talked to her after her mother left. She said it was difficult to talk to her, but she kept thinking about what you two talked about and that she made you a promise that she would try,” he said.

“I’m glad, Philip,” Courtney said feeling proud of Kianna.

“I’m sorry, Courtney. How are you?”

“Good,” she replied.

“And how is my girl, Sabrina? Why didn’t you bring her in when you brought Kianna home?” Philip asked.

“She’s fine. She was upset with me because she wanted to see you,” Courtney said.

“Courtney, I don’t care what’s going on around me, if I’m close by I want to see Sabrina.”

Chapter Eleven

Philip had to work late Friday evening. He asked Courtney to get Kianna from school and let her go with her mother who would be waiting outside. When Kianna got into her mother's car, she looked at the back seat that was filled with groceries.

"I thought, we could make a special dinner for your daddy tonight," Bria said. "Do you have homework?"

"No," Kianna replied.

Bria and Kianna made homemade cookies and brownies while cooking dinner. Philip called home later that evening to let them know he had to work a little later than planned. After Kianna and her mother ate dinner they watched a movie. Kianna was still a little uncomfortable with her mother. As the movie was ending Bria touched Kianna's long hair that was in a pony-tail hanging down her back.

"Do you want me to do your hair for tomorrow?" Bria asked.

"No," Kianna replied swiftly and firmly.

"Who does your hair anyway, your father?" Bria asked.

"No," Kianna replied again and then she chuckled.

"What's funny?" Bria asked smiling.

"Daddy, doesn't know how to do girls' hair. Either my grandma or Aunt Laura does it. Most of the time it's my mommy, Courtney, who does my hair," she said proudly.

Bria didn't say anything as she folded her arms together while shaking her head to herself. She couldn't believe what Kianna said to her. Philip got home around midnight. When he walked in the house, Bria had the lights dimmed and jazz playing in the background while sitting on the couch looking through some photographs.

"Bria, I'm sorry," Philip said, as he put his briefcase down. "I didn't know it was going to take this long. I didn't want to go into the office tomorrow."

"No problem," Bria said, while putting the pictures away.

"Is Kianna asleep?" He asked.

"Yes. A couple hours ago," she said, in a lax mood.

"You mean 10:00 p.m.!" Philip cried.

"It's not like she has school tomorrow. She didn't mind," Bria said, nonchalantly.

"I bet she didn't." Bria smiled. He took off his jacket.

"I really had a great time with Kianna. I think she's getting used to me. I have your dinner on the stove," she said.

"No, thanks. I don't eat this late at night or have you forgotten?" he asked, as he sat on the edge of the couch. Then he put his elbows on his knees as his head came down to his hands.

"No, I haven't forgotten," she said, as she got behind him. "Sit back a little." Then she started massaging his shoulders.

"Mmm that feels good," he said, as her hands were kneading areas of his shoulders.

"See, I haven't forgotten some things. Philip, you are really tense. Why don't you let me release the rest of the tension from your body," she said in a sexy tone.

"I feel relaxed now thanks," he replied, as he stood up from the couch.

"Relaxed enough to dance with me? Come on," she said, as she turned the music up a little with the remote. As she began to slow dance with him she looked into his eyes, "I must have been crazy leaving all this. I'm really sorry."

They continued to slow dance. Towards the end of the music they looked into one another's eyes then she kissed him. The kisses between the two were getting hot and steamy making Bria wanting more and more of Philip. Then all of a sudden he stopped and shook his head as something ran across his mind.

"Feels good doesn't it?" She whispered.

"I was thinking of something," he said, as he looked at her with sincerity.

"So was I," she said. Then she kissed him again.

Later that morning, Kianna's room was chilly. She got up and put her window down. She noticed her mother's car was still parked in the driveway. She put on her slippers and robe. She tried to open her father's bedroom door, but it was locked. She knocked on the door and there was no answer, so she knocked a little harder.

"Who is it?" Philip asked, drowsy.

"Daddy, it me," Kianna said.

"Sweetheart," he said, as he opened the door a little, "it's five o'clock in the morning!"

"Daddy, why was your door locked?" Kianna asked, as she tried to look in his room.

"Honey, lower your voice. Your mother is in the next room."

"Can I sleep in your room?" She asked.

"Yes, but you have to go to sleep, please. Daddy got home late last night from work," he said, as Kianna got into her father's bed.

"Daddy, you locked the door again," Kianna said.

"I'm sorry honey, I did it by accident again. I'll get it later. Goodnight, sweetheart," he said, as he covered himself with the covers.

"Don't you mean good morning, daddy?" Kianna asked chuckling.

"Yes," he said. Then he closed his eyes.

"Daddy?" Kianna asked.

"Yes, Kianna?" He looked up at the ceiling.

"Are we as in you, mommy Courtney, Sabrina and me going to the black circus today?" she asked.

"Yes, Kianna. Now go to sleep," he said, as he looked at

her with candor. Then he turned over and went back to sleep.

At the circus they took some pictures. Then the girls wanted their parents to take a picture together. Philip put his arm around Courtney's waist.

"Miss, why don't you snuggle up a little more to your husband," the cameraman said to Courtney. "Okay one more picture," he said, as he looked through the camera lens. Then he looked at Philip, "Why don't you kiss her. Come on," he said in an encouraging tone of voice, "don't act like strangers."

"Yes, I know what you mean," Philip said agreeing with the cameraman.

Courtney gave Philip a staid look and he began to grin. He bent down to Courtney's shoulder then they took a picture together with their faces side by side.

After they left the circus they went over to Courtney's house for dinner. Philip cooked. The kids played, took baths, and then they were ready for bed. Philip read to the girls while Courtney relaxed downstairs. After Philip was done, he came downstairs and watched a movie with Courtney on television. An hour later the movie went off then a commercial came on stating what will be coming on next.

"That should be an interesting movie. I wonder how it's going to end," he said, bright-eyed and lying back comfortably in the chair.

"Philip, what's on your mind?" Courtney asked.

"Nothing," He smiled. "Just relaxing."

"I can tell you have something on your mind."

"Nothing, I'm probably tired,"

"I know how that feels," she said, hoping he would get the hint that she was tired and ready to go to bed.

An hour later Courtney looked at her watch, then she put her head down on the chair hoping that Philip would get the obvious and go home. She wound up falling asleep on the couch. As she was sleeping, she jerked and woke up then she looked over at Philip who was asleep.

"Philip. Philip, wake up," Courtney said, while turning off the television. "It's 11:30, I have church tomorrow."

"I'm sorry. Let me get up," he said, not moving.

Courtney went to the kitchen to get some water. When she came out, he fell asleep again. She went back into the kitchen to get him a glass of cold water. She walked over to the chair calling Philip's name and then she tapped him on the shoulder. He sat up on the edge of the chair as she handed it to him.

"Thank you," he said, as he took the glass. Then he drank some water. "I don't know why I'm so tired. I'm sorry for keeping you up."

"You want to go outside to get some air?"

They stood outside as the cool but pleasant night air swept across his face making him more awake. He drank the rest of the water. Then he had a faraway look on his face.

"Are you going to tell me what's on your mind?" Courtney asked.

"Why do you think something is on my mind?" he asked looking directly at her.

"Number one, I thought, you don't care for old movies and number two, you have never spent this kind of time with me and the girls together."

"You and I haven't hung out in a while so, I'm making up for lost time," he said, smiling while passing Courtney the empty glass.

"You're lying."

"But it sounds good," he said, as they both smiled. "However, there is something I want to ask you. I have front row seats tickets to a musical play called Prince Cammolott: First Love. I think we would enjoy it. It's in two weeks on a Saturday evening."

"I don't think I have anything plan. I'll let you know," Courtney said, as she smiled.

"Fine. I'll see you tomorrow. Go into the house and lock the door so I can go home and get some sleep. I have to go into the office tomorrow," he said.

"Goodnight," Courtney said.

When Philip got home Bria was parked in his driveway.

"Another late night at the office," Bria said getting out of her car.

"What are you doing here, Bria? I told you, Kianna and I had plans out all day," he said.

"Hey, I missed my family," she said, smiling. "Where were you?"

"I'm not going to entertain your interrogation," he said, getting angry from being tired. "You need to get back into your car and go home. It's late. No lady should be out here this time of night."

"Philip, I want to spend the night here with you. Don't turn me away, please," she said. She attempted to entice him while touching his smooth face. "Since I've been around you, you seem to be more at peace with yourself."

"I see one thing hasn't changed, you give yourself too much credit," Philip said, chucking to himself. He couldn't believe how arrogant she sounded. "Now Bria," he said as he became serious, "you are really pushing it! Please leave." He opened her car door for her to get in.

"Why are you doing this?" she asked, as she shut the door moving closer to him. "I'm reaching out for you. Don't you want me?" she asked seductively looking up at him batting her eyelashes. Then she put her arms around his neck.

"Next time call like you used to before you become too comfortable," he said, while gently pushing her back. "I'm going into my house alone. Goodnight," he said firmly. Then he walked away from her.

When he got to his room ten minutes later, he looked out his window and Bria was still parked outside his house. He went to bed.

Later that night, Philip dreamed that Bria tricked the alarm to get inside his house. In his dream, he was in a deep sleep and he couldn't wake up. Bria was dressed in a white lingerie with matching stiletto heel slippers. She used a drill to get into his locked bedroom door. In his dream, she walked into his room and he woke up.

"You didn't think I was going to give up that easily?" Bria asked in his dream. Then he looked at the window and it shut down by itself. "You are going to give me what I want that has always been mine from the beginning. Doesn't this bring back memories?" she asked, in his dream as she walked towards him kicking off her shoes. She blew a kiss at him and then his hands were handcuffed to the bed and his feet were spread apart tied to the side of the bedpost. "After I'm finished with you, you won't make me wait again and that's a promise," Bria said boldly in his dream. Then she kissed him as her right hand moved down to the side of his stomach then to his back with her fingernails pressed against his skin.

Philip woke up from his dream sweating and his heart beating a mile a minute. He felt something pressing against the side of his back. He felt for it and it was a remote. He looked at his bedroom door that was wide open that he knew he left that way before he went to sleep. He got up, looked outside one of his bedroom windows, and saw Bria's car was gone.

Days later, Bria called Philip and apologized for her behavior the other night. She explained that she had been drinking and about time she got to his house, she was kind of tipsy. That's why she was acting irrational. She didn't want to cause an accident or to be pulled over by a cop trying to get home, so she didn't leave Philip's driveway until she got herself together.

As time went on, Bria felt by spending time with Kianna and helping Philip even more with small things around the house, that she had invested enough time to want more from him. Bria was helping Philip put away groceries.

"Listen, Philip, I need a commitment," Bria said, as she put something up in the cabinet.

"What do you mean?" Philip asked perplexed.

"You need a woman who can take care of your needs and look after Kianna," Bria said candidly.

"You talk about Kianna as if she is a stranger and not your own flesh and blood daughter."

"No, that's how you interpreted it. I want to be your woman then later become your wife again and we can have all the babies you want," she said smiling.

"Why are you ready to give me something that I haven't asked of you?" he asked, as she seductively walked over to him.

"Don't forget," Bria said boldly. "I know your dreams, desires and what you could never get out of your system. That's me! Think about what I said," she stated, as she looked into his eyes. She saw that Philip was not going to respond to her affectionately. Then she smiled. "Well," she said stepping back from him, "I'll have Kianna back home in a couple hours so you can take her over to Miss Perfect's place." Then she handed something to him, "Here you can put this away yourself." Then she walked away. Philip turned around and watched the kitchen door shut behind her.

Philip took Bria on one of his long Saturday drive that he likes to do sometimes to relax. They stopped at country stores where they brought fresh fruits and vegetables. They looked at different style of antique furniture and drank fresh water from a brook. They lost track of time picking Kianna up from Courtney. He called Courtney on her cellular phone since she wasn't home.

"Courtney, please forgive me," Philip said. "I'm about five hours away. Can Kianna stay with you tonight? Hold on," he said, laughing. "Stop!"

"Philip, are you with Bria?" Courtney asked.

"Yes," Philip replied smiling at Bria. "You can bring Kianna home tomorrow after you get out of church."

Then Courtney heard Bria in the background.

"If she is going to bring Kianna home tomorrow, we can

spend the night here," Bria said to Philip while he was on the phone with Courtney.

"Courtney . . . Courtney," Philip said. "Hello. . . . hello, Courtney!" Then the call ended.

"What happened?" Bria asked Philip.

"We were disconnected," Philip replied, as he looked down at his phone seeing that there was no signal failure.

Philip tried to call Courtney back but she didn't answer. Courtney was at Ashley's house.

"Courtney, you should have answered that call. It could have been important," Ashley said.

"I don't believe, Philip!" Courtney said, getting upset.

"What?" Ashley asked concerned.

"He's out of town with Bria," Courtney said distinctly with an appalled look, "and since Kianna is staying at my house tonight, Bria wants Philip to come home tomorrow."

"Wait a minute," Ashley said, surprised at her sister. "Are we jealous? I'm sure you don't mind keeping Kianna overnight."

"I'm not jealous," Courtney said, as her voice changed to a higher pitch. Ashley turned around as if she was looking for something while smiling. Then she turned back around to look at Courtney concerned. "I can keep Kianna for eternity. The point is Kianna was looking forward to seeing her father," she stated in a sad tone.

"Let's see," Ashley said. Then she walked to the back door of her house. She smiled as she saw Kianna running around with the other children, "Kianna, come here please."

"What are you doing?" Courtney asked, as Ashley walked back to the room.

"Yes, Aunt Ashley," Kianna answered, as she walked into the room.

"Come here," Ashley said. Then she put her arm around Kianna's shoulder. "Your father called, you will be spending the night at your mommy's home tonight."

"Yea!" Kianna said. Then she walked over to Courtney and hugged her then she ran out the room.

"She didn't look disappointed to me. You are the one who was looking forward to seeing Philip," Ashley said teasingly. "The only thing you had to say, Philip, I want to see you," she said in a sexy tone. Then she smiled, "Why don't you admit it, you really like him!"

"Shut up, Ashley! You don't know what you are talking about," Courtney said, with attitude.

Four and a half-hours later, Courtney got a phone call from Philip.

"Courtney, I got back in town about twenty minutes ago after I dropped Bria off at her place. Is everything okay?"

"Yes, Philip everything is fine," she replied.

"Do you want me to come over and get Kianna?" he asked.

"No, Philip. I don't want you to wake her out of her sleep this time of night," Courtney said.

"What happened earlier on the phone?" he asked.

"What do you mean?" Courtney asked in a puzzled tone, knowing what he meant.

"When I was talking to you earlier today it seemed we had a clear connection and the next thing I know you were gone. I tried calling you back but there was no answer. I got your voice mail. What happened?" he asked.

"I hung up on you because you couldn't decide who you wanted to talk to. When you called back, I didn't want to answer the phone," she replied, adamantly and honestly.

"I understand," he said as he smiled nodding his head. He appreciated her honesty because he knew that's what it was. "Goodnight, Courtney. I'll see you tomorrow."

Chapter Twelve

It was a Saturday afternoon and Courtney was at home setting up Sabrina's pool for a party that her daughter was having for her friends. The water was coming out effectively through the special hose Courtney had hooked up to the pool. The pool was half full of water when it stopped running. Courtney kept trying to figure out the reason why the water shut off.

"Mommy, what's taking so long to fill the pool?" Sabrina asked.

"Sabrina for some reason the water won't come through," Courtney replied puzzled.

"Mommy, you have to do something," Sabrina whined.

"Sweetheart, we might have to get buckets of water and pour it into the pool," She said.

"That's not going to work," Sabrina said boldly. "If we do it that way it won't get the special affects from it while we're in the pool."

"Aunt Courtney, you still can't get the holes to work?" Zakeya asked, while working the camcorder.

"No," Courtney replied, smiling at the camcorder.

"I like your hair style." Zakeya said, while she was still recording.

"Thanks," Courtney said, smiling again with a pose, as she ran her hand through her hair. "I went to the hairdresser last night."

"My party is going to be ruined!" Sabrina said, upset. "I told all my friends that they would be able to swim in my pool and what neat things it does."

"Honey, mommy, is trying," Courtney said calmly.

Sabrina walked away upset. Philip walked to the back yard with Kianna.

"Sabrina, why the sad face?" Philip asked, concerned as Kianna went over to Courtney.

"Mommy, can't get the water to run into the pool," Sabrina said disappointedly.

Philip walked over to Courtney holding Sabrina's hand.

"Look at you," Courtney said to Philip smiling. "You look very handsome."

"Thank you. I'm going to a cook out," Philip said. "Let's see what the problem is," he said, as he let go of Sabrina's hand and reached for the hose in Courtney's hands.

"Philip, that's okay. I don't want you to get your clothes messy," Courtney said, as she tried to look down the hole.

"I won't. I'm a man who knows how to take care of things like this without getting messy," he said boldly, while taking the hose from her. Courtney gave him a disgusted look.

"Mommy, can I change into my swim suit?" Kianna asked, as she hugged Courtney around the waist.

"If you want to but the party won't start for another two hours," Courtney said, as she rubbed Kianna on her arm.

"Come on, Kianna, let's go in the house so we can change into our swimwear," Sabrina said.

Philip told Courtney to hold the hose. This was no regular hose. It was a little smaller than the fire department hose. Philip turned the waterspout off. He tried to figure out what would stop the water from running through. As Philip shook the holes in different sections the girls came out of the house playing. No one was paying attention to the two divas dressed in their swimwear with their sunshades on walking like women as they came back outside. Sabrina was thinking she was helping out by turning the waterspout off like she saw her mother did earlier, but she actually turned it on. Then the girls went back into the house for something.

Philip told Courtney again to hold the hose over the pool. Each time he believed he was turning the waterspout one way, he was doing the opposite. Meanwhile, Zakeya was working the camcorder recording Philip and Courtney by the pool. What Philip was doing to the hose didn't seem to work. The girls came back outside to see if the pool was finally working. Then Philip and Courtney were trying to look down the holes again when the water suddenly shot up in full force. As the water hit Courtney's face, the metal part of the hose hit her nose. Philip tried to pull it from Courtney as he lost his balance falling backwards then Courtney tried to grab him and they both fell into the pool with the hose. Philip helped Courtney to stand up in the pool.

"Are you okay?" Philip asked, as Sabrina ran over to the waterspout and turned it off.

"I think my nose is broken," Courtney said, frightened as she touched her nose lightly.

"Why did you let go of the hose?" he asked.

"Because it hit my nose," Courtney replied, as Philip helped her out the pool.

Courtney walked to the house with her head back. She didn't see any blood, but it certainly felt broken. Philip hooked the hose outside the pool and turned the water on.

"Here you go, Philip," Zakeya said. "Have one of the little kids' towels," she said humorously trying not to laugh.

"Thanks," he said, as he took the towel from Zakeya. Then he looked at her, "You can go ahead and laugh."

"No," Zakeya said, trying to refrain from laughing. "I'll wait until you go into the house," she said, smiling.

Philip went into the house and got a bigger towel for Courtney. She was standing in the bathroom looking at her nose in the mirror.

"Let me see your nose," Philip said, as he turned her around to him.

"I don't think my nose is broken," Courtney said, in a

whisper.

"I know it's not," he said, as he took his hand and lifted her chin up to look at her nose more closely. "You just have a small nip on the side of your nose," he said, as he wiped her face gently with the towel. He noticed how curly her hair was when it's wet.

Courtney continued to look up at Philip as the water came from his hair line down his eye brows and how his thick eye lashes held some of the water for a couple of seconds before dripping down his face. Courtney took part of the towel and wiped his face then they both begin to laugh. Philip opened the drawer in the bathroom and took out a couple of cotton balls and alcohol to nurse her nose.

Philip went home to change out of his drenched clothes and he unexpectedly came back to help out at the party. Courtney's hair was in a ponytail which made her look even younger. She was in good spirits walking around making sure that the guests felt welcome. Ashley and Preston had Philip cooking on the grill from time to time. Sabrina's party was a success. Zakeya stayed over at the house to help Courtney and Philip clean up.

Philip and Courtney watched the water run out the pool. Then Philip stopped watching the pool and stared at Courtney, unaware of what he was doing.

"What?" Courtney asked.

"I'm sorry. I wasn't looking at you. I was day-dreaming," he said.

"You look more tired than I am."

"I'm a little worn out," Philip admitted.

"Let's go inside. I don't know how I'm going to church tomorrow but I'll press my way. I'll get Zakeya to watch the girls for me. Did I tell you that I joined one of the choirs at my church."

"No," he replied.

"I did. I have rehearsals every second Saturday," she said sounding happy.

"Courtney, why is church so important that you have to go every Sunday?"

"Church is where my foundation begins for me every week," Courtney replied. "I want to give something back to God. I love to spend time with my family and friends and I feel God deserves at least a day. I owe it to myself to give thanks to Him in songs and getting to know Him better through the good word that the reverend delivers every Sunday."

As they walked inside the house they heard Zakeya laughing hysterically at the television.

"Zakeya, what are you laughing at?" Philip asked.

"Let me rewind the tape. Watch this!" Zakeya said. She showed them part of the tape where Philip and Courtney fell into the pool. Then they all laughed, but Zakeya was laughing the hardest. "I have to make copies of this. Goodnight!" she said breathlessly, turning off the VCR. Then she got up and walked with her hand on her stomach to the stairs case still chuckling. When she got to the fifth step, she stopped and laughed more bending down then she continued on up the stairs again. By this time Philip and Courtney didn't think it was funny any longer.

"I'll make sure that this tape mysteriously disappears by morning," Courtney said, assuring Philip. He smiled nodding his head.

Chapter Thirteen

One weekend, Courtney was out doing some errands and the last thing she had to do was to drop something off at Philip's home.

"Here you go, Philip. I'll talk to you later," Courtney said at the door. Then she turned around to walk away.

"Hey, Courtney, are you in a rush?" Philip asked preoccupied, as she turned back around to him. "I want to talk to you about something."

"Oh, okay. Sure!"

"Come in, please. How much do I owe you for the dry-cleaning of Kianna's uniforms?" he asked, as he hung the clothes in a closet.

"Don't worry about it. What do you want to talk to me about?" They walked into the living room.

"As you know Bria has been around here for months now. Kianna is not totally comfortable with her but she seems to," then he paused. "Let's see, what word am I looking for?" he murmured to himself.

"Tolerate," Courtney said, as she looked him in his eyes.

"No. How about adjusting to Bria. Anyway, I feel in due time Kianna will come around. Bria has made positive efforts to make up for some lost time with Kianna. It's like Bria is trying to work towards an acceptance from us. Nothing serious has happened between Bria and I. I mean, I'm not in love with her but something is missing from Kianna and my life. Bria wants us to try again as a family. She is willing to give me more children that I always dreamed of having, Courtney.

What do you think? Should I allow her back into my life that has been cut off all of these years?" he asked. Courtney didn't say anything as she looked away from him and then back at him not believing what he was asking her. "Courtney, what do you think?"

"I think you are a fool!" She said rudely.

"A fool?" he asked, astounded. "No one has ever called me that since my mother and I believe I told you about that."

"And you know what?" she asked harshly. "I see why your mother said it! I guess since Bria was gone for so many years that these last two or three months she decides she wants to visit supposed to erase broken hearts overnight. Don't sell yourself short. Most importantly don't sell Kianna short. You and Kianna came through a stressful and painful time during Bria's period of being a responsible adult. If that's what you want to call it. Does she really love Kianna as a mother should and is she willing to make her life more difficult having children? How long do you think the good times are going to last between you two before she becomes bored again and she gets a new vision of her life. Then it happens all over again she's gone. Vanished! The woman who put on an act that won her an Emmy before to get you and the same performance is going to do it again, right? The woman you want is not in Bria.

Philip, I can see it now," she said, sarcastically. "When she turns 45 or 50-years-old, she will probably still be wearing mini skirts, thinking life is passing her by. She will be showing all of the goods that the Lord blessed her with to other men. Then Kianna and whatever brothers and sisters she has will suffer, but Kianna is a smart girl. Maybe she will tell her siblings about one of many experiences with her mother's disappearing acts and how she survived it. But as I think about it, Philip, maybe I'm getting a little ahead of myself because she hasn't survived the first one. Kianna is still dealing with the hurt and she still has dreams of being left.

As for you, why do you keep spending time with women

that you don't care about? They are not willing to know the real Philip Edward Franklin Jr.," Courtney said.

"How did you know my middle name?" he asked.

"That's not important, Philip. What's important is you and who you are inside here," she said, as she pointed to his heart. "You are impatient. You want things when you want them. Doesn't it matter to you if it feels right or just okay is good enough for you? You want to spend precious time with someone you know doesn't have the same interests as you or prefer the same person who took you through the mud more times then you care to admit.

Could you have seen this coming before you married Bria?" she asked, as Philip turned around from her upset. "Or were you so blinded by her beauty that you couldn't see how hideous she was inside. Well, next time you may not be so lucky.

Philip, why don't you love the people who are right in front of you," she said, as he turned around to her. "You have Kianna, your close family and friends. Eventually everything will fall into place when the time is right. Don't rush it! You are too special of a person for that," she said.

"You have nerve!" Philip said, looking at Courtney angrily as he took a couple steps towards her. "Telling me that I spend my time with women that I don't care about. Well, at least I'm willing to take a chance! You hide behind Sabrina, your job, and church when it comes to your true feelings about a special man being in your life."

"Oh, no, you didn't go there," she said, stunned.

"You act as if you have so much going on and you are not ready for a relationship. Do you know what your problem is?" Philip asked forward without being apprehensive. "You have hypnotized yourself for so long, you believe your own lies." Courtney's eyes widened as her mouth dropped down some from shock. "At least I'm honest about my feelings. I want someone to love me and I want to love the right person that is for me. Can you honestly say that Courtney and be truly honest with yourself?

So you were hurt eight years ago by one man," he said, as he held up one index finger for a couple of seconds, "and you go into a shell like a turtle. Everyone makes mistakes! You learn from them and move on. There is a whole world out there," he said with enthusiasm, "but you won't enjoy it. Why don't you stop punishing yourself for something that is history!"

"You don't know what you are talking about!" she angrily said, walking a few steps away from him.

"Yes I do. I see it, Courtney," Philip said boldly, as Courtney looked at him. "I see it in your eyes and at times in your body language," he said compassionately, walking to her. "You should stop acting like your heart is made out of stone. I'm sure the church you attend expresses that you shouldn't be selfish with your love. You should share it. Especially with the people who share their love with you."

"If you think I'm going to put my heart out there to be crushed, you're nuts!" she said.

"This is great!" he said sarcastically, as he threw his hands up in the air. "Now you have down-sized me from a fool to a nut. I know what you are trying to say. I'm not saying you should sleep with every man you meet. You know how to establish a friendship because you did it with me, Courtney. You don't know what's out there and you are cheating yourself."

"If that's all, I really have to go," she said, calmly. "I've said all I had to say about your matter."

"Yes, that's it. Thanks for bringing Kianna's uniforms by," he said gently.

"Don't mention it," she said softly, as she walked around him to the front door.

Courtney was so upset it took all her will power not to slam the door behind her as she left Philip's home.

Later that day Bria stopped by Philip's place. She could tell something was on his mind because he was quiet and preoccupied during dinner. When Bria walked into the living room

Philip was standing up staring at a picture on the wall. His mind was a million miles way. She walked over to him.

"What's wrong, Philip? You didn't eat much at dinner," Bria said concerned.

"I'm tired. I really need to turn in early," he said calmly, as he looked at her.

"You are stressed. Let me make it better for you," Bria said in a seductive tone, as she put her arms around his neck.

"Bria, do you always resolve situations with sex?" He removed her arms from around his neck. "I haven't and I won't sleep with someone for convenience. I did that before I became a family man. I won't allow my life to become difficult by any means."

"What is your problem tonight?" she asked, wondering if it was something that she had done.

"I need to be alone."

"Fine! I'll be back tomorrow to see my daughter," she said getting her purse off the chair as she left.

Courtney was at Ashley's place that evening talking about Philip. Ashley was sitting down in the family room nipping on her last cookie while watching her sister's hand motions while she paced the floor, ranting on and on.

"I couldn't believe Philip. He asked for my opinion and when I gave it, he jumped all over me. Why did I even give it? And, what's wrong with my life anyway? I like it," Courtney said agitated.

"I agree with you, Courtney. You like your life the way it is," Ashley said while dipping the rest of her cookie into a half of glass of cold milk. "It's not a crime to be alone. For some people true love comes once in a lifetime. Then, you have those people who are blessed with second chances to love again. You haven't truly been in love but if you turn it away that's your business." Then she ate the cookie.

"Do you want to tell me something about you and Philip?"

"What do you mean?" Ashley asked puzzled.

"You two stick up for each other all the time. Maybe he's your brother and I'm the friend of the family," Courtney said upset.

"I don't know what you are talking about. Have you been talking about me to Philip? Don't answer that, I know you have. He's your best friend and I know he wouldn't tell you something inappropriate. Listen, I think you both meant well and maybe it didn't go over the way it was meant to be taken. Things will work itself out. You guys will probably be talking before this night is out."

Courtney went home and put her foot up on the centerpiece table in her living room drinking a cup of tea and thinking about what Philip said to her. She found herself getting angrier saying to herself what she should have really said to him.

Philip went to bed upset, thinking about what Courtney said to him. He was listening to classical music on the radio and he heard a piece that was played at one of the performances they had seen together. Then at that moment he realized something about Courtney that really stunned him, but he thought he could be wrong about it. He cast the thought away believing it was crazy!

The next day Bria came over to Philip's house to see Kianna. Bria walked into the house with a nonchalant attitude as she cut her eyes at Philip.

"Bria, I'm sorry about yesterday. I meant what I said but how I said it wasn't right. This is not going to work with us," Philip said openly.

"What's not going to work with us?" Bria asked, hoping that Philip wasn't giving up on wanting another relationship with her.

"Pertaining to you and me personally. I've been thinking about it, the life I want and what you want are two different things. You want to live my dream but you won't be happy with it. Kianna is your daughter and you can see her as often as you wish. I know you told me that you don't like for her to call Courtney mommy. I can talk to Kianna and eventually she will call Courtney by her name, and you will be addressed as her mother only."

"Isn't that being unfair to Kianna?"

"Yes," Philip stated, "by stopping Kianna from calling Courtney mommy would be harsh to her. Courtney has been there all this time for her. She got through to Kianna in ways that neither my family nor I could. However, out of respect to you, I'll do it. Even though there is no future for us, you have a responsibility, Bria. If you are going to be in her life, I expect 100% from you like she gets from me. If not, I want you to tell me before disappearing again."

"Fine!" Bria said upset. "I'm going upstairs to see my daughter."

"You know where her room is," he said, as he walked away.

Bria went to Kianna's room. She tapped on the door as she entered.

"Hi, Kianna. What are you doing?" Bria asked.

"Hi, mom. Playing with my dolls," she said, while braiding one of the doll's hair.

"Kianna, would you stop playing with your dolls for a moment," Bria said, as she sat on the side of Kianna's bed. "I need to talk to you about something important. I know in time your father, you and I will be together again as a family. Wouldn't you like that?" She smiled. Kianna didn't say a word, as her eyes dropped down to her doll lying on her lap. "Until then, I'm going to do my best to be here for you. If you ever need anything let me know. I'm your mother, all right?"

"Yes," Kianna replied, looking at Bria.

"Good!" She smiled proudly at Kianna feeling that they were becoming closer. "So, is there something that I can do for you? Just ask me."

"I want you to leave my family alone," Kianna said,

boldly.

"What?" Bria asked, in shock. "I'm your family, Kianna. I'm your mother!" she said distinctly.

"Only by birth," she said bluntly, "I heard my daddy telling you that when you came back months ago. I just want it to be my daddy and me. Everything was perfect until you came back and interrupted our lives. That's what I want from you. To leave us alone."

"Kianna, you hurt my feelings," Bria said brokenhearted.

"This is my doll Shiann," she picked up another doll on her bed and handed it to Bria. She showed no remorse of what she said to her mother. "When I feel bad I hug her then I feel better. Here try it."

"I'm okay," Bria said discouraged, as she held the doll in her hands thinking. "For once, Kianna, I'm going to honor your feelings, your request. I'm going to leave," she said, as her voice cracked. She looked up taking a deep breath, "This has been a hard day for me." Then she looked at Kianna, "Can I at least get a hug from you?"

Kianna hugged her. Bria went downstairs. Philip saw tears in her eyes as they stood at the door as she was about to leave.

"Bria, what's wrong?" He asked concerned.

"Our daughter has become a little woman," Bria said. "She definitely says what's on her mind."

"She takes after her mother. What did she say?" Philip asked.

"Nothing really. We just had a little girl talk. Please don't get on her; she was being what I could never be, which is herself. I'll talk to you later."

The next day Philip put his house on the market to be sold and he had a realtor draw up the contract on the house he wanted to buy.

As the days went by Philip and Courtney spoke to one another strictly about the girls. Because of their stubbornness neither one of them mentioned anything about the intense discussion that they had that Saturday afternoon at Philip's home. The girls still spent a lot of time with each other. When Philip would call Sabrina, Courtney would race her daughter to the telephone just to hear Philip's voice say, 'Hello, Courtney. How are you?'

Philip and Courtney talked to the girls together about his decision to move and how they wouldn't be going to the same school any longer. Philip's house was sold in two weeks but he couldn't move for another two weeks when his interior decorator would have his new home ready to move in. He didn't need any ideas of how he wanted in his new house to look. He just stated the specifics and it was taken care of.

The day of the move, Kianna woke up early putting the rest of her dolls in the empty boxes in her room. There was a tap on her door.

"Come in, daddy." She said downhearted.

"Good morning, sunshine." Philip kissed his daughter's forehead.

"Good morning, daddy. I'm finished packing my dolls."

Philip picked her up in his arms. She put her arm around his neck while looking sadly into her dad's eyes.

"Honey, I need you to be a big girl for me. I know you don't want to move because you will be further away from your friends."

"And my sister Sabrina and my mommy Courtney."

"I know but you will still get to see them on the weekends. The only thing will change soon is seeing them everyday at school. Daddy lived in this house for 11 years and it's time for us to move on. I promise this will work for all of us. I need you to be the happy little girl I'm used to. I can't be happy if you're not. Okay?"

Kianna nodded her head.

"Aunt Lauren is here. I'm going to put some of your stuff that you don't want the movers to handle in her car. Then she's going to meet us at our house. Meanwhile, I want you to get dress and have breakfast before the movers get here."

"Yes, daddy," she said sadly.

"Kianna, please smile baby."

"I love you, daddy." Kianna said, then she hugged her father. When she looked at him again she smiled. Then he blew big kisses on her cheeks, the shoulders of her robe, and on her hands as she covered her face while laughing. Lauren smiled as she walked past the staircase hearing her niece giggling louder and louder.

Bria stopped by the house while the movers were putting things on to the truck. She began to reminisce while walking through the house when she and Philip first moved in and the times she visited. Deep inside her, she felt those days of popping in and out of the two people's lives was over. She thought that God gave her the perfect gift, which was her family and she gave it all up for vanity. Since Bria didn't see Philip she went to Kianna's room.

"Kianna," Bria said.

"Hi, mom!" Kianna said, walking from the window.

"Are you excited to be moving?"

"Yes and no. I'm going to miss my sister Sabrina," Kianna said. She looked sad thinking about her friend. "We won't be taking classes together too much longer but we still get to see one another on the weekends."

"That's good. Kianna. I'm leaving town for good. There is nothing here for me, really. You and your daddy are doing fine. I need to find a life for me now. I wanted to say bye. I'm going to keep in touch. If I write you will you write back?"

"Yes, I will," Kianna replied.

"I think that will be sort of fun getting letters in the mail from one another. Kianna, if there is ever anything I can do for you, I want you to let me know. I know I have a strange way of showing it but in my own way I do love you. See you later," Bria said sadly. Then she turned around to walk out the door.

"Mom," Kianna said.

"Yes," Bria answered, as she turned around to Bria.

Kianna walked over to her mother and hugged her around the waist. Bria wanted to burst into tears, but she kept telling herself she had to be strong.

"Thanks and don't forget to write," Kianna said.

"I won't. That's a promise I'll keep," she said, firmly.

"Here, you can have my doll Shiann," Kianna said, as she took the doll out of one of the boxes.

"Thank you, Kianna. Every time I look at this doll, I'll think of you and imagine," Bria said, as she closed her eyes, "I'm hugging you everyday of my life."

Bria went downstairs looking for Philip. She walked to the kitchen.

"I should have known you would be in here," Bria said smiling.

"Hi. I'm making sure all the cabinets are cleared out. What are you doing with Shiann?" he asked.

"Our daughter gave her to me. I'm leaving for good, Philip," Bria said.

"Why?" he asked concerned for Kianna.

"I don't like to stay anywhere I'm not wanted," Bria said. "I used to be wanted once upon a time long, long ago, but I'm no longer the apple of either you or Kianna's eye."

"You are needed as a mother to Kianna. Other personal feelings shouldn't matter," he said.

"Well it does. I can only be me, right?" she stated rudely, then she stopped for a second. "Sorry," she said, as she somewhat smiled. "I made a deal with Kianna, we're going to write each other and I'll call once in a while to hear her voice. Once I settle down, I'll call you with a phone number. If you need me, you know my Uncle Melvin's phone number and my mother's of course."

"I'm sorry things didn't work out the way you hoped," Philip said. "Especially for Kianna's sake."

"Me too. I know this is going to sound crazy to you but

this place was like a little haven to me like home. Now all that's gone. If only I would have came back a year ago, I probably would have had a chance with the family I used to have. No need to cry over spilled milk especially when you keep doing it over and over again. Take care." Bria said, as she hugged him with regrets. "Whomever you share your life with Philip will be one happy woman. Goodbye, Philip."

"Goodbye, Bria," he said, as he let her go. She turned around and walked away.

That was the first time Philip ever said goodbye to Bria and actually felt it. Philip went upstairs to check on Kianna and to get the rest of the boxes of stuffed animals. When he opened the door to Kianna's room it was only two boxes left for him to take. Kianna was sitting in the center of the room in Indian-style playing with two dolls.

"Are you okay, Kianna?" He asked, as he bent down to her then he kissed the side of her of face.

"Yes, daddy," she replied.

"Are you sad that your mom won't be around?"

"No, daddy. I have you." He smiled. "Are you sad about mom?"

"No." They both smiled at each other. "The movers are finished; we're ready to go."

"Daddy, I'll be right down," Kianna said, as they both stood up. Then she went into the bathroom.

"Kianna, I'll be in the car. I need to set something outside," he said loudly, while carrying the boxes down the stairs.

Philip waited in the car for five minutes then he came back in the house. Kianna was still in the bathroom posing in the mirror.

"Courtney, what are you doing up there? Let's go now!" Philip demanded.

Kianna came down the stairs laughing.

"Daddy, you are funny," Kianna said.

"Why is that?"

"Because you called me, Courtney." Then she put her hand over her mouth giggling.

"No, I didn't," Philip said, not believing he would do that.

"Yes you did, daddy. You said, Courtney," she said trying to sound like her father, "what are you doing up there? Let's go now!" Then she laughed again.

"Come on, sweetie. I made a mistake," He said, as he opened the front door for his daughter. She took her father's hand walking to the car.

"This is the second time you called out mommy's name. You called Aunt Lauren, Courtney too when you were talking to her earlier on the phone."

"Kianna, would you please get in the car," he pleaded. "Put on your seatbelt." Then he shut the car door, smiling at his daughter.

Chapter Fourteen

Philip hired a housekeeper name Patricia who would also take care of Kianna's needs during the weekdays. Sometimes she would work on Saturdays when the girls were together at Philip's place while he was gone into the office for a few hours.

The girls had one more week together in school before Kianna started her new school. On her last day at the school her home room teacher had a cake, punch, and a card signed by her classmates and the faculty. While everyone was mingling in class, Sabrina was standing off by herself looking out of a window feeling very sad.

"Why are you over here by yourself, Sabrina?" Kianna asked.

"I don't want you to go," Sabrina said, as she looked at Kianna. Then she began to cry.

"I don't want to go either," Kianna said, then she started to cry.

When some of the kids saw them crying they started crying too because they knew Kianna since kindergarten. When their teacher saw them crying, she stopped what she was doing and talked to them as she wiped their faces with tissues.

The girls told their parents they didn't want to go to school that Monday morning without one another. What kept Kianna going that first week that she knew Sabrina would be coming over to her house for the first time since her and her father moved. Courtney brought Sabrina over to Philip's home on Friday night.

"Hi, mommy," Kianna said, excited hugging Courtney.

"Hi, sweetie," Courtney said, happy to see Sabrina as she hugged her. "Hi Philip," she smiled.

"How are you?" Philip said candidly to Courtney. Then he looked at Sabrina and smiled, "Hi, Sabrina."

"Hi, daddy," Sabrina said, as she walked over to him and hugged him.

"Wow! This place looks great," Courtney said, as she looked around.

"Thanks," Philip said, "It not completely finished. As you will see I listened to some of your suggestions. Let me show you around."

When they all got to a particular room, Philip told Sabrina it was hers but she had to close her eyes first before she could see it.

"Go ahead, Sabrina, close your eyes," Kianna said, excited.

"I love surprises," Sabrina said, while closing her eyes with anticipation.

Philip put his hands around Sabrina's eyes while Kianna opened the door.

"Okay, Sabrina, open your eyes now," Philip said, as he smiled removing his hands from over her eyes. Sabrina's eyes lit up like a Christmas tree as her mouth opened. They walked into the room and he stooped down next to her. "Do you like it?"

Philip had her pink and white colorful room decorated in her favorite cartoon characters. The king size bed was wrapped in a big white bow with her name printed in pink. There was also a night stand with a soft pink phone, an alarm clock radio with tape and CD player, and a small picture frame of Kianna, which was Kianna's idea. The entire corner of the room had a pink rose garden canopy with a round play table inside of it with chairs and a tea set. The other side of the room was a 4ft. doll-house with small dolls and furniture for her to decorate it as she pleased. There were all kinds of stuff animals and different kinds of art work for her.

"Oh, you are the best daddy in the whole wide world!" Sabrina said, as she kissed and hugged him.

"Philip, that is so kind of you," Courtney said, sort of speechless as she looked around in the room smiling. "This room is beautiful."

"Thank you. I wanted Sabrina to know she has a place in our home," Philip said, as he was so pleased that Sabrina liked her room.

The girls ran on top of the bed and jumped on it while holding hands.

While Kianna was in Sabrina's room showing her how to work the remote to her bed, Philip and Courtney chatted a little downstairs for the first time since they last talked at his old house. Then he walked her to the car and watched her drive away until he couldn't see the taillights of her car. When Courtney got home, she went straight to bed with a book then the telephone rang.

"It's Philip. I wanted to make sure you got home safe," he said.

"Thank you, Philip. Yes, I'm fine," Courtney replied, as she put her book down.

"From now on if the girls have to get together after day light, I'll be the one to drive over to your place to pick Sabrina up. I don't like for you to drive out here in no man's land when it's pitch dark."

"Okay. I appreciate that," she said.

There was a long pause between the two. Courtney opened her mouth to say something like she missed him but the words wouldn't come out. She became nervous.

"I have to go, Courtney. Goodnight," Philip said.

"Goodnight, Philip."

Courtney held the receiver to her chest wanting to talk to him more. She didn't have anything important to talk to him about but she just wanted to hear his voice and his laugher.

Philip hung up the telephone taking a deep breath missing his best friend. A friend that he never had before her and knowing he would never find it in anyone else again.

One afternoon, Philip was at home in his library reviewing several contracts and acquisitions from his attorneys concerning business. Courtney was at home stretching from a long run before taking a hot deserved bath. They both were listening to the same classical radio station when they heard that Cammolott's First Love would be performing again at the Pavilion. They purchased tickets online thinking they were going to ask one another to see the play.

Philip stared at the telephone wondering how to ask Courtney out. He kept telling himself he had plenty of time. Courtney picked up the receiver, dialed only four numbers and then hung up the phone telling herself she would call tomorrow.

One evening after work, Courtney went to pick up Zakeya from the studio where she took voice lessons. Since Courtney arrived at the studio a little early, she got a chance to hear her niece sing. She sat in a chair listening and smiling at her niece thinking how wonderful she sounded. As she listened to the words of the song she became sad. Courtney hardly said a word to Zakeya while walking to the car.

"Aunt Courtney, did I sound bad in the studio? You looked at me as if I was hitting a bad note." Zakeya asked.

"No, not at all," Courtney said, as she put her arm around Zakeya. "I loved it! I'm sorry. I'm a little tired."

"Just think next month, I'll be sixteen and I'll be driving myself around to voice lessons, swimming practice, school games, and shopping at the mall with my friends!"

"Don't rush it, young lady," Courtney said as she smiled.

Courtney drove Zakeya home. As they walked in the house Zakeya called out for her mother. Ashley yelled that she was in the kitchen. Preston was in the kitchen fixing a salad for dinner.

"Are you staying for dinner, Courtney?" Ashley asked. "Look, I made your favorite lasagna."

"No thank you. I'm tired. I'm going home and get some rest," Courtney said, looking uneasy.

"Are you okay, Courtney?" Preston asked, concerned.

"Yes," Courtney replied, preoccupied. "I'll talk to you all later," Then she walked out the kitchen. Zakeya walked Courtney outside to her car.

"What's wrong with Courtney, Ashley?" Preston asked.

"My poor sister is in love and she isn't even aware of it," Ashley replied, as her husband walked over to her.

"Well don't you go telling her. Let her figure it out for herself," Preston said, looking suspiciously at his wife.

"Too late. I told her that some time back but I used another word instead of love because I didn't want her to bite my head off," Ashley said, as she smiled at her husband.

"I know one thing," Preston said putting his arms around Ashley. "I find myself falling more and more in love with you every day. I'm glad we're spending the rest of our lives together."

"I feel the same way, honey," Ashley said.

Preston and Ashley began to kiss then Zakeya walked into the kitchen.

"Mom! Dad! Come on! Can Cameron come over for dinner?" Zakeya asked, with one arm behind her back.

"Your boyfriend was over here last night," Preston said, smiling looking into his wife's eyes.

"Is it okay, please?" Zakeya begged.

"Sure," Preston replied.

"Thanks. As you both were," Zakeya said smiling, as she removed her arm from around her back with the cordless telephone. Then she pressed a button as she walked out of the kitchen. "It's okay, come on over."

Preston and Ashley continued to kiss.

Since school was out for the summer Preston and Ashley made plans to take all the children to Walt Disney World for a week. Philip dropped Kianna at Ashley's place Saturday morning since they were leaving on the plane that afternoon for the trip. Then Courtney dropped Sabrina off.

"Did you see, Philip?" Ashley asked. "He just left here."

"No, I didn't. Preston is putting the girls' luggage in the van. Are you sure you don't need me to go with you guys to the airport?" Courtney asked.

"No. We can manage." Ashley looked at Courtney concerned. "When are you and Philip going to sit down and talk this thing out? And don't give me a smart answer telling me you do talk to him. I'm talking about your relationship."

"Our relationship is good. We're still best of friends," Courtney said impassively.

"No, it's more than that. You know, I left him in here by himself for a few minutes to do something and when I came back, he was holding this picture of you," Ashley said while taking one of the picture frames sitting on the mantle piece of the fireplace holding it up for Courtney to see and then she sat it back down, "He was tracing something with his finger. Maybe it was your face. I'm not sure. I know he really misses you."

"Why do you have to read into everything?" Courtney asked frustrated.

"I don't have to read into everything, Courtney," Ashley said boldly, "It's as plain as the nose on your face. Both of you need to stop being stubborn. I know you really like Philip. No, let me change that. I know you love Philip. I don't understand why you two are willing to let happiness pass you by."

"So, Ashley, how did your doctor's appointment go?" Courtney asked, in a calm tone.

Seven days later it was the night of the performance. Philip and Courtney went to the performance alone, sitting one aisle away from one another. Of course when the play got to a certain scene Courtney was in tears. Philip smiled as he remembered how she responded to each act. He looked up at the ceiling praying in his mind to God about something as he took a deep breath. They missed each other twice that night, once in the huge lobby of the Pavilion and again leaving the parking lot in their cars.

The next morning Courtney went running, worked out with a videotape, and went grocery shopping. Later that afternoon the doorbell rang as Courtney came down the staircase. She opened the door.

"Hi, Philip," Courtney said, surprised to see him.

"How are you, Courtney?" Philip asked candidly.

"Fine! Fine. Please come in," Courtney said smiling and feeling flustered.

"I need to talk to you," he said, as they walked to the living room.

"Sure, but hold that thought. I need to take some clothes out of the dryer. It's laundry weekend for me. I'll be right back then we can talk. So don't go anywhere," she said, smiling.

"Sure," he said, as he watched her walk away.

As Philip walked to the couch, he noticed an unused ticket to the last night's performance sitting on one of the end tables. He smelled something cooking in the kitchen. He went to see what Courtney was cooking.

"Here you are," Courtney said, as she walked over to him. "As you can see I can't do two things at the same time. Especially cooking," she said, laughing nervously.

"We just need to turn the burner down some. If you don't mind, I'm going to set the frying pan to the side. I really need you to listen to what I have to say to you," he said, sounding serious.

"That's fine," she said, as she leaned back on the kitchen counter. "You want to talk here or in the other room?" she asked, as they walked to the table in the kitchen.

"Here is fine." He said. Neither one wanted to sit down.

"You have my undivided attention. What is it you want to say to me?" she asked. Then she quietly took a deep breath and having a stern look ready to take on anything that he had to say to her.

"The last time we talked about the situation concerning

Bria I don't know what I was expecting you to say. I thought it was going to be sugar-coated. You brought some very important matters to my attention that I some how had lost sight of. You were right, I would be a fool to let Bria back into our lives," he said.

"No, Philip. I shouldn't have said that," Courtney uttered, sorrowfully.

"Courtney, please let me finish. Please!" Philip said, as she nodded her head. "I went to bed upset that night. In fact, I couldn't sleep because you colored a picture that my mother has been drawing all along. I wanted Bria in our lives because I wanted Kianna to have the opportunity to say she had a mother who loved her and she would be there for her no matter what. I wanted Kianna to have a mother who would bake cookies with her, take her by the hand walking down the street like I see women do with their daughters, rubbing her on the head telling and showing her love. When she turns an age when she needs to be told about the fact of life, I want her mother and me to do it together. I wanted the mother of my daughter to see Kianna's needs first before ours.

The other women I've dated haven't fit what I wanted in a woman. I was taking the easy way out like some people do. Courtney, I don't want to do that. While thinking about our conversation that night, I realized something that I couldn't believe. I had to stay away from you until I could see things more clearly in the right frame of mind. I still wanted Kianna to spend as much time with you as possible and I wanted to be the very best dad in the world to Sabrina. When I moved, I believed my thoughts and feelings would change about us but they didn't. I respect my mother to the utmost. I've never said this about any woman, but Courtney, I respect you in the same way as a woman, a mother, and as my best friend. You are an example of what I want my daughter to be someday in life.

True genuine friendship is not easy to come by. It's like a diamond in the rough. I thought about everything that we did as a family and as friends. I remember the times when we would be doing something and we would accidentally brush up against one another, turning the ropes while the girls jumped double dutch and our talks any and everywhere. When we go to a musical or plays together I get exhilarated watching you enjoy what many people take for grated. I see the opera world in a different light now through your eyes. Courtney, everything we did had some significant meaning to me. It was a seed that was planted in my stony heart and then you watered it with your smile and honesty.

You said that I should love the people who are in front of me. I love my Kianna very much. She's my heart. I love Sabrina, she's the baby of the family and sometimes she comes to me and gives hugs just because she wants to. And as for you, I just don't love you as a best friend but I realized I'm in love with you, Courtney," he said, with such meaning.

Courtney was surprised as she tried to stay calm and in control of her emotions.

"Oh, I see," she said smiling nervously, as she folded her arms.

"I need you to be honest and tell me how you really feel about me," he said.

"Okay," Courtney said, as she cleared her throat while unfolding her arms. "I've been putting up walls around me lying to myself believing this was the best for me. I was scared to love again so I lied to myself saying I don't need love. You saw through my walls. Inside, I truly wanted to love someone and I wanted to be loved someday. I felt I wasn't worth the chance because of my fear of being alone again. I made myself believe that it would never happen again so I accepted it, but once in a while that feeling would change into maybe it could happen. Isn't that strange? I only felt that way when I was around you, Philip," she said, as he smiled. She continued, "Again, I would manage to justify it and then remembered what happened before that would bring me back to reality. I wanted to live my life alone like my mother being content with myself. It seemed that life would be simpler that way. The only difference between my mother and me is that she knew what true love was and she wasn't alone.

I thought you were going after Bria and believe it or not, I was hoping the best for you and Kianna. Kianna is a wonderful child that I'll always see as my daughter and always love. I felt a special bond with her the first day I met her. You both deserve happiness for the rest of your lives.

I had my nerve to tell you to love the people before you something that my mother always told me. I couldn't do it at first myself when it comes to loving a man. When I see you, I just don't see a man by his genitals, but a wonderful man who is truly my soul mate," she said, as her eyes became watery. "Philip," she said with such meaning, "I missed not talking to you and seeing you like we use to. I knew I was in love with you," she said boldly as Philip's eyes widened. Then he smiled at her as he nodded his head with assurance and confidence in what she was saying to him, "when we went to the circus together I felt secure with you for the first time in my life. It was like something clicked when you put your arms around me while we were taking pictures. I don't know how long I had felt this way about you but when I realized it, it was a new, strong, wonderful and vibrant feeling that I experienced for the first time in my life. I can't and I don't want to fight the feelings any longer."

"Do you truly love me, Courtney?" He asked, as if his eyes were piercing through hers.

"Yes, Philip, I truly love you." She smiled. "But what really got me, I fell in love with you. I can't believe that I'm saying this," she said, not believing the words coming out of her mouth. "But it's true."

Philip got even closer to her. He puts his hands around her face looking into her beautiful brown eyes and sexy cinnamon voluptuous lips. She placed her hands on his wrist while looking into his dreamy eyes and his pecan lips. He brought her head forward to meet his and he kissed her slowly, savoring every moment as if it was the air he was breathing and each kiss had an emphatic meaning. They melted into each other's arms. Then they looked into each other eyes again for the first time in a different light.

"I bought something three years ago and I finished paying on it last year," Philip said, smiling. "When I brought it, I wasn't dating anyone at the time. I saw it and I wanted to give to it to the special lady in my life one day. But if it never happened, I was going to give it to Kianna who would get married one day and have my grandson and he would give it to the special lady in his life," he said. Philip took out a black velvet box. "But now, I don't have to do that because I'm in love with you," he said, as he opened the box. "Courtney, will you marry me?" he asked. He opened the box, took the ring out, placed the box on the table, and then he took her left hand and placed the two sizes too big on her finger.

Courtney looked at Philip, stunned.

"Philip, I can't believe this," she said, as she held his hand. "Yes, I'll marry you."

"Yea!" he said, in shock not believing his ears.

"Um hum, yea," Courtney said in English, "*Si*," she said in Spanish, "*Oui*," she said in French, "*Hai*," she said in Japanese, "*Shi de*,'" she said in Chinese, "*Enyow*," she said in Fante and, "*Ja*," she said in German nodding her head forward. "All that means yes!"

He kissed her again and then he stopped for a moment with such calmness thinking how beautiful she was. She opened her eyes and smiled as if he removed the poison apple from her lips and replaced it with a Prince kiss.

"You have made me the happiest man in the universe!" he said with enthusiasm, as they hugged one another. Tears began to flow down their faces.

Courtney put her hands around his face while taking her thumb wiping his tears. He caught her left hand as she removed it from around his face and kissed the palm of her hand then he wiped her tears replacing them with a kiss.

"One last thing, Courtney," he said.

"What is it, Philip?" She asked, wondering to herself what else could it be.

"I want to adopt Sabrina if it's okay with the both of you. I want the two special ladies in my life to have my last name."

"I can't believe it! Philip that would be great. We would have to ask Sabrina. I know she would love that," she said, as she hugged him again. "I'm so happy." Then she pinched him.

"Ouch! Courtney. Why did you pinch me?" he asked, laughing.

"I wanted to make sure you weren't dreaming," she said, as she laughed. "I thought I would do it backwards."

"I would rather kiss you instead to see if I'm dreaming."

Then they kissed again.

Philip and Courtney went over Ashley's place all smiles. The girls couldn't believe it seeing them together again.

"Hi. You two came to get the girls?" Ashley asked.

"Yes and no. I mean, I know you told us we could get them tomorrow. Where is Preston?" Courtney asked.

"He had to go into one of his offices," Ashley replied, somewhat preoccupied.

"We came to give you some news. Ashley, what is it?" Courtney asked, as Ashley looked perplexed.

"I just got off the telephone with my doctor. I'm two months pregnant," Ashley said, in a daze.

"Again. Wow!" Courtney said.

"Congratulations," Philip said.

"Yes, kid number nine. I'm sorry, you had something to tell me?" Ashley asked, as she tried to focus on what Courtney and Philip had to say.

"Have a seat, Ashley," Courtney said.

"Fine, I'm sitting down. What's going on?" Ashley asked looking at her sister and Philip.

"I realized something about your sister," Philip said looking at Courtney. "I'm in love with her and to prove it, I asked her to marry me and," he smiled, as Courtney finished the statement.

"I said yes!" Courtney squeaked, showing her ring.

"What did you just say?" Ashley asked, looking totally confused.

"Philip asked me to marry him, Ashley and," Courtney said.

"And you said yes!" Ashley said, as she jumped out of the chair running over to hug them. "I can't believe it. Okay!" she said, excited fanning herself trying to calm down, "Okay when is the wedding?"

"In six months," Philip said.

"In six months? " Ashley asked. "How about eight months? By then I will have the baby and my stomach will be flat as a washboard. This will also give us more time to organize the wedding plans. I want everything to be perfect. I know the best caterers and bands in town. To accommodate your wedding, I know the perfect church to have the wedding. I'll take care of everything!" Ashley said, as she was making plans already in her head.

"I don't want all that, Ashley. Philip and I can go to the justice of the peace," Courtney said.

"Justice of the peace!" Ashley said in shocked. "Oh, no," she said, as she sat down looking like she was about to faint.

"Ashley, are you okay?" Philip asked.

"I'm fine if my sister can stop talking crazy. Justice of the peace, Courtney!" Ashley said not believing what she was hearing.

"Okay, we will go to a preacher's house," Courtney said. "The reverend would be glad to do it," she said, as she looked at Philip.

"A preacher's house? Courtney!" Ashley said, panicky.

"Courtney," Philip said, turning to her, "you should have

a church wedding. I've done this before, but you haven't. For the first time, we should do it up. So how about a church wedding?"

"Right," Ashley said, nodding her head in agreement with Philip. "Yea, right." She said watching her sister closely waiting for the right answer.

"Okay, we will have a church wedding," Courtney said, smiling. "Actually, I would like an April wedding." She looked at Philip, as he smiled at her.

"Thank you, future brother-in-law," Ashley said, as she walked over and hugged Philip again. "I have dreamed of planning my sister's wedding."

Philip and Courtney told the girls together. They were very ecstatic and Sabrina loved the idea of being adopted by Philip. Then they went to Philip's mother's house. As they were driving up, Lauren and her husband were getting into their car. Kianna and Sabrina got out of their car and ran to Lauren.

"Aunt Lauren, daddy and mommy are getting married," Kianna said smiling.

"Really, Kianna," Lauren said, in disbelief getting out of the car.

"It's true," Sabrina said, smiling.

"Kianna, I wanted to tell them myself," Philip said, while putting his hands around the Kianna and Sabrina's mouths. "Why is it you two can't keep anything a secret?" The girls as they giggled.

"So, it's true? You and Courtney are getting married?" Vince asked smiling.

"Yes, it's true," Courtney said.

"Oh, Philip," Lauren screamed running to the other side of the car hugging him in tears. "I don't believe this, Courtney," she said, as she held out her hand to Courtney. "I know you and my brother couldn't resist each other for the rest of your lives as just friends. I saw something between you two when Courtney came over here for the first time for dinner." Then she hugged

Courtney.

"What's going on?" Beverly asked walking out of the house. At the same time all four of them said to Kianna and Sabrina to be quiet! Everyone walked into the house. "Lauren, I thought you and Vince were leaving."

"We were, mother," Vince said, smiling.

"Mother," Philip said, as he took his mother by the hand while holding Courtney's hand with the other. "I asked Courtney to marry me and she said yes."

"Honey, that's wonderful!" Beverly said, as she hugged both of them.

"Let's see your ring," Lauren said to Courtney.

"We have to go to the jeweler to get it fitted," Philip said.

"I remembered when he showed me this ring," Lauren said. "Philip had no one in mind to give it to. I thought he was crazy for buying it but I see there's nothing wrong with a little faith, right, brother?"

Lauren and Philip hugged.

"That is some ring!" Vince said impressed. "Have you two set a wedding date?"

"Yes," Courtney said smiling, "the first Saturday in April," She said, as Philip, Lauren, and his mother smiled at each other.

"Mom," Lauren said, "you and daddy got married on the first Saturday of April," she said, as tears came down Beverly face.

"That's a wonderful day to get married," Beverly said pleased.

"That's not all, Grandma. Daddy is going to adopt me so I'll have his last name too," Sabrina said ecstatically.

"This is great!" Lauren said. Tears ran down her face while hugging the girls.

"I believe that God put you girls together in order to bring your parents together at this time and for the rest of their lives," Beverly said, as she hugged the girls again with so much joy. "I love you!"

Later that night after Courtney put Sabrina to bed, she sat up in her bed staring at her diamond ring. A girl's best friend. The telephone rang.

"Why don't you get some sleep," Philip said to Courtney on the phone.

"Hi, Philip. How did you know I was up?"

"Because I can't sleep either. This has been some day for all of us," he said.

"Yes, a day that I'll cherish for the rest of my life. Thank you."

"No, thank *you*. I called to say I love you, Courtney Marie Kennedy."

"I love you too, Philip Edward Franklin, Jr."

"I love you mommy and daddy," Kianna said on the telephone.

"Kianna!" Philip said, surprised.

"Kianna," Courtney said laughing, "why aren't you asleep?"

"Mommy, I had to get some water and I saw the red light on the telephone that indicated the phone is in use. I thought maybe a phone was off the hook," Kianna replied.

"Courtney, I'm going downstairs to see what she's doing. I'll talk to you tomorrow," he said.

"Okay, get some sleep," Courtney said. "Kianna, I love you."

Chapter Fifteen

A few days later, Courtney went to her mother's gravesite. She placed some flowers at the foot of the tombstone. She stood up and looked at the writing on the tombstone while taking a deep breath. She thought to herself how only last year her mother was alive and then she felt the void and the loneliness again of her mother.

"I know you are not here but I feel better coming here from time to time. You are not going to believe this," Courtney said, as she looked down on her mother's grave, "Philip and I are getting married. I have loved him for a while, but I wanted to be sure that it wasn't anything else that could cause us to lose out on a good friendship," she said, as she looked at her left hand with a wire twisted like a ring that Philip put on her finger at the jewelry store. She smiled, "I just left Philip at the jeweler. We went to get my ring fitted and he proposed to me again with this paper clip. People in the jewelry store smiled and congratulated us. You told me a long time ago when Sabrina was one year old that when the time is right, love will happen for me. But my heart has to be in tune to wanting to be love. I couldn't see it but you did. Philip is going to adopt Sabrina, however, I have to get her father's okay on that. I'm going to believe it will all work out with God's help.

I miss your presence. Sometimes, I try to remember how your cheek felt when I kissed you, I try to remember your voice, hugs, and of course no one can cook like you and most of all when you use to tell me that you loved me. I would give anything to experience all those things I had once from you. I'll always love you mom," Courtney said, as she smiled then she left.

By the beginning of October, Ashley had already planned half of Courtney's wedding. Lauren asked Courtney and Ashley if she could help with the preparations of the wedding, which they didn't have a problem with. Due to Courtney's busy work schedule, it was mid-November by the time she chose her 15 bridesmaids and the wedding colors. She wanted white with royal blue trimmings. The 100-person guest list turned into 300 when it got to Ashley and then Courtney compromised at 275. Lauren had one of her dear friends design the wedding dress and shoes. They flew to New York City a couple of times to make sure everything fitted perfectly.

When Philip and Courtney were around each other their hands were like magnets. Every time they were close to one another their hands automatically connected without thinking about it. One evening Philip was at Courtney's house watching a movie snuggled up in one another's arms. He would rub on her arms and at times he would kiss her soft cheeks. Then they looked into each other eyes and began kissing. Philip placed his hand on the side of her stomach and she felt his hand moving up little by little.

"Philip, I can't do this," Courtney said as she sat up. "I don't want to sleep with you. Not now."

"Okay," Philip said. Then he got up and walked into the kitchen to get some water.

A few moments later, Courtney walked into the kitchen. She took the glass out of his hand and drank out of it.

"Philip, I'm not trying to be arduous," Courtney said.

"Shh, Courtney, listen to me, I don't think that. I respect your feelings. It's best to wait," he said and then he kissed her nose. "We shouldn't be alone like this. We have four more months to go before we get married and if we keep this up, we would be in bed together before we say I do."

"I agree," she said.

"I'm going to leave. What time are we leaving for church tomorrow?" he asked.

"Sunday school starts at 9:00 a.m." She smiled.

"All right. I'll be here for my future bride at 8:30 in the morning," he said. Then he kissed her goodbye and left.

Ashley encouraged Courtney to talk to Sabrina's father concerning the adoption soon since time was approaching and it takes time to process the paperwork if he agreed to it. Courtney dreaded the call to Sabrina's father that Wednesday afternoon.

"Hi, Jeff, this is Courtney," she said, calmly on the phone.

"Courtney, hello. How is my girl?" Jeff asked, in a friendly tone.

"She's fine. Jeff, we need to talk," Courtney said straight-forward.

"Is everything okay? Anything wrong with Sabrina?" Jeff asked intensively with concern.

"Everything is fine. Can we meet tomorrow for breakfast?" She asked. "I have something I want to talk to you about."

"That will be fine. How about we meet 10:00 a.m. at Lou Mitchell's Restaurant on West Jackson Boulevard?" Jeff asked.

"That's fine. I know where it is. I'll see you then."

The next day Jeff walked into the crowded restaurant. As the host approached him, he noticed Courtney seating at one of the beige booths. The host welcomed him to the establishment and he responded with a demeaning look, as he went passed her over to the booth. Courtney looked up at him and put away her planner in her purse.

"Courtney, hello," Jeff said, as he sat down. "I'm still in shock that you called wanting to meet for breakfast. How is my girl?" He asked, as he smiled.

"Sabrina? She's fine. She's the reason why I wanted to see you," Courtney said candidly.

"Are you sure everything is fine with my daughter?" Jeff asked in a protective tone.

"Yes," Courtney replied. Then the waitress came over to get their order.

"That is some rock that you have on your finger there," he said, as he gazed at her ring.

"I'm getting married."

"I can't believe it after all these years and now you finally decided to say yes to a lucky man," he said.

"Jeff the reason why I wanted to see you, my fiancé Philip wants to adopt Sabrina. Sabrina wants him to adopt her," Courtney said in a soft tone. Jeff looked at her in a weird way, "In other words, we need you to sign a legal document giving up all rights as being Sabrina's father."

"Wait a minute, Courtney," Jeff said. "I can comprehend well. I know what adoption means. This is a surprise that you would ask me to do that. I don't know what to say about it, Courtney," he said, not liking the sound of his daughter being adopted by some other man. Then the waitress brought Courtney a small glass of orange juice and Jeff a large black coffee.

"Can I get you anything else?" the waitress asked both of them.

"No," Jeff said condescending. "Like we told you earlier that's it. Thanks," he said rudely wanting her to leave.

"Jeff, this is important to all of us," she said.

"I'm sure it is! I don't know, Courtney," he said hesitating. "Sabrina is my firstborn."

Courtney was thinking a lot of impolite things she could have said. She waited for a couple of seconds before she responded.

"Sabrina will always be your firstborn child, Jeff. She is old enough to know who her real father is. I know this is an enormous request that I'm asking of you. However, this isn't about you, me, or even Philip. Think about Sabrina. She wants this very much," Courtney said with sincerity.

"You have really changed, Courtney," Jeff said looking smug.

"What do you mean?" she asked puzzled.

"If you were the same person you were eight years ago, you would have brought out the obvious facts that I haven't paid the first child support payment even though you told me you didn't need my help. And you probably would have brought up the fact that I haven't even visit Sabrina in years. The only reason why I haven't seen her in some time because I know she probably hates me for not being there for her."

"Sabrina, doesn't hate you. She doesn't know you."

"Well," he said setting back in the booth with one arm spread across the back seat, "that's neither here or there. I know that I failed her as a father and I can't face her. But, thanks anyway for trying to make me feel better. Whoever this Philip is he has really changed you," He said, sarcastically smiling.

"You have that wrong, Jeff," Courtney said boldly, as she looked him in the eyes. "I'm not trying to make you feel better concerning your responsibility to Sabrina. I was stating the facts, and as for you giving credit to something that you don't know anything about, I've changed myself through the grace of God and my mother's help."

"Speaking of your mother how is she? Is she still holy as ever?" Jeff asked ferociously.

"Jeff, my mother died over a year ago," She replied softly.

"Oh, Courtney, I'm really sorry," He said feeling bad, as he set upright in his seat. "I didn't know."

"How could you have known that Sabrina lost the only grandmother she ever known?"

"Sure, I'll help. Whatever I can do to make Sabrina's dream come true. I know you want the best for our little girl," he said.

Courtney opened her purse, taking something out. "Here is the card of the attorney's office that is handling our case," she said, passing Jeff the card. He glanced at the card looking unsure of what he really wanted to do. "They will inform you of what needs to be done. Thank you, Jeff. Have a good day." She got up to leave.

"Thank you for being honest and seeing how I felt about this, Courtney. You have always been a lady. Philip is one lucky man. Congratulations," Jeff said, as he rose to leave as well. "I really mean it." Courtney took out her wallet. "I'll pay the check. That's the least I can do."

Courtney went to work tense. She didn't know what to believe from her meeting with Jeff. Will he really sign over his rights as Sabrina's father or will she have to call him in a couple of weeks to talk to him again about it or will he change his mind all together?

Later that evening Philip came over to Courtney's place after he left the airport from flying in from a business trip. The girls were excited to see him. Later, Courtney was standing outside on the porch looking straight ahead. Philip came outside and stood behind her as he wrapped his arms around her waist. Then he slowly began to rock her from side to side as if they were dancing to music.

"What's on your mind?" Philip whispered in her ear.

"I met with Jeff this morning for breakfast," Courtney said, feeling nervous and worried. "Oh, by the way, I missed Clinton's call and when I called his office his secretary told me he was in court all day. His secretary stated it would be okay to page him, but I didn't want to bother him. Since Clinton didn't say on my voice mail that it was urgent, I thought I could reach him later at his office. Now, I regret not paging him."

"Clinton called me too. He wanted us to know that Jeff came by his office today and signed the necessary documents for Sabrina to become my baby legally," he said pleased.

"What?" she asked, turning around to him. "You're not pulling my leg are you, Philip?"

"No, Courtney," Philip replied smiling, as he ran his thumb across her chin. He looked into her beautiful brown eyes, "I wouldn't joke about something like this."

As Courtney hugged Philip she felt a weight lifted from her shoulders.

"Thank you, God!" she said with relief as she looked up. She had been praying all day that Jeff would do the right thing for his daughter.

"What did you say to him to make him move so swiftly?" Philip asked.

"Nothing. It took prayers and kindness."

"Well it worked."

"I'm truly thankful to God for how things worked out," Courtney said. "but I thought he would want to see how Sabrina really felt about being adopted or meet you and ask some questions. I know you wouldn't have handled a matter like this with Kianna."

"You're absolutely right. Jeff and I are two different people like day and night."

"Yes that's true. I'm glad that Sabrina is experiencing the day instead of night," Courtney said, as Philip put his head to her head.

A few Sundays later, Philip joined the church. Courtney was so proud that Philip became a member of her church. The Reverend and some of the church auxiliary members shook his hand welcoming him to the church family.

Philip and Courtney spent a lot of time at Ashley and Preston's home when the girls weren't around them so they wouldn't start the honeymoon before the wedding day. The children of Courtney's family were already calling him Uncle Philip.

The girls celebrated their birthdays together again. This time the birthday party was at Courtney's home. The 100 guests had a great time and Courtney had an even greater time since everything was catered.

Philip and Courtney were getting pre-marital counseling. Everything was going great until Philip assumed that Courtney would give up her career once they got married. Philip couldn't see what the big deal was since he was financially stable. Courtney felt it wasn't about money but the principle. One night after the kids went to bed they had a heated discussion about her career.

"Are we going to let this stop us from getting married?" he asked, Courtney concerned.

"No, Philip," she replied preoccupied, "but we have to come up with some kind of agreement. I love working. My career is my life. Then on the other hand, I know you don't want a nanny raising our children and I agree."

"We will find a way to work it out," he said, as he hugged her. "It will be all right."

Bria flew into town without Philip and Kianna knowing about it at the time. She didn't want Philip to think she was trying to start trouble. She called Courtney to meet with her at a restaurant.

"Thanks for meeting me," Bria said, as Courtney sat down.

"What can I do for you, Bria?" Courtney asked tentatively.

"Listen, I know I started off on the wrong foot with you when we first met. I'm sorry about that. I heard through the grapevine that you and Philip are getting married soon. Congratulations," Bria said.

"Thanks. Bria, I'm due in a meeting in the next hour. I'm sure you didn't ask me here to congratulate me on my engagement to Philip. What's on your mind?"

"Since I won't be part of Kianna's life, I'm asking you woman to woman to really take care of my baby," she said, as tears rolled down her face. Courtney felt compassion for Bria as she squeezed her hand. "I'm sorry. I told myself, I wasn't going to get upset," She wiped her face with a Kleenex.

"It's okay. I'm sorry that things haven't worked out for you and Kianna in the way you wanted. You need to give Kianna more time and one of the ways to do that is to be around her."

"I know and you are right," Bria smiled. "You remember

the old television show called Wonder Woman? I think I was five when that show was on. I would watch it religiously and I would see my mom as a pretty wonder woman who could do anything and protect me from any evil with her life. That's how Kianna sees you, Courtney. When she looks at you, her eyes light up. When she says mommy to you, she says it with meaning and enthusiasm. On the other hand, when it comes to me, she say mom because it's the proper thing to do.

I also know if it wasn't for you, she wouldn't even be speaking to me. At times, Kianna and I talk on the telephone. Of course I do all of the talking but like you said I need to give it more time.

Please continue to be a mother to my baby because I lost that chance years ago with her. I was in those shoes that you fit so well. Could we be friends, Courtney?" Bria asked with her hand extended to Courtney.

"Sure," Courtney said, smiling as they shook hands.

Ashley had her baby two weeks early February 14th. Her new daughter's name was Juliet Lynn Harringston. Her weight was eight pounds seven ounces.

One Saturday afternoon, Philip and Courtney were ready to leave to take the girls to an early movie. Philip received a telephone call regarding an important fax he was about to receive. They had to go to a later movie. While Philip was faxing documents, Courtney walked into his library.

"Come on in," Philip said. "I'm almost done. I'm sorry about this."

"It's okay. The girls and I understand. Philip about our honeymoon," she stated and then Philip interrupted her.

"I know, I can't wait!" He said, humorously in a seductive tone.

"Philip," Courtney said, candidly, "I'm not that experienced when it comes to satisfying one's sexual desires." He looked up at her; he noticed tension in her voice. "Jeff was my first love and I haven't been with anyone since. I don't know if

I can satisfy you," she said nervously. "It's been over ten years since I've been with a man."

"Courtney, where is this coming from?" Philip asked

"I was just saying. I don't know what you are expecting from me."

"I'm not expecting anything from you. I wish I could say I was with only one woman in my life time but I can't. I'm very fortunate to get a woman that hasn't been fondled, poked, and glanced at as if a doctor was examining her. You are a special jewel. Sweetheart, that's nothing to concern yourself with. Okay, that's faxed," he said, as a conformation sheet printed out on the fax machine. "Let's take the girls to the movies." He took Courtney's hand and left out the library, eager to leave.

After the movies, Philip was driving Courtney and Sabrina home. Philip and Courtney were chatting. Sabrina was in the back of the car asleep. Kianna unbuckled her seatbelt.

"Daddy," Kianna said, putting her arms around her daddy's neck.

He rubbed her arm with one hand, "Baby, you should be in your seatbelt." Philip said.

"I thought you were asleep too," Courtney said to Kianna.

"Daddy, I want to ask you a question," Kianna said, sitting back down and putting on her seatbelt.

"What is it, sweetie?" Philip asked.

"Can mommy adopt me like you are adopting Sabrina?" Kianna asked.

Philip and Courtney looked at each other.

"Honey, we are a family. When I asked Courtney to marry me and she said yes, I wanted Sabrina to have my last name as well."

Courtney turned around in her seat to Kianna, "Honey, I don't have to adopt you to know you are all mine. You are in here," Courtney said, as she put her hands over her heart. "You're not going anywhere. We have our own understanding of how we feel about each other. The love that you and I share makes us mother and daughter. Okay?"

"Yes," Kianna replied. Minutes later she got up and hugged Courtney from the back and kissed her cheek. "Thank you." Then she sat back and put back on her seatbelt.

Courtney reached back to Kianna and squeezed her hand. Then Courtney eyes became watery. Philip held Courtney hand as she looked at him. He smiled and blinked his eye. When Courtney looked back at the girls a few minutes later, she saw Kianna asleep.

Two months before the wedding, the wedding party had to take dance classes for the wedding reception when the bride and groom have their first dance. Courtney was getting a little more nervous, knowing her wedding was not so far away.

The following week, Philip had a get together at his house to celebrate Sabrina's adoption. He was so proud to be gaining a precious little girl who loved him so much. Kianna was happy herself, feeling like more than ever they were sisters.

One month before the wedding, Lauren and Ashley had the wedding dinner rehearsal. Then two weeks later the wedding rehearsal at the church then the bridal shower.

The following Sunday Reverend Solomon unexpectedly asked the choir to sing a song after his sermon. The director of the choir called Courtney to help him lead a song called 'Oh Happy Day.' She felt she wasn't ready to sing it. She was quiet shy at first. Courtney looked over at Philip as he winked at her nodding his head smiling while holding Kianna and having his arm around Sabrina. After the choir finished singing the entire church was up clapping.

It was a week and one day before the wedding. Courtney was up late Friday night still packing boxes of things she wanted the movers to take to Philip's home tomorrow. As Courtney was putting paper in the bottom of a box, she all of a sudden stopped and looked around her living room seeing boxes all over the place that Ashley and Zakeya helped her pack earlier that week.

She realized even more that she was getting married and nothing would ever be the same again. The life she once knew would be just a memory. A speck. It wouldn't be just her and Sabrina anymore. "God what's wrong with me?" Courtney asked, as tears rolled down her face. She felt overwhelmed but at the same time wonderful knowing that there was a man that loved her so much that he wanted to spend the rest of his life with her. On the other hand, she felt fear and second-guessing herself whether or not she was truly ready to give herself to a man that she only knew as a friend. She walked to the front window and looked at the sold sign in the front yard of her house. She reminisced when she brought her house eight and half months pregnant with Sabrina. She thought about some of the bad and good times she had from then until that present time. The telephone rang. "Hello," she said in a still voice.

"Hey, baby, how is the packing? Are you ready for the movers in the morning?" Philip asked.

"Yes," she replied walking back over to the box.

"What's wrong? Is it hitting you that we are getting married in almost less than a week?" Philip asked. She didn't answer as she wiped her eyes. He knew from her silence that she was experiencing some concerns as he was as well. "If it makes you feel any better, I'm getting a reality awareness myself of us getting married. My stomach feels kind of unbalanced. At first I thought maybe it was Patricia's cooking," he said humorously, and Courtney smiled. "The truth of the matter it's my nerves. Sometimes the unknown of life can be exciting of what you believe it could be. It also can be intimating at the same time of what the truth really is."

"We will get through it, Philip," Courtney said in a cheerful voice.

"Thanks, baby. I needed to hear that from you," he said, as he felt more excited for next weekend. "Even though it's not my first marriage, but it is the first time to marry the woman that is for me. Since last month, I have prayed a special prayer everyday that God will give us strength to get us through this time, and once we've said our vows, He will lead and guide us in our marriage. I love you so very much, Courtney."

"I love you so very much too, Philip," she said, as her uncertainty turned into joy of expectancy.

The following morning Philip parked his car by the sidewalk of Courtney's house as the moving truck parked in the driveway. Philip walked to the door and as he was about to knock on it Courtney opened the door with a radiant smile.

"Good morning, honey," she said.

"Good morning, my future Mrs. Philip Edward Franklin Jr.," he said, as he smiled. Then they hugged.

Hours later after the moving truck left then another truck came soon after to move furniture that Courtney was donating to the Salvation Army.

Lauren had Philip and Courtney's picture in the newspaper announcing their wedding day from Sunday through Saturday.

Three days before the wedding everyone was at the church. People were becoming irritable towards one another. Everyone seemed to be getting on each other's nerves.

"Okay, everyone, we're going to take it from the top again," Lauren said. "We're going to pretend that David has already sung The Lord's Prayer."

"Good! I could almost sing that song backwards," Ashley said, as Lauren looked at her with a repellent look.

"You know, Ashley, you can have a seat. I've got this!" Lauren said, in an abusive tone. "James, would you please start playing the organ for Kianna and Sabrina to come down the aisle. Thank you," she said, as the man smiled and began playing again. Then she looked at Ashley and faked a smile.

After everything was supposed to be over, Lauren wanted the bridesmaids to march in one more time to make sure they got their steps right.

"Lauren, we don't need to march down the aisle again. Tiffany and Toni are the ones who have big feet that keep stepping on our heels," one of the bridesmaids said.

"No, that's not true. The rest of you walk too slow like you are the ones getting married," another one of the bridesmaids said.

Then the other bridesmaids started arguing. Ashley and Lauren got into it when Ashley mentioned she should have coordinated the wedding by herself. Then the make up artist, whose twin sons were the ring bearer and the chest carrier, started arguing with the lady who designed the wedding dress concerning how Courtney's hair should be done. And to top it off, Kianna and Sabrina started arguing over how they should light the candles. The men were looking around at the women arguing and laughing to themselves. By this time Courtney's nerves were shot.

"Wait a minute, everyone," Courtney said, as she raised her voice. Then it seemed everyone was getting louder, "Everybody shut up!" she shouted. Then suddenly it was silent in the church as everyone looked at her. This was the first time that anyone ever heard her raise her voice. "We have been told we were only going to be here for two hours which it has been three hours and a half. We have walked these aisles at least ten times. I think everything is perfect. It can't get any better then this. Ashley and Lauren this is my wedding not yours. I feel that we're doing a runway for a fashion show not preparing for the most exciting day of my life. My wedding!

Look at all of you," Courtney said, looking around, "you are turning vicious toward one another for little small things. At this moment, I don't even care if Philip and I don't have a wedding. Maybe we should have eloped like we started to. I'm surprised at all of you!" Courtney said. Then she walked out of the church. Everyone looked at one another again stunned and then the ladies started feeling ashamed for the way they were acting.

"Well, she didn't say she didn't want to marry me," Philip said, as he smiled, then he went after Courtney.

"We can march in again," one of the bridesmaids said to

Ashley and Lauren.

"Everyone take five," Ashley said "Lauren, I'm sorry. Courtney is right. As I think about it we haven't been fair to her. I'm going to talk to her."

"Ashley, please let me talk to her," Lauren said. "She is going to be my sister-in-law and I want to get in practice cheering her up. I won't be long."

Lauren walked outside. Philip had his arms around Courtney talking to her.

"Excuse me, Philip. Can I have a minute with Courtney," Lauren said. Then she took Courtney by her hand and they both sat on the church step.

"I'm sorry, sis," Lauren said. "Ashley and I were trying to make your wedding day better than ours. We never really asked you what you wanted and what you thought about all of this.

You know days before my wedding, I felt like you did. I was on pins and needles. I would take a drink in the morning to have something to boost me up and at night to help me sleep. I remember it as if it were yesterday," she said, as she smiled. "Philip caught me one night about to have a drink and he was very upset with me. I was trying to explain how I was feeling and I just needed something to calm my nerves. He felt it was an excuse. He said, by me knowing that I'm about to marry someone who loves me and I love him should be enough to boost me in the mornings and help me sleep restfully at night. He also told me, it's more than a wedding that is filled with glamour, the trends, family, friends and gifts. He hoped one day to be where I was. Courtney, you are giving my brother something he always wanted and that's you."

"Thank you. That's means a lot," Courtney said, as they took each other by the hand.

Ashley came out with Zakeya.

"Everyone did great," Ashley said.

"Aunt Courtney," Zakeya said, "I know that Lisa won't be able to sing The Prayer at the wedding. I want to sing it and I know I can do it."

"I don't know, Zakeya. Lauren has already removed the selection from the program and some of Philip's friends who will be playing the instruments, won't have to play The Prayer now." Courtney said.

"Well, Courtney just so you will know," Lauren said, "the programs won't be printed until tomorrow morning when I call the printers to give them the okay."

"I talked to Uncle Philip, he doesn't mind listening to David and I sing it. Would you give me this opportunity to sing your favorite song?" Zakeya asked.

Courtney agreed. Everyone sat down in the sanctuary to listen to Zakeya and David sang the song. They both sounded wonderful together as if it were Celine Dion and Andrea Bocelli singing it themselves. After they finished singing, Courtney was in tears as she hugged Zakeya and David. Even Preston was impressed. For the first time, he really heard his daughter talent. He walked over to his daughter and hugged her.

Chapter Sixteen

The day before the wedding Philip was scheduled to be off from work but he found himself at the office before day break. The security personnel had never seen the president come to work before 9:00 a.m.

One of Courtney's girl friends named Trish allowed Courtney to use her house for the ladies day out. Ashley kept everyone busy for a while getting manicures, pedicures, and waxing and then five handsome well-built men came to the house to give the ladies massages.

Later that evening they had a catering service to come to the house and serve food and drinks. All the helpers were men, no women workers were allowed on the premises.

Zakeya watched Sabrina and Kianna after school at Ashley's place. The girls whined so much about how they wanted to be with their mother that Zakeya brought them over to the house where the ladies were staying.

Much later that evening Jack came to Philip's office to pick him up to celebrate his last day as a single man. Later that night, all the men met at a place called "Sports Bar." It was a place where people go to play cards, pool, checkers, chess, and watch all kinds of games on big wide screen televisions. There were about seventy men there that Philip knew and more of them were coming as time moved on that evening. There were some ladies there trying to talk to Philip but he wasn't interested in carrying on a conversation. However, his cousin Jack didn't mind taking Philip's spot. Later, Philip received a page from Kianna who wanted him to pick her up from the house where Courtney was staying. After Lauren finished complaining on the telephone to her brother about how she should have known better to get Jack to set up a respectful bachelor party, she stopped for a second and thought that's not what he called for. She felt terrible as she apologized to Philip. He didn't take what Jack did to heart. Lauren promised Philip she would have Kianna home by the time he got there so he wouldn't take a chance picking Kianna up and seeing his bride the day before the wedding. Philip stayed at the Sports Bar for another hour mingling with the guys and he sneaked out.

Later on that night Philip called Courtney on her cellular phone that she had under her pillow. They talked for hours.

Finally it was the day of the wedding. A couple hours before the wedding, Courtney and the ladies that were in the wedding party arrived at the church where their wedding attire was. They were in a huge room talking and laughing as the ladies got dressed. An hour later, Trish had everyone to leave the room except for the hair stylist who was getting Courtney ready. After Courtney was all dressed she requested some private time with Ashley. Courtney reached for Ashley's hand.

"I'm scared," Courtney said. "It's really hitting me now more then ever, I'm really getting married today anytime now," she said excited.

"It's okay," Ashley said, as she smiled. "Let me ask you a few questions like mom asked me on the day of my wedding. This is how she said it," she said, as she tried to sound like their mother, "Now I want you to think about this but don't answer until I'm finished asking you these questions. Are you having second thoughts about this wedding because if you are, you can call it off, it's not too late. It doesn't matter about the time and money that was put into it. Never mind your family and friends who are here to give you their blessings they will understand. Are you sure without a shadow of a doubt that Philip really loves you and not lusting for you? Can you see yourself growing old with him no matter what? And most importantly are you in love with him? What is your answer, Courtney?"

"No, yes, yes and very much yes!" Courtney exclaimed.

"Something else mom said to me. Whatever you go through in your marriage let it be between you, your husband in this case Philip and God. No third party. Not friends, not your brothers, or even me. But if you both can't come to an understanding make sure you two come together to someone with experience and wisdom in marriage," Ashley said.

"That was beautiful, Ashley. Thank you," Courtney said, as she smiled.

"Has dad talked to you already?" Ashley asked.

"Yes, he took me out to breakfast this morning. We had a lovely time."

"Dad is wonderful isn't he? Look, we're running late," Ashley said looking at her watch. "Are you okay now?" She was becoming a little nervous herself.

"Yes. You and Lauren go ahead and get my wedding started. Have you seen Philip?" Courtney asked.

"Yes. He arrived here an hour ago. He's holding his own just like you are. See you later," Ashley said, as tears rolled down her face. "I love you, Courtney." Then they hugged.

When it was time for Courtney to make her entrance into the sanctuary her father tapped on the door for her then someone inside the room opened the door for Courtney to come out. Her father was speechless as she smiled at him. She was absolutely breath taking.

"Baby girl, you look just like Jackeé. Your mother would be so proud of you if she saw you right now," Courtney father said.

"Thank you, daddy," she said. He proudly reached for her hand as she walked out the room.

As they walked down the aisle three little boys carried the train of Courtney's dress. Courtney was so nervous she could hardly see Philip's eyes but as she got closer she saw his smile more and more. When Courtney got to the second row of seats from the front she looked to her left and saw Sabrina and Kianna smiling at her. Courtney moved her lips to say she loved them as Sabrina wiped her eyes. Courtney and her father stopped at the end of the aisle. Reverend Solomon instructed everyone to sit down. Kianna and Sabrina sat on the edge of their seats holding hands, forcing their attention on their parents. Reverend Solomon said a few words then he looked at Courtney and her father.

"Who giveth this woman away?" Reverend Solomon asked.

"I do," Courtney's father answered boldly, as he looked at his daughter. Then he turned around to her as she smiled at him. "I love you, Courtney. I'm here for you." Then he lifted up her veil and kissed her cheek. Then he walked her up to Philip. Philip reached for Courtney's hand. Courtney's father took her right hand and placed it in Philip's left hand. "Take care of my baby girl."

"Yes sir, I will," Philip said as he looked at Courtney's father sincerely.

Courtney's father looked at her again and sadly walked away to his seat. When he sat down his wife held his hand to comfort him. During the ceremony, Philip and Courtney had something personally they wanted to say to one another.

"At this time, Mr. Philip Edward Franklin Jr. has something to say to Lady Courtney," Reverend Solomon.

"When I first met you, I had no idea you would be my four seasons," Philip said in his vows to Courtney, "For Winter witty; for Spring experiencing new love you giveth every day; for Summer my sunshine; and for Fall laughter to the end of time. You are my best friend that will become bone of my bone and flesh of my flesh. I'll cover you, I'll love you, and I'll bless you in all areas that you need and ever want from me in your life. Since we carried our friendship in the right way that God wanted us to do as single adults, I know our union will be blessed by Him."

"Now, we will hear Ms. Courtney Marie Kennedy's vows to gentleman, Philip," Reverend Solomon said.

"Philip," Courtney said candidly and then they smiled at one another, "I was lost because of the wrong choices I made in my life. God has sent you the light to my world to show me the right way. There is such a thing called love, because I love you. I thank God for giving me a second chance when you came into my life. I'll love you with every being of my soul. I'll happily obey you in God's eyes, I'll cover you and love you for the rest of my life," she said with such feeling. "As long as we have God centered in our lives, we will make it!" she said, as she and Philip smiled again.

One of the bridesmaid's broke down in tears as well as some of the guests, Ashley, Lauren, Beverly, and Jack who took his hand and wiped his tears. With Jack no one could tell if he was in tears from the moving words of Philip and Courtney's or from his hangover from last night.

When the Reverend ended his part of the ceremony, he told Philip that "he may kiss his bride." They both kissed as if they were breathing life into one another. Everyone stood up cheering and clapping their hands.

The photographer must have taken over hundred pictures at the church. The make-up artist kept checking Courtney's face to make sure she wasn't sweating so the pictures would be crystal clear and flawless. Lauren was sitting in the limousine as Courtney got in to help her with her dress.

"Would you get out of here Lauren so my wife and I could have some privacy," Philip said, smiling.

"Sure thing brother," Lauren said, laughing. "Listen, I have some handkerchiefs over here and Courtney your lipstick is in this case. See you two at the reception."

"Thank you, Lauren," Courtney said, as Philip knocked on the window for the chauffeur to open the door for Lauren.

"Okay! Okay! I'm getting out," Lauren said. "You guys look so handsome together," she said, as they smiled.

Philip and Courtney looked at one another without saying one word then they kissed over and over again riding to the hotel where the reception was.

The wedding reception was wonderful. The food was so good, it melted in your mouth, the band played and sang great songs, the wedding cake was designed so beautiful that it was a shame to cut it, and countless gifts. It was something to remember for everyone. Zakeya caught the bouquet and her boyfriend Cameron caught the garter belt. When it was time for Cameron to put the garter belt around Zakeya's leg, he was grinning from ear to ear while getting on his knee. Zakeya's father walked behind Cameron and squeezed his shoulder and gave him a stern look. Cameron put the garter belt around Zakeya's ankle saying that was as far as he could go. Everyone laughed.

Philip and Courtney were driven to the airport where Ashley and Preston met them.

"What are you two doing here?" Courtney asked glad to see her sister.

"We wanted to make sure both of you are okay," Ashley said while walking away with Courtney.

"I'm so nervous about our honeymoon, Ashley," Courtney said, as she squeezed her sister's hand.

"Courtney, let me tell you this it's like riding a bike. You never forget. Believe me you will not need any training wheels," Ashley said, as they laughed.

As Ashley and her husband watched Philip and Courtney walking through a gate to abroad the plane, Ashley eyes became watery.

"Honey, are you all right?" Preston asked.

"I can't believe my sister is married. I wish that mom could be here to see how beautiful she was today and how happy she is." Preston took his handkerchief and wiped her eyes.

"Your sister is fine."

"I know now." Ashley said, as she and her husband put their arms around each other and began to walk away. "How about our new cousin Jack. He seems to be—" her husband quickly interrupted her.

"Happy with his life and can manage to change his lifestyle if he wants to. So stay—"

Then she quickly responded.

"Honey," Ashley said, as she covered her husband mouth. "I'm just kidding!" They both laughed. Then Preston looked at his wife wondering if she was really kidding.

Philip and Courtney flew to the Island in Maui. They arrived at the hotel late that night. When they got to the suite Philip carried Courtney inside.

"This suite is lovely," Courtney said. "It's still early, you want to go out? While you were checking in at the front desk, I looked at the hotel brochures. There are plenty of places we can go."

"Courtney, it's 10:30 at night." Philip said.

"Okay, are you hungry? I can order room service," Courtney said nervously.

"No, I'm not hungry but I can call for room service for you. What would you like to eat?"

"I'm not hungry," she said, as she found herself getting fidgety. Then she walked to the telephone, "I'm going to call the girls to see how they are doing. I know they must be wondering if we have arrived here safely."

"Courtney," he said, as he took the receiver from out of her hand. "you know the girls must be asleep by now. You called them twice on the plane."

"How did you know that? I thought you were asleep," she said.

"You know the old saying, every eye that is shut is not asleep and every goodnight is not gone. Why are you treating me like a stranger? We've been alone before and you've never acted like this," he said smiling.

"Tonight is different," Courtney replied, as she folded her hands in front of her.

"Honey, I'm not going to hurt you. Gentle is my middle name," he said, as he kissed and hugged her.

Minutes later they received a bottle of wine to their suite. While Philip was showering, Courtney tried to unpack all of their clothes. Philip managed to get her to finish unpacking a little later. Courtney must have showered for forty-five minutes or more that seemed like fifteen minutes to her. After she put on her lingerie, she sat in a chair in the bathroom with her eyes closed.

"Baby, are you okay in there?" he asked, as he tapped on the bathroom door.

"Yes. I'm putting on the finishing touches. I'll be out," she said, through the closed door.

"I guess I can wait another minute or two. I waited an hour and ten minutes already," Philip said. Then he smiled walking away.

Courtney laughed out as she stood up.

"It's hasn't been that long," she said. Then she said to herself nervously, "Not long enough."

Courtney took a deep breath while opening the bathroom door. In the bedroom the lights were dimmed, the balcony door was opened with a cool breeze coming in. She could hear the waves of the ocean outside. Philip walked to her telling her how beautiful she looked. She saw how wonderful his body structure was built. Philip definitely had a six- pack.

"Nice birth mark," Courtney said, smiling as she glanced at his right shoulder.

"Thank you," he said, as he hugged her. He felt her body trembling. "Let's have a glass of wine."

Philip stared at her as she took a little sip of the wine then smiled. He excused himself to go to the restroom. Before the bathroom door shut, Courtney drank all of her wine. Then she poured another glass of wine swallowing that down then she started drinking from the bottle. When she heard the water running in the bathroom, she poured some more wine into her glass and quickly sat the bottle down. He came out the bathroom and picked up his glass.

"You're still sipping on the wine?" Philip asked, as Courtney looked at him smiling. He looked down at the bottle and couldn't believe his eyes. "Courtney, you drank almost the whole bottle. You are going to get sick!"

"No, I won't," Courtney said, as she began to drink from her glass. "I'm sorry, I'm nervous."

"I can tell," he said, as he took the glass out of her hand. "It's okay."

They went outside on the balcony with their arms around one another. As Philip talked to Courtney, he rubbed her back.

"Excuse me," Courtney said, as she ran to the bathroom. She threw-up over the toilet seat. Afterward, she splashed some water on her face then Philip wiped her face. "I'm sorry about this, Philip."

"It's all right. I knew you were going to get sick from drinking all that wine so fast. Let me help you to bed," Philip said.

Courtney laid her head on Philip's chest while they played with each other's fingers as her eyes grew heavy.

"I know this is not what you expected," Courtney said drowsy.

"Just knowing you are Mrs. Philip Franklin is enough for me. Go to sleep, my bride," he said, as he rubbed her arm.

Philip couldn't sleep so he went downstairs to watch television. Hours later, Courtney woke up. She freshened up then came downstairs to where Philip was.

"Hey baby! How do you feel?" he asked.

"Wonderful!" She replied.

"Good. You want to watch television a good movie is about to come on," he said.

Courtney picked up the remote and pushed a button to turn the television off.

"No," she replied, smiling. "I want to get to know my husband."

He reached for her hand as he stood up and then they went to their room.

It was a good thing that they had a two weeks vacation because the first three days they did a lot of staying in.

A week later, Courtney went to bed thinking of the song that Zakeya and David sung at her wedding. She dreamed that she and Philip were on the plane heading home. All of a sudden there was such a vibration on the plane that drinks, food and other things were falling to the floor of the plane. One of the flight attendants told everyone calmly to put on their seatbelts right away. The plane starts to jerk. People were screaming. Philip asked the flight attendant what was going on, she stated it was turbulence. Philip took Courtney's hand looking scared as she was. The plane went upside down as it began to fall. People were screaming. Courtney turned her head to look out the window of the plane and saw nothing but clouds as the plane fell even faster. Then she heard the song "The Prayer." As she awoke she jumped up from her sleep sweating and breathing hard.

"Courtney, what wrong? Baby, it's okay. It was just a dream," Philip said, as he wiped her face.

"I know. It seemed so real," she said, panicky. Then he kissed her cheek.

She went into the bathroom to splash some cold water on her face. Philip came in with her.

"You okay?" Philip asked.

"Yes," Courtney replied. "I'm sorry I woke you up."

"It's all right. What was your dream about?"

"I dreamed we were on our way home and our plane was about to crash." She said, concerned. "It seemed very real and scary."

"It was just a dream, sweetheart," he said, as he kissed her forehead. "Come on let's go back to bed."

She couldn't go back to sleep. Five hours later it was morning and she was still up. She went running. As the day went on the feeling she had from the dream was getting stronger. It was as if she was afraid to ride on the plane home. Later that evening they were coming from dinner and they were riding on the elevator to their floor.

"Philip, let's stay here another day," Courtney said.

"If we do that we will have to transfer planes and we won't get home until late Sunday night. I want to spend some time with my girls before they go to school on Monday. You are still thinking about that dream you had last night?" he asked, as they walked off the elevator.

"No. I mean yes," she answered regretfully.

"Everything is going to be okay," he said, as he put his arm around her.

"You think I'm being silly don't you?" She looked at him.

"No," He replied looking into her eyes. "You are letting that dream get the best of you."

The next day Courtney took a nap. She dreamed, she was on the same plane again. From the corner of her eye she saw Philip's hand but she couldn't turn all the way around to see his face. A flight attendant told everyone to put on their seatbelts. A lady was screaming out because of her ten-week-old-baby. The woman was bending over her child calling on God. She got out of her seat and gave her child to a woman asking her to take care of her baby. The woman who took the baby was Courtney's mother.

"Mom!" Courtney said, in disarray in her dream. "Philip it's my mother! Mom is that really you?" Courtney asked, as she tried to unbuckle her seatbelt but it was stuck. Courtney reached for her mother's hand but she couldn't stretch out anymore but her mother could.

"Courtney, I can't touch you right now," her mother said, in her dream.

"Why? Please try!" Courtney cried.

"No! Listen to me, Courtney. You have to be careful," her

mother said in a puissant tone in her dream. "You shouldn't have gotten on this plane. It's not too late!"

The lights went out on the plane as it turned upside down. Everything went black. You couldn't even see the clouds because they were black as well.

Courtney heard something like a loud crashing sound as she woke up crying in her sleep. She called the airlines right away to change their return date back to the States and she made sure that they could keep the suite for another day. At that point it didn't matter if they didn't have anywhere to sleep. She didn't want to be on that plane. Philip came in from his run and took a shower and sat on the bed while Courtney dried off his back.

"Philip, I need to tell you something," Courtney said.

"What is it?"

"I changed our reservations at the airport for the following day to leave here," she said.

Philip stood up from the bed while turning around and looked at Courtney puzzled.

"Courtney, I told you I didn't want to do that," he said, getting upset.

"I know," she replied sadly.

"So that doesn't matter to you?" he asked firmly.

"Philip!" she said softly, "Do you love me?"

"Yes," he replied quickly, "but what does—"

She wouldn't let him finish his questions, "Philip, please trust me on this one," she said. "That plane may not even crash. Lord knows I hope not. Let's leave a day later, please!" she begged.

"This is really important to you isn't?" he asked, as he stroked the side of her face. He looked at her with concern not truly understanding her fear.

"You have no idea how important." He hugged her.

Philip was disappointed because he really wanted to leave on that day in order to spend some quality time with his girls.

The morning when they were supposed to leave they spent

most of the day in the suite. Philip decided that night he wanted to get something for them from the market for their dinner. Courtney took a nice long shower. Her sister and her mother-in-law called the suite but there was no answer. By Philip and Courtney not answering the telephone at the hotel they thought that they changed their mind and took the original departure as planed to come home. The family left Courtney and Philip an urgent message to call them just in case they hadn't left.

Philip was standing in line at the market and it was on the news that an airplane crash happened that afternoon. Philip left the items on the counter and drove back to the hotel. He ran in the hotel as the desk clerk called his name waving urgent messages at him. Philip ran into the suite calling Courtney's name. When she heard him it was a sound that she never heard before. She ran out the bedroom and they met on the step.

"What's wrong, Philip?" Courtney asked timorously.

"You were right about the plane that we were supposed to be on. Courtney, the plane crashed this afternoon!" Philip said, as he hugged her scared. "It was on the news. Baby, you saved our lives," he said. Then he gave her big kisses all over her face. Then he stopped and they stared at one another as they thought about what they would have left behind. They both went down on the steps in tears.

"Did the news media mention anything about a baby?" she asked concerned.

"Yes," Philip replied. "There was a six-week-old baby that was getting adopted by someone in the States."

Chapter Seventeen

Being married was new for Philip and Courtney. They enjoyed waking up together in the morning and cuddle up together at night. They were not only thinking of one's self as in mine but ours as in one plus one equals two. That was easy for them since they were accepting one another's responsibilities before friendship even started.

Courtney loved the words Mrs. Franklin and Philip became all smiles every time when someone asked him, 'How is your wife?'

One Tuesday evening, Philip was assisting the girls with their school projects. They had to do a show-and-tell at school the next day. Sabrina had an ant and snail farm. They had them in separate plastic glass cases built on one another so people could watch the ants and the snails at the same time. Kianna had a small turtle. The day before the show and tell projects at school, the girls discussed with their parents about getting a puppy. They were told no at that time because Patricia was unable to take on another responsibility. Philip and Courtney didn't have the time to make sure the puppy would be well taken off.

The girls did great on their projects. The teacher kept some of the projects like Sabrina's ant and snail farm, but anything like a turtle or rabbit had to be taken home. Kianna and Sabrina were sitting on the school bus talking to their friend Robert about his cute puppy. The girls decided to exchange the turtle for Robert's puppy for a day. The girls sneaked the puppy carefully into the house then they took it to Kianna's room. They did a good job hiding and feeding the puppy without anyone knowing it or being suspicious of something going on. Sabrina and Kianna took their baths earlier that night without being told. They wanted to sleep in the same room together. Before their parents came in to kiss them goodnight they put the box where the puppy was in with his toy in the closet with a flashlight shining so the puppy wouldn't make any noise. When their parents came into the room to kiss them goodnight, Kianna told them how tired she was while Sabrina tried to yawn discreetly. Before Philip and Courtney walked out the room, he turned around again thinking to himself how adorable they looked and how proud he was to be their father. Kianna acted as if she couldn't keep her eyes open another second. Then Sabrina asked Philip not to turn off the lights because sometimes would wake up at night thinking about the bogeyman. After Philip shut the door the girls waited several seconds before they got out of bed just in case their parents came back in to check on them again. Then they looked at each other and smiled. They jumped out of the bed and brought the box out the closet. They stayed up playing with the puppy. When they became sleepy they sat the box to the side of the room and only left one lamp on.

Later on that night Sabrina got up to go to the bathroom and when she came back into the room she didn't shut the door tight. The puppy managed to turn the box over and he ran out into the hall. He walked down the hall a few times sniffing around things then he looked down the long staircase. He tried to take his time going down the steps but he lost his balance and fell all the way down without hurting himself.

Philip and Courtney were still up. Courtney went downstairs the back way to the kitchen to get them something to drink. As she picked up the glasses she saw something running across the kitchen floor but she only saw the end of a tail. She dropped the glasses and ran quickly up the stairs, terrified. She told Philip there was some kind of wild animal downstairs, like a raccoon, in the kitchen. Philip went in the kitchen with a bat. Courtney stood midway on the stairs telling Philip to be careful because of the broken glass that's on the floor. Seconds later he called Courtney down to the kitchen while holding the puppy that didn't even resemble a raccoon.

The following morning Sabrina woke up smiling calling Kianna's name telling her the alarm was going off and it's time to get ready for school. Sabrina looked in the box and was surprised that the puppy was gone. The only thing that was in the box was the puppy's toy. They called the puppy's name softly while looking under the bed and in the closet for the puppy. They didn't know where he was. They thought to themselves, since the box was sitting straight up and the door was shut when they woke up, what could have happened to it? Courtney knocked on the door and the girls almost jumped out of their skin while pushing the box into the closet while closing it.

"Both of you should be in the bathroom washing up," Courtney said. "Come on, you don't want to be late for school."

"Mommy," Kianna said, looking pitiful, "I can't go to school today because I have a tummy ache," she said wanting to stay home and look for the puppy.

Then Philip walked up behind Courtney.

"You're not feeling good, Kianna?" Philip asked, as Kianna shook her head while slowly rubbing her stomach. "Stay home and I'll have Patricia take you to the doctor. It's time for your annual check-up and after they take your blood test."

"Blood test for a tummy ache, daddy?" Kianna asked perturbed.

"Well, it's not only for that, sweetheart, but like I said it's time for a check up. Instead of getting it done next month, you can get everything done today," He said.

"I probably just need breakfast," Kianna said upbeat, as Philip and Courtney looked at one another knowing that Kianna was faking an illness. "I'll go to school."

"Good. Come on girls. We'll see you downstairs," Courtney said, as she and Philip walked out of the room. The girls looked at each other concerned and wondering what they should do.

After the girls were fully dressed in their school uniforms they needed to go downstairs for breakfast. Kianna went down the back stairs and Sabrina went down the main staircase. They didn't run down the stairs like they generally do, they took their time going down each step looking around and hoping to see the puppy without their parents or Patricia seeing it. The girls hardly ate their breakfast while looking at each other gloomy across the table. Courtney was already gone to work. When the girls got ready to leave for school, Philip walked with them to where they wait for the school bus with the other kids. The girls walked outside with Philip hand in hand and that's when they saw the puppy playing with a small ball. They froze for a second then looked up at their father.

"We're going to talk about this later," Philip said, looking down at them.

"But daddy," Sabrina said.

"No." Philip said boldly. "Sabrina, I don't want to hear from either one of you. I want you to think about what you did by sneaking a puppy in this house without asking me or your mother first. You were both wrong and your mother and I are disappointed in both of you."

Sabrina's eyes became watery as Kianna looked sad. Philip walked them to where the school bus was waiting. He kissed them as he helped them on the bus.

The puppy was wearing a collar therefore Philip knew who he belonged to. He returned the puppy to Robert's family and apologized for the girls' behavior. Robert's parents apologized as well and returned the turtle to Philip. The girls were punished. For two weeks the girls had to be in their own rooms an hour early and no television on a school night. On the weekends they could watch television until 6:00 p.m. instead of 8:00 p.m. During their two weeks of discipline they did a lot of reading and playing board games.

Philip and Courtney talked to Patricia about her employment with them. Patricia's health was worsening before he married Courtney, so they made an agreement once he got married she would only work three times a week. Philip didn't want to let Patricia go since she was such a good worker but for the girls' sake, he was willing to hire someone else full-time. Philip liked Patricia the first day he met with her to take care of Kianna during the week. Patricia loved being around the girls and they loved her company as well. Two days a week, Courtney would be at the house when the girls got home from school.

Courtney knew how Philip felt about someone other than her raising the girls, but he never said a word because of their understanding before they became husband and wife that she would give up her career if something drastic happened to the girls or once she started having children.

On the days Courtney had to be home for the girls, she would barely make it there in time. Patricia called Courtney at work one morning to remind her she had a doctor's appointment that she couldn't miss. Courtney assured her that she would be home before the girls got there.

Courtney had an alarm clock in her office that would go off at a certain time just in case she became too engrossed in her work. She worked on several articles that day and the last thing she had to do was to help an associate by reviewing a column that had to be ready to print in the newspaper the following day. Instead of Courtney reviewing the column in her office, she worked at another person's office while they were gone to a meeting. This also saved her time from going back and forth retrieving information where she had everything she needed in that office. At that time, it had been five hours since Courtney talked to Patricia and time was moving fast as she worked diligently. Two hours later, the girls got off the school bus and walked to the house.

"Patricia's car isn't in the driveway and mommy doesn't seem to be home," Kianna said to Sabrina while walking to the house.

"Maybe mom parked her car inside the garage," Sabrina said.

They tried the door but it was locked. They rang the doorbell and knocked, but there was no answer.

"Mommy is probably on her way home," Kianna said. They played on the swing, seesaw and the sliding board for an hour. "I'm getting thirsty. Let's try our key."

"We can't, the alarm will go off," Sabrina said.

"Maybe not," Kianna said. "Patricia, probably left the alarm off knowing mommy wouldn't be home," she said. She unlocked the door. "So, far so good!" she said, with the door ajar. As she pushed the door opened the alarm went off. Kianna shut the door back quickly. The girls jumped up and down panicking.

"Oh, no!" They both said.

The police cars showed up in minutes as the siren rung loudly. The girls were down the steps holding each other with teary eyes. One of the officers talked to the girls as the other officer talked to the alarm company to reset the alarm. The officer called Courtney's job but no one could locate her. They believed she already left for the day. Then the officer called Philip's office. Philip's secretary had to interrupt his meeting. Philip had to reschedule his meeting and told his secretary not to leave before he got back. While Philip was driving home, he tried calling Courtney himself but he was unsuccessful in reaching her.

Meanwhile Courtney looked at her watch as she stood up quickly from the desk. She rushed to her office to get her purse. When she got on the main highway it was traffic city due to a couple of automobile accidents.

When Philip pulled up in the driveway, he got out of the car as the girls ran up and hugged him. The girls apologized for setting off the alarm. He comforted them as he talked to the officer. Thirty-five minutes later, Courtney drove up to the house as she saw a police car pulling away. Her heart began to really race. She walked quickly into the house.

"Honey, I'm really sorry about this. Are my babies okay! What happened?" Courtney asked concerned, as the girls came down the steps and hugged her around the waist glad to see her.

"Kianna and Sabrina, go upstairs to your rooms and change your clothes." Philip said. He waited a couple of seconds to make sure the girls were upstairs. He looked with disappointment into Courtney's eyes. "You want to know what happened? Our daughters got off the school bus and no one was home. They sat outside and played for over an hour, Kianna used her key hoping the alarm wasn't on, but the alarm went off, and the police cars showed up scaring them," he said getting upset. "One of the officers called you at work, but no one there seemed to have any idea where you were. Your office even tried paging you. Then the officer called my office. I was in the middle of a meeting and here I am. That's what happened. What in the world were you doing that you couldn't be here for our children? Suppose I was out of town," he said disgruntled.

"Honey, I feel really bad about this whole thing," Courtney said, sincerely. "I was working on something at someone's desk and I lost track of time. I'm really sorry!"

"You don't have to apologize to me, Courtney because I see my family more important than my career," he said straightforward.

"That's not fair, Philip. I see my family more important than my career," Courtney said, firmly.

"Your apology should be directed to the girls. I'm going to hire someone full-time to be here because I can't and I won't go to work thinking are you at home or stuck at the office. I'll see you later. I'm on my way back to the office."

Philip left. Courtney stood in the foyer starring into space as her purse slid off her shoulder on to the floor. She washed her hands thinking very seriously about what Philip said as she started dinner. She went into the girls' room to talk to them and apologize for what happened. While dinner was cooking, she helped the girls with their homework then after dinner she played a game with them. After she put the girls to bed, she continued to think about Philip and what he had said to her earlier.

It was getting late and Philip wasn't home yet. Courtney kept looking out the window and watching the clock. She practiced in her head what she was going to say to him. She finally saw headlights coming down the road. She met Philip at the door.

"Hi. Do you want me to get you something?" Courtney asked.

"No thank you," Philip replied, tired. "I'm fine. I'm going to bed," he said, as he walked up the steps.

Philip looked in on the girls then took a shower. Usually when Philip would take a shower, she would help him dry off. When he came out of the bathroom, he was dressed for bed. As he walked to the bed, Courtney said, "Philip," as she took a deep breath, "I'm really, really, truly sorry for what happened today."

"You already told me that. I told you what you should do," Philip said, checking the alarm clock.

"I talked to the girls. You don't have to hire someone full-time. This will never happen again," she said with assurance.

"Good." Philip got into bed and turned off the lamp on his side of the bed. "Goodnight."

Courtney moved closer to him and wrapped her arm around him.

"Courtney," he said, "I'm not trying to be mean, but I had a long day and even a longer one tomorrow. I need to get some sleep."

He turned over to kiss her and then he turned back over on the bed.

Courtney woke up around 2:00 a.m. unable sleep. She got up, went downstairs and got on the computer.

Later on that morning everyone was in the kitchen. Philip was talking and playing with the girls then he kissed Courtney and left for work.

Later on at work, Courtney was in Pete's office who is one the senior executive chief editors of the newspaper. He was praising her for an excellent article she critiqued the day before.

"Thank you," Courtney said. "That means a lot coming from you, Pete. Here you go this is for you."

"What is this? Oh, I left something on your desk. I know you saw it. I want you to help Shelby with a little glitch. I need you to turn a 1,500 word article into 500. I feel there are still some important factors omitted that should be mentioned. I need to see your revision by noon. I know you can do the impossible," Pete said. Then he read what Courtney gave him. "Oh, no, Courtney!" he said in a surprised tone, "You are resigning?"

"Yes. I think it's time," Courtney said.

Courtney didn't say anything to Philip that night about her resigning as the senior editor of the paper because she wanted to get used to the idea first.

Philip had to go out of town for a few days. It seemed everything was getting on Courtney's nerves. Philip would call the house to make sure Courtney was there with the girls. She became so frustrated because she felt Philip didn't trust her completely when it came to her being at home in time for when the girls arrived home from school. She went to the bathroom, locked the door, ran the shower and cried for almost an hour. She wished again that she could talk to her mother.

A couple days later at work, Tiffany one of the staff writers walked into Courtney's office and sat down in from of her desk with a disappointed look.

"Tiffany, what's wrong? You want my opinion on something?" Courtney asked, as she looked at files in Tiffany's arm.

"I heard the news of you resigning. I'm going to miss you as my boss."

"You're sweet."

"No, Courtney. It's the truth. I'm not just saying it. I've learned so much from you. Some of the editors around here can be difficult to work with. But you are more personal and you come across helpful with your suggestions not insulting because of your knowledge of how to do things accordingly due to your experiences. Why you haven't told us?"

"I have three weeks more here and I'm not ready for this kind comments such as the wonderful words you just said. I don't want to get teary-eyed." Courtney smiled. "When we have our meeting on tomorrow, I will announce the news of my resigning. You are a wonderful writer! After you obtain your masters in journalism, you will be able to a get a job anyplace in the news world."

"I hope I can master half of what you have already done. I know you only have three weeks left, but I want to give you a hug now."

"Sure," Courtney said smiling standing up from her desk as Tiffany walked over to her. After they hugged, Tiffany walked away with tears in her eyes.

Courtney sat down in her chair feeling emotional herself but she was determined that she wasn't going to cry. Then someone stormed into her office and shut the door.

"I can't believe it!" Martin said fanning himself, as he flopped down in the chair. "Courtney, I'm going to miss you terribly. Why are you leaving?"

"Who told you?"

"I don't know who told my source about you leaving. You know how it is, we can't reveal our sources," he said, as they both smiled. "Sometimes, when you hear of a person leaving or even dead, you're all smiles!"

"Martin, that's not nice."

"You know how I am Mrs. Franklin. I tell it like it is! But, when you hear of someone leaving such as yourself, I wish it wasn't so and," he said moving to the edge of the seat, "do you think if I applied for your position, I will get it?"

Courtney looked at him puzzled then she smiled knowing he had to be kidding and then they both laughed.

"Martin, thanks for making me laugh. I needed it."

He stood up and walked around her desk and took the trashcan to dump it outside the door on to his cart. Several seconds later, he came back in.

"You know the Bible said, ask and you shall receive," Martin said.

"Right. But you have to be in the position to ask in order to receive. Martin, you told me when you first started working here, what five years ago?" Courtney asked, as he nodded his head, "that you wish you could be a gossip columnist. I have encouraged you for so many years to take the basic college courses. Even if it's one course a seminar; it's better then nothing. Think about where you could be today."

"Your right. I just don't have the time. I feel I'm not smart enough for college. I wasn't the smartest person in school as you can see what I'm doing now."

"That's no excuse. You have embedded that lie in your mind for so long and now you feel that your self-worth is nonexistent because of your occupation. There is nothing wrong with what you do for a living if that's what you want to do. I could have said, I want to be an editor someday. Then I sell newspaper on the streets, read the paper from front to back, and give my opinion from the sideline of how I could have written columns better but, it won't get me closer to my dream. There are a lot of people that felt they weren't academic in school but they took a chance and succeeded in the midst of obstacles that turned into triumph. So, you shouldn't ask God for something that you're not ready to work for yourself and to have the knowledge to maintain it. Believe in yourself no matter what fear you maybe facing and do something about it."

"I'm going to miss our talks like this. One day I'm going to college and I'll follow my dreams. See you later, dear."

"Have a good day, Martin."

The following week, Courtney was at home in the bathroom drying off Philip's back.

"Honey," Courtney said. "I'm resigning from the paper in

two weeks. I gave my letter weeks ago. I would have told you sooner, but I needed to adjust to it myself. I'm ready. I think it's time for me to be home where I'm really needed."

Philip turned around to her.

"Sweetheart, are you sure this is what you want to do? I don't want you to regret this later. It's not the end of the world to hire someone full-time to be here," Philip said.

"But it will be the end of our world and our dreams. Philip, what made us husband and wife one, because we were friends first. Two, we still have the same beliefs and dreams. That hasn't changed for either one of us. And finally, I love you, our girls, and our future children to come. So now is the time to start preparing. It's not going to be easy, but I'll get through it," Courtney said.

"No. We're going to get through it together. This is great!" He said pleased, as he picked her up turning her around.

Philip and Courtney told the girls the news together. They were very excited about having their mother being home in the near future like the other children at their school.

A week later, Courtney's manager called Philip and Ashley to see if they could attend a surprise luncheon the following Friday in honor of Courtney's dedication to the paper.

When Courtney woke up Monday morning in bed, she thanked God for seeing another day and then she thought four more days before her career ends. That Thursday afternoon the company had a catering service for anyone whom wanted to come to say farewell to Courtney. Some people that worked for the company was there but surprisingly a lot of clients also came. This was another way to throw Courtney off track concerning the luncheon.

Friday morning, her last day at work, her manager told her about a future accountant that he wanted her to interview along with him for his department at a hotel for lunch later that afternoon. Martin tapped on Courtney's door. She looked from her work.

"Hello, Martin. Come on in," she smiled.

"I'm not going to hold you up. I just want to give you this." he said, handing her an envelope. "Don't open until I leave. I wish you weren't leaving."

"Thanks, Martin." Courtney said. Then they met each other around the desk and hugged. "I'm going to miss you."

"I just want you to know that all the talks we had were special just like you. It's all in here," he said, as he pointed to his head, "and hopefully one day you will be proud of me. I should be going before I do something I haven't done in a long time." A tear ran down his left cheek. Then he left.

"I'm not going to do it," she said, to herself turning around to her desk not wanting to cry. She opened the card and read the moving words inside of it. Then she opened a folded paper. It was a copy of Martin's class schedule that listed two courses he would be taking in the evenings at a university beginning Monday. She couldn't believe her eyes as read it again. She shut the door, locked it, sat at her desk, and grabbed the tissue box.

When Courtney and her manager arrived at the hotel, he had her sit in the lobby while he checked on something at the front desk.

"Okay, Courtney, our appointment is already here." She walked behind him looking at a dummy report asking questions about the interview they were about to do. When her manager opened the door telling her to go on in, she didn't look up. She walked in slowly talking about the report then everyone screamed, "surprise!"

They scared her so bad that she jumped turning to her manager.

"I don't believe this," Courtney said, laughing wiping her eyes.

The manager hugged her. "Come on; let's go to your table. Shall we." he said.

People were standing up clapping as she walked to the head table. After the food was served, people were coming up to the podium giving praises to Courtney's work. She and Philip were holding hands smiling. Then the president of the paper, Andrew Edward Tillmanson, came up with beautiful flowers to give to Courtney and words about her.

"I remember when Courtney first worked here as a volunteer at age 14," Andrew said, as he smiled at Courtney. Then he looked over the ballroom. "One of the associates at the time knew her father, the prominent Judge Frederick Stephen Kennedy, who recommended that she work at my company. And one day, she wanted to be an editor for a newspaper company. The day she came on board, she informed me of her writing experiences since she was six years old taking at a writing class at a writer's center. She also told me about the books she has read on American history, agriculture, politic and how she felt about it. She also wrote for her high school newspaper as well in college. I was impressed with her and ready to hire her on the spot to take over some of the positions here where I was paying top salaries to, but her adolescent face reminded me she was just a youngster. She started off running errands within the building with a smile. The following year she worked as a receptionist. She had that kind of voice that was very soothing to the heart. When people came into the office they were looking for a woman but saw a lady with many characteristics of beauty. At that time, she was going into her second year of college.

How I knew this lady was gifted, one day she looked at an interesting project that was in my office and she asked my permission to review it and to give me her perception of it. I'll never forget it, she reviewed several tapes and notes on Afghanistan in Asia and how the Jews were treated in the 1930's. I also remembered for two days she spent countless hours of her time in our library gathering more information on the subject. When I reviewed her findings, I couldn't believe it, she was only 16 years old and she was writing like an experienced reporter. I knew then that she would always have a job here. After she graduated from Preston University, many companies offered her jobs, even the ones she wasn't quite ready for at the time, and she turned them all down. When I asked her why, she stated she wanted to start at the bottom first. Just in case she falls down, she would have something to land on.

After so many exceptional years she had with the paper, she was offered opportunities of moving up the ladder that would have consume more of her time with the paper and of course abroad. I even recommend that she work for one of my good friends who owns his news station in New York City because she was good at the news, and I could see her being more then just a senior editor. She hasn't only worked for me, but she also did some contracting work for other newspapers establishment for other states. However, she also turned down so many opportunities to advance in her career for two reasons, which are very rare these days when something is handed to you or you don't have to struggle too much to get where you want to be. Her reasoning number one she loved what she did and number two, which is the most important being a mother is her first priority.

Courtney," Andrew said, as he looked at her so proud and sad at the same time that she was leaving, "we here at Revolution of the World newspaper love you and appreciate you greatly. You have been an asset to me as a friend and as well as a wonderful employee," he said. Everyone clapped as Courtney stood up and hugged Andrew. He said something in her ear and she laughed. As she sat down, he came back to the microphone, "Philip, I told your wife if being a housewife doesn't suit her, she will always have a career with us," he said as everyone laughed. Then he left the platform.

Ashley had a little something at Courtney's place to continue the celebration. Ashley could tell that Courtney wasn't totally happy with her decision of resigning from the paper. Ashley tried to cheer her up, but it seems Courtney was getting agitated.

After Philip finished talking to some people outside he came in the house and turned off all the lights thinking Courtney was upstairs. He looked in on the girls who were asleep, but there was no sign of Courtney. He came back downstairs looking for her. He walked through the kitchen then he saw the slide door cracked. Courtney was standing up outside with her arm around a column.

"Courtney," Philip said.

"Yes," she answered, as she turned her head half way around to him.

"Why are you out here?" he asked, as he stepped outside.

"Getting some air. Thinking. You go ahead up I'll be in soon," Courtney said, sitting down on a step.

He came down the steps and sat next to her.

"Courtney, I want you to look at me," he said.

"I'm fine, sweetheart," Courtney said not looking at him. "See, I'm just getting some air," she said. Then she took a deep breath and exhaled.

He turned her head to him as tears rolled down her face.

"Talk to me," he said while wiping her tears.

"It's not that I don't think my family is not worth me giving up my career because I felt I have proven that. I have been so independent for so long. I always said my prince charming would come along, but I never thought you would come. I always saw myself retiring from the news world. I'm sorry, Philip. I didn't want you to see me like this."

"Don't apologize," Philip said and then he kissed her. "I know this was a sacrifice for you." He took her hand.

"I don't want anything to happen to our babies or to my prince charming," she said, as she looked like a woman who was in love with her husband. "You know if I could change anything during my transition period of resigning it would be that tie you wore at the luncheon."

They laughed.

"I know. Ashley told me about it as soon as I sat down at the table. I wasted coffee on the other one that I wore to work."

They became serious as they looked into one another's

eyes and kissed.

Slowly but surely Courtney was adjusting to being a housewife. She decided to wash and to iron Philip's shirts instead of sending them to the cleaners. One morning, Philip must have changed his shirts five times because they were all wrinkled.

"Look at this!" Philip said, disgusted. "Honey, I need to change cleaners. This is ridiculous!"

"Why?" Courtney asked, as she looked at his shirts not seeing anything wrong with it.

"My shirts that go with my suits look terrible. It looks like I slept in them," he said, as Courtney had a strange look on her face. "Honey, what's wrong?"

"I've been ironing your shirts, Philip. They don't look wrinkled to me," she said. Then she smiled because she thought she did an impressive job.

"Honey, I appreciate your efforts, but please let the professionals handle this. I have some shirts at the office. I'll change once I get there. Thanks for trying though. I'll see you this evening," he said, as he walked over to her and kissed her. Then he rushed out the room ready to leave for work.

One day Patricia helped Courtney clean and cook fresh greens and to make barbecue chicken. Courtney wanted to make homemade rolls from scratch without any assistance from Patricia. Later on that evening the family was sitting at the table eating dinner. Courtney came out of the kitchen.

"Okay everyone, here are homemade rolls," Courtney said, proudly while putting a roll on the girls plates. "I'm sorry that they weren't ready when you began dinner. Honey," she said to Philip, "I was thinking this Thanksgiving you, Lauren and I should make some homemade rolls then we could see whose taste the best," she said. Philip noticed how hard the roll sounded when Courtney put it on his plate. Sabrina took her folk and knife and began to beat on it like it was a drum. "Sabrina, honey, don't play with your food."

"Mommy, I'm full," Sabrina said not wanting her roll.

Philip looked at Sabrina and Courtney then smiled as he finished eating his delicious barbecue chicken.

Kianna took a big bite of her roll and then her eyes got wide. Then she started talking strange as if she had a mouth filled with tissues.

"Look!" Kianna said muttering, as she got up from the table. "My tooth came out," she said, as she took the tooth that embedded in the roll showing it. Courtney gasped, as she put her hand over her mouth in shock. "Now I don't have to go to the dentist."

"Kianna, come here," Philip said. "It's okay," he said to Courtney. "Kianna's tooth has been loose for over a week, it was only a matter of time before it was going to come out. I'm going to take Kianna upstairs and wash her mouth out. Honey, I'm done with dinner. Thank you."

"Excuse me, mommy, I'm done too. I'm going upstairs to see about Kianna," Sabrina said, pushing her chair under the table.

Courtney sat at the table for a few seconds looking at the food taking her fork hitting her somewhat hard roll. She wondered what happened since she went by the cook book instructions. Courtney put everything away off the table. Then she went upstairs to check on the girls before going to the bedroom.

"Go ahead and laugh," Courtney said to Philip feeling bad about Kianna, as she walked into the bedroom.

"I already did," he said while holding a book up to his face then he started chuckling.

As she walked away from the bed he jumped up and pulled her onto the bed then kissed her.

"This housewife thing isn't working," she said sadly.

"Baby, you can't expect to be Mrs. Homemaker in a month or two. Take your time."

"I guess you're right. Kianna seems to be all right," she said.

"Yes she is. She said the next time she has another lose

tooth, she wants you to make homemade rolls," he said, jokingly laughing again.

Courtney grabbed a pillow and began to hit him with it. Then they had a pillow fight.

As time went on Courtney's cooking improved with Ashley, Patricia and Philip's help. However, she never learned the proper way of ironing Philip's shirts without burning or having watery prints on them. She finally decided to leave all dry cleaning to the professionals like her husband suggested.

Courtney would sometimes go with Philip on business trips, luncheons and dinners parties. As time went on she volunteered her time at a local charity in the mornings. Because of Philip's busy schedule, he would sometimes call Courtney from the office asking her out on a date just the two of them.

It was a Saturday afternoon of thunderstorms. There was no hope of sun in sight. Lauren came to the house with sunshades. She handed Courtney something in a bag.

"Lauren, why don't you take a load off. It's raining really hard out there," Courtney said, as she helped Lauren with her raincoat and umbrella. As they walked up the steps to the second level of the house, Courtney talked about the rainstorm that happened last weekend. Lauren's mind was a million miles away not hearing what Courtney said.

"Where is my brother?" Lauren asked, as she entered the living room then she walked over to one of the windows looking at the raindrops.

"In the library. I'm sure he wouldn't mind the interruption from his sister. Why do you have on sunshades?" Courtney asked Lauren.

"Nothing. I'm sorry I forgot to take them off," Lauren said, as she removed her sunshades with her back still turned to Courtney.

Courtney walked over to Lauren and turned her around.

"Why are your eyes red? You have been crying? What's wrong?" Courtney asked, concerned.

"I just wanted to drop the package off that I have been promising you for weeks," Lauren said trying to smile, "and I needed the long ride out here. I'm fine. I really have to go. Tell the girls I said hello."

"They are not here, but I'll give them your regards. Come on Lauren talk to me. Don't leave like this."

Philip walked in the room.

"Hey sis! I thought I heard the doorbell," Philip said, as he smiled. Then he noticed she wasn't herself, "Lauren, what's wrong?"

"Honey, would you give us a second. Please," Courtney said to Phillip.

"Fine," Philip said. "Lauren, don't leave before I see you." He walked away.

"Come on, Lauren," Courtney said. "Have a seat. What's wrong?" She asked as she and Lauren sat down on the couch.

"You are so lucky," Lauren said teary-eyed, as Courtney looked at her puzzled. "I found out at the doctor's yesterday, due to medical reasons, I can't have children," She said. Then she got up wiping her eyes. "Can you believe that! Vincent wants children and I can't even give him one child. I know what you are going to say I can adopt. Well, that's not good enough."

"Have you told Vincent what the doctor said?" Courtney asked.

"Yes," she replied, as she frowned feeling hopeless. "He was wonderful about the whole thing, but I see the disappointment in his eyes. I don't feel like a woman right now. I feel useless, ineffective and unproductive. Courtney, I can't have children." Then she broke down in tears.

Courtney walked over and hugged her.

"It's going to be okay," Courtney said, as tears came down her face feeling sorrow for Lauren. "I know you don't see it now, Lauren, but you are still blessed even with this unpleasant news." Then she looked Lauren in her eyes, "You have a family that loves you and we will see you through this. Most of all you have a husband that loves you unconditional and understands life complications. There is always healing or a remedy to all situations. You have a wonderful alternatives, you can adopt and love that child as if it's your very own."

"You're right and I know that. But the fact remains the same. I'm sure as time goes by my feelings about this will change. You know what my husband did after I told him the news?" Lauren asked, as she smiled a little. "He wants to wine and dine me tonight at our favorite restaurant. He even wants to go dancing. I couldn't believe he wasn't upset."

"Why would Vincent be upset? He knows that this matter is out of both of your hands," she said, as Lauren shook her head to Courtney in despair. "I know you probably want to disappear, but don't forget the love of your life. If Vincent can accept it and move on so can you, right?"

"Yes," Lauren responded. "I'm glad I talked to you because I wasn't planning on going out this evening with Vincent. I do have a lot to be thankful for, but I'm still disappointed. Is it possible to be thankful but disappointed at the same time?"

"Yes, but it's our attitude towards the disappointment that makes the difference," Courtney said. True

"I'm going to see Philip and then I'm going to leave," Lauren said. "I'm not going to tell him what I talked to you about. I'm not ready to freely talk about it yet. Only you and my husband know about this."

Philip got it out of Lauren. He talked her into getting a third opinion. She did what he suggested, trying to be hopeful. However, the doctor came with the same conclusion as the other physicians, she was unable to bear children.

The holiday season was back again in full force. Philip and Courtney went to his mother's for Thanksgiving. They were not only thankful to see another Thanksgiving, but to celebrate an addition to the family. Lauren and Vincent adopted a three-week-old baby boy name Christian.

Philip, Courtney and her in-laws celebrated Christmas at

Ashley's home. As usual Ashley loved to go all out from Christmas morning until midnight trying to make sure everyone that came to her house had a great time.

On New Year 's Day everyone was at the church witnessing Beverly's marriage to Dr. Edwin Nicholas Hammond. God blessed Lauren's womb and she became pregnant. Her due date was in seven months. The miracle was a blessing for all of them. A few months later, Edwin retired from his practice and he and Beverly moved to the islands. Beverly promised that she would come back a few weeks before Lauren had the baby.

Chapter Eighteen

Philip made plans months ago to celebrate their first wedding anniversary in Bermuda.

Philip was lying in bed one night talking to Courtney while she was brushing her hair. He decided to tell her something that he really dreaded.

"Courtney, I need to tell you something about our trip to Bermuda," Philip said.

"We can't go, right?" Courtney asked, as she stopped brushing her hair while turning around to him.

"How did you know?"

"I could tell from our conversations about work in general. Your enthusiasm about the trip had diminished," Courtney said.

"Baby, I'm really sorry about this. This is not a good time to go because of a project I'm working on."

"It happens. I guess, I'll go to the Bermuda alone," Courtney said with a straight face teasingly, as she turned back around to the mirror bushing her hair once again.

"Right," he said, laughing. "I'm going to make it up to you. Don't take my promises lightly. One other thing honey, we're going to have house guests for a week."

"Who?" Courtney asked, as she turned around to him again.

"Mr. Jiang Keon and his wife Yang. They are from Beijing. He's a prominent business man that I have known for many years. I went to a big social dinner with Mason, a good friend of mine, who knew that Mr. Keon was going to be there. I read every business magazines and new articles whether it was native or foreign on Mr. Keon's business and his wisdom on success. When I met him I was impressed and at the same time intimated. I could tell he wasn't interested in what I was telling him about TELCOM. I barely had two minutes with him before he politely bowed his head and walked away with his associates. While mingling with the crowd, I over heard Mr. Keon telling someone that he was going to this well known country club to play golf the next morning. After the function was over that night, I had Mason showing me at his home 11:00 at night how to use a golf club. It wasn't like being taught on an actually golf course but I just wanted to look like I knew a little something." Courtney smiled. "Since Mason was a member of the country club and his best friend's father's brother is one of the owners of the establishment; Mason made arrangements for me to come to country club as a guest since he couldn't bring me himself due to a meeting he had to attend."

"There's nothing like networking," Courtney said smiling.

"That's right. The next morning, I was at the country club with Mason's golf clubs. An hour later after Mr. Keon noticed me, he asked me would I like to join him and the fellow players. He noticed I wasn't a player so he taught me some things and he was surprised how quickly I caught on. We were on the golf course for a few hours and then we had lunch. Mr. Keon wasn't interested in TELCOM but he liked me and we kept in touch from time to time. I met his wife one year when I was on travel. We were staying at the same hotel. She's a sweet lady."

"Amazing. I never knew you like golf."

"Baby, I don't. I haven't picked up a golf club since then." They laughed. "Mr. Keon and his wife will be coming to the States for two weeks. Washington, D.C. will be their first stop and then they will come here. The reason why I want them to stay here is because family is very important to Mr. Keon. He believes if a man or a woman has a successful business their family should be as equal. Wholesome. That's his culture, so I asked him to stay here with us.

I've been trying to get Mr. Keon's business for years. I thought we could give him and his wife a tour of our city, if he likes we can play as much golf as he wants," Courtney smiled, "and I'll of course present accurate facts of how TELCOM would be a wise choice for his business. Courtney, if I get Mr. Keon's account, we will be on our competitor's heels. They would be nonexistent in five years or less. Mr. Keon has chump change of $99 trillion dollars to invest in order to reconstruct his business for his company and other areas that we can give our expertise for the millennium."

"That sounds great, Philip. So they are leaving for the States next week?"

"Yes," Philip replied, as he got up. He walked over to Courtney and took the brush out of her hand. He began to brush her long black hair. "Are you upset?"

"Disappointed, sort of, but upset? No," She replied, as she smiled at him in the mirror.

He moved her hair to the right side of her shoulder. Then he kissed the side of her neck. "Come on let's check on the girls."

Philip hired a full-time housekeeper and a cook that specialized in Chinese cuisine while Mr. Keon and his wife were in town. Mr. Keon and his wife fell in love with Philip's family. Mrs. Keon taught the girls some Chinese while the girls attempted to teach Mrs. Keon Spanish and Italian.

Courtney spent some time with Mrs. Keon after her run in the mornings. They would walk several miles chatting. Then they would go to the market and other stores as well.

One morning Courtney was smiling from ear to ear as she approached the breakfast table while listening to the girls talked to Mr. Keon and his wife in Chinese. Philip had to correct the girls from time to time in their pronunciation, but they were doing very well learning the language. Later that morning, Mrs. Keon and Courtney walked the girls to the school bus since Mr. Keon and Philip began to talk business at the breakfast table.

A couple of days later, Philip walked into his office feeling terrible because he and Courtney were supposed to be in the Bermuda celebrating their wedding anniversary. When he opened his briefcase, he saw a package wrapped in brown paper sitting on top of his newspaper. He opened the brown envelope. It was a paper card that Courtney had made for Philip that had all kinds of designs that read,

Philip:

Happy Anniversary, Sweetheart. I love you so very much. This has been the happiest time of my life and it's all because of you. I hope you enjoy your anniversary gift.

Love you always, Courtney

Philip smiled as he opened his gift that was wrapped in brown paper. He opened the box and saw a white photograph album trimmed in gold around the edges with a cassette tape mounted into the cover. The inside of the album consisted of pictures and beautiful words of how Courtney felt about him during the first year of their lives together as husband and wife. He continued to browse through the album as he played the tape. It was Courtney singing "You Are So Beautiful To Me" and "You Light Up My Life." Courtney went to a recording studio to perform the songs that had different instruments playing in the background. Philip called Courtney at home, he was speechless. The only thing he could say was thank you and he loved her very much.

Later on that afternoon Philip called Courtney telling her something came up at the office and he would meet her, Ashley and Preston at the restaurant. When the limousine came to pick her up she was surprised that Ashley and Preston weren't in the limousine as planned. Courtney picked up the telephone in the car to speak to Oscar the driver.

"Oscar, were you told to pick up the Harringstons first?" Courtney asked.

"Yes ma'am, but I received a call from Mrs. Harringston

stating that they weren't going to join you and Mr. Franklin this evening."

"Thanks," Courtney said, puzzled. Then she called Ashley in the car. "Ashley what happened? Why can't you and Preston make it? Are the children okay?"

"The children are fine. Sis, I'm really sorry about canceling on you and Philip at the last minute. Are you on your way to the restaurant?" Ashley asked.

"Yes. I don't understand what could be so important that you and Preston can't come."

"Courtney, I really have to go. Tell Phillip I said thanks for the invitation, but we won't be able to attend. We will make it up to you two. Okay? Happy Anniversary!"

Courtney hung up the telephone.

"Great," she said to herself. "Philip is running late and our family bailed out on us at the last minute."

When Courtney arrived at the restaurant she was escorted to a private dinning area. As the host slid the doors apart, Courtney heard the piano playing the song, 'You Light Up My Life.' She couldn't believe her eyes as she saw a portrait that someone had drawn of them on their wedding day hanging over the fireplace. There was a table set for two.

"Mrs. Franklin, happy anniversary," the host said.

"Thank you," Courtney said, as she smiled.

"Someone will be right with you, ma'am," the host said smiling. Then he stood out side the doors and slid them together.

Philip walked out from behind a statue.

"Courtney," Philip said, as he walked over to her. She turned around, and he kissed and hugged her.

"I thought you were working late," she said, smiling.

"That's what I wanted you to believe. I wasn't going to let anything spoil our evening together. I just wanted to have you all to myself."

"So this thing with Ashley and Preston," Courtney said.

"It was all planned this way," he said, as he kissed her again. They walked to the bar and Philip poured a non-alcoholic champagne.

"You can drink as much as you want of this," Philip said, as they laughed. "It won't make you sick."

Everything they ate and drank out of was made out of paper. A gentleman came in later and played a couple of songs on his violin. After dessert the waiter brought out another serving tray.

"Honey, what is this?" Courtney asked. "I can't eat another thing."

"Let's see what it is," he said, as he stood up and removed the top.

It was little pieces of white paper rolled up on top of one another from the edges of the tray building up like a mountain. Then a paper box was sitting in the center of it. Courtney opened it and it was a carbon ring made like her wedding ring but the center of the carbon ring had a white diamond in it. Philip took it out and put it on top of her ring finger as he said his wedding vows again to her. Someone came into the dining area to take their pictures.

When they got home, Ashley, Preston, Mr. and Mrs. Keon, and the girls were there waiting for them with a cake and vanilla ice cream, Philip's favorite.

Later on that night while Courtney was getting into her lingerie she was thinking of the wonderful evening she had with Philip. She walked out to the bedroom and took off her wrap and got into bed. Philip was sound asleep. Courtney leaned over and kissed him on the check.

"Goodnight, my prince," she whispered.

Minutes later, Philip rolled over to her and put his arm around her waist. He kissed the back of her neck as he cuddled up even closer to her.

"Happy anniversary, baby," Philip said and then he fell back to sleep hugging her.

Late one morning, Courtney rode with Mrs. Keon to the airfield to meet her husband to return back to Beijing. They expressed their gratitude for the hospitality not only at TELCOM but especially at the Franklin's household. Philip and Courtney had their arms around one another watching the jet take off. Philip felt very pleased with his meetings with Mr. Keon, however, Philip still had a long way to go to get Mr. Keon's business.

Philip kept his promise to his wife. Two weeks later, on a Thursday afternoon, Courtney met her husband at the airport believing they were going to the Bermuda. As the plane was taking off, Philip whispered in Courtney's ear that they were going to Paris instead to celebrate their delayed wedding anniversary.

One morning after Courtney walked the girls to the school bus, she ran three miles. She came home feeling pretty good and more energetic than ever. When she got out of the shower she felt dizzy. She sat down on the bed then she blacked out. When she came to she couldn't remember falling asleep. The following weekend Courtney, Ashley, and Preston took the kids to the circus. When they got to her house Courtney went to the kitchen to fix a pitcher of lemonade. Ashley and Preston came into the kitchen talking and laughing. Ashley put the ice cubes in the glasses while Courtney was putting the pitcher of lemonade on the table. As Courtney turned around from the table, she felt dizzy again then fainted.

Preston picked Courtney up from the floor and carried her to the couch in the family room. Kianna and Sabrina were upset as they called out for their mother but she didn't respond. Zakeya took the girls to another room where their nephews and nieces where playing. Ashley put a wet towel on Courtney's forehead while calling her sister's name and gently stroked her cheeks. Seconds later, Courtney opened her eyes slowly feeling as if she was waking up from a deep sleep. When Philip got home from the airport that evening the girls told him what happened as he was trying to get in the house. Courtney was in the kitchen cooking dinner.

"Courtney," Philip said concerned, as he walked over to her.

"Honey, you're home," she said, as she kissed him. "I missed you."

"I missed you too," he said, as he put his arms around her. Then he put his face to hers to see whether or not she had a fever. She felt normal. "What's going on? The girls told me you fainted earlier today. Are you okay?"

"Yes. It's nothing. I guess I'm tired," Courtney said casually. "I'm glad your home."

"Has this happened before?"

"What do you mean?" she asked trying to act clueless, as she took a pot off the stove.

"I hate when you do that, Courtney. Has this happened before! Have you fainted recently?" he asked agitated.

"Yes!" Courtney replied. "About a week ago. It happened after a run. I sat on the bed then later I found myself waking up."

"What? Courtney!" Philip said upset.

"Honey, it's nothing. I probably over did it running that day when I blacked out. I've alternated my daily run to speed walking twice a week. Maybe I'm tired for some unknown reason. It will go away," she said, as Philip shook his head to her, "I don't want to argue about this, Philip."

"No, we're not going to argue. I want you to make a doctor's appointment."

"Philip, I've been thinking about that. Ashley must have called me five times since she got home encouraging me to see my doctor. I will soon. I promise," she whispered, as she smiled. "Dinner will be ready any minute."

After dinner the girls wanted their parents to watch a movie with them that was coming on the Walt Disney channel. Philip and Courtney were sitting on the floor with their arms wrapped around one another. Courtney fell asleep watching the movie.

"Baby, the movie is over. Let's go upstairs and get ready for bed," Philip said. As Courtney stood up, she became light headed again. She stumbled back some as Philip put his arm around her waist. "Come on we're going to the emergency room tonight."

"Honey, we will be there all night. I'm fine," Courtney said, laughing it off not wanting to go to the hospital. "My legs were asleep that's all."

"Why do you lie?" Philip asked upset.

"I'm going to the doctor first thing Monday morning," Courtney said, as the girls looked at one another worried. "While you were upstairs changing before dinner, I called the doctor's office and I got an appointment, someone had just canceled minutes before I called. I really want to wait to see my own doctor," she said. Then she looked at the girls who had a serious concerned look on their faces. "Really, I'm okay. Mommy is okay."

After the girls changed into their nightclothes they knocked on their parents bedroom door wanting to sleep in their bed. Philip told them they couldn't talk but to go to sleep. Both of the girls slept in the middle of the bed. Kianna was lying next to Philip and Sabrina was next to Courtney.

Later that night Kianna looked over at Sabrina.

"Wake up," Kianna whispered to Sabrina, as she nudged her. "You're supposed to be watching mommy."

"I am," Sabrina said, as she rubbed her eyes.

"Sabrina!" Philip said.

"Sorry, daddy," Sabrina said softly, as she put her index finger over her lips to Kianna while lying back down.

Sabrina turned over to her mother and put her finger near her mother's nose then she accidentally touched the tip of her nose.

"Sabrina, what are you doing?" Courtney asked, rubbing her nose.

"Courtney, I'm trying to sleep," Philip said.

"Me too," Courtney said.

About a minute or two later Kianna whispered to Sabrina to let her lay next to Courtney.

"What are you two doing?" Philip asked, as the girls switched places in bed. "No! Everyone go to their own beds now," he demanded, as he turned on the lamp.

"But daddy, we want to make sure that mommy is breathing. We don't want her to die," Kianna said sadly.

"You girls are so special. Mommy is not going to die. Well not tonight," Courtney said, as she smiled at the girls. "I know all of you are concern about my fainting spells, but I'll be okay. Come on give mommy a hug before you go to your rooms."

Philip walked the girls to their rooms. He came back to bed and held Courtney in his arms.

"Honey, please go to the doctor on Monday. To be honest, I'm really concerned about you," Philip said, as he wrapped his arms around her.

"Now you all have me worried too," Courtney said rubbing Philip's arms around her.

On Monday morning Courtney went to the doctor. The doctor advised her not do any running or working out until he had her test results back from her annual exam and blood test. However, he wanted her to rest more until the test results were back in a few days.

The doctor called Courtney the following evening asking her to come to the hospital the following afternoon. He wanted to talk to her between his rounds at the hospital. He didn't want to wait until Friday to see her at his office. Philip took off from work for a couple of hours to go with Courtney to the appointment. Courtney's heart was beating a mile a minute as they walked into the office to meet with the doctor.

"Courtney, let your heart rest," the doctor said, as he could see how worried she looked. "I'm not going to tell you and your husband something deadly."

"What's wrong, doctor? Why did you want us to come

here to see you?" Philip asked.

"When something like this happens, I don't want to say it on the telephone and hang up, but this is something very serious and I want to start preparing immediately," the doctor said. Then he looked at Philip, "Courtney, told me she needed to know her test results as soon as possible, which is understandable when one is experiencing an unusual symptom in the body."

"Doctor, I can handle it. What is it?" Courtney asked, taking a deep breath.

"Congratulations, you and your husband are going to have babies," the doctor said.

"What! A baby?" Courtney asked smiling.

"He said babies, Courtney," Philip said not believing his ears.

"Yes. Babies. Twins! Courtney, you are eight weeks pregnant. I could tell when I did your exam that you are pregnant but I wanted to have all the facts first."

Philip got up and hugged the doctor.

"I'll be going on vacation for three weeks and I didn't want to wait until I came back to go over general things you should and shouldn't do. Number one, Courtney, you told me that your eating habits have changed. You have to eat more than once a day even though you eat a lot of fruits and vegetables. You will have to change your eating habits back to three meals a day with your normal snacks, fruits and vegetables, like carrots. Then once your pregnancy progresses, you will have cravings and so on. Secondly, no running. However, walking will be good for you and the babies," the doctor said, as his pager began to beep. "Please excuse me, I'll be back."

Courtney was in shock. Philip got on his knees in front of her.

"We're pregnant," Philip said, proudly.

Courtney touched her stomach.

"Yes, we are," she said, excited.

Sabrina and Kianna were excited about the news of their

mother expecting twins. Courtney allowed the girls to help her choose decorations and furniture for the babies' room.

When Courtney got into her sixth month of her pregnancy, Philip would go with her to the doctor's office. Two months later, Philip and his associates from his company flew to Beijing for several weeks to meet Mr. Keon and the members of his board. Philip was concerned about Courtney because she was having false labor pains in the beginning of her eighth month.

Philip met Mr. Keon's 23-year old beautiful daughter, Kym Su Keon, who was on travel when he met with her father in the past. She was a very attractive woman, her height 5'6, small built, and shoulder length brunet hair. She graduated from high school at the age of 14 and graduated from college with a master of science at age 19. Kym was very impressed with Philip in seconds when she met him. She noticed his wedding ring as she bit her bottom lip wishing he were single.

Philip and Kym were inseparable at Mr. Keon's company. They had plenty in common concerning the business world. They would work early in the mornings to late at night. One evening Philip finished up his conversation with Kym concerning a strategy of how they were going to handle a competitor in China.

"Philip, we worked very hard in the last few days," Kym said, as she locked her briefcase. "Let's call it a day while there's still day light and go out to dinner. If you want we can continue our conversation of the progress report at the restaurant."

"I don't know about you, but right now my sleep is more important than eating. We talked enough about this report. We can continue with this discussion tomorrow," Philip said, as he put on his jacket.

"Very good. Until tomorrow," Kym said, as she smiled.

Philip was missing his family more than he ever had. Instead of him calling Courtney twice a day, like when he was at home, he would call home at least four times a day. Once in the morning before the kids left for school, twice during the day and sometimes at the hotel if it was not too late just to hear Courtney's voice.

Early one Saturday morning Kym arrived at Philip's hotel room to pick up some charts that she wanted to review on their day off. Philip just came from running at the time. He was sweating and his clothes were stuck to his body that revealed his muscular physique.

"You are really fit, Philip," Kym said, as she watched him smiling. "That's good! Plenty muscles indeed."

"Here you go, Kym," Philip said not responding to her comments. "Everything is self explanatory, but if not you know the number here."

"Thank you," she said, as she took the report out of the envelope. "Fine," she said, as she scanned over the pages of the report. "I better leave now. I have some other things to do."

"Have a good day." He opened the door for her.

"What are your plans for the day?" Kym asked turning around from the door.

"I'm not sure, but I'll find something. Bye, Kym," Philip said straightforward.

Days later they were looking over a proposal and Philip was leaning over the side of Kym's shoulder. Kym found herself looking up at Philip more times then she had to while they were discussing some figures. Philip left the office for a second when Courtney called.

"This is Ms. Keon," Kym said, in Chinese.

"Hello," Courtney said, in Chinese. "May I speak to Mr. Philip Franklin."

"He's not available right now. May I ask who's calling?" Kym asked, in Chinese.

"This is Mrs. Franklin. His wife," Courtney said, in Chinese.

"I'm sorry, Mrs. Franklin," Kym said, in Chinese. Then she spoke in English. "We can speak in English. Hi, my name is Kym Keon. I work along with your husband. If you would hold on, I'll get him for you. Actually, he just walked in. Please hold on," she said and then she covered the receiver passing it to him. "Philip, it's your wife. If you need me, I'll be in my office."

As Kym walked out of the office closing the door slowly, she listened to part of his conversation.

"Sweetheart," Philip said with enthusiasm to Courtney. "I miss you so very much. How are my girls?"

Kym walked away from the door.

It was Thursday morning in China, when Philip and his associates gave an excellent presentation to the board, private investors, and the attorneys. Kym was able to answer some of the questions that the members of the board had concerning their corporation regarding Philip's presentation. There were no questions that Philip and his associates had to get back to Mr. Keon, or the investors or even Kym about later. Everything was understood. Kym learned a lot from Philip in the short time she spent with him.

Later on that evening Kym and Philip went out to dinner.

"Philip, why didn't you take my parents up on their invitation to stay at our home while you were here," Kym asked.

"Why? Did your parents say anything to you about it?" He asked.

"No. Nothing like that. They understood you wanted to be close to the airport if your wife needed you to get home in a case of an emergency because of the pregnancy. Actually that was impressive to my father. However, he could have accommodated you."

"I know but it's not necessary. However, I enjoyed my visits to their lovely and impressive home," Philip said. Then he put some food in his mouth as Kym smiled at him.

"Philip may I ask you a question? It's personal," Kym said, as she sat her chopsticks down.

"What's the question?" Philip asked, as he looked at her.

"Are you truly a happily married man?" Kym asked boldly.

"Yes." Philip answered, without hesitation. "Not only am I a happily married, but I'm in love with my wife. She is the only woman for me and the only one I would give my life for," he said gently with such meaning.

"That's good. I hope one day I'm that lucky if I would give a man the time of day."

"Well you have to give them the time of day if you expect to meet someone special," Philip said. "You are a very bright and ambitious young lady. I see why your father loves to run things by you first before he presents it to the members of the board. You have plenty of time for happily ever after. You have more successful avenues to cross first."

A couple days later while Philip was waiting on Mr. Keon's decision at the office, Philip received a call that Courtney was having contractions two weeks before her due date. Courtney never remembered being in so much pain with Sabrina. She wanted to have a natural birth. Philip called the hospital.

"Courtney," Philip said. "I'm going to be there as soon as possible. The secretary here is trying to get me an airplane reservation. How do you feel?"

"Fine. The contractions are not so painful now. Then again that's not true. Oh!" Courtney said, as she screamed in pain.

"Baby, I'm going to be there soon," Philip said, as his heart went out to Courtney.

"Philip, no. If you can't make it I understand. Ashley is here," Courtney said, as her sister whipped off her sweaty head.

"I know but I want to be there. Courtney,"

"Yes, Philip," she answered in pain.

"I love you. I'll be there before you know it," Philip said.

Philip called the secretary at Mr. Keon's company. The next plane wasn't leaving until 7:00 a.m. the next morning. Hours later, Mr. Keon called Philip into his office. When Philip got there Kym was in the office waiting as well.

"Philip, I know how excited you are about your wife having the babies. I had my secretary cancel your airplane reservation. My driver is on his way to pick you up, take you back to your hotel to get your things, and then take you to one of my jets. You should arrive back home in 15 hours max. That's our gift to you. Actually, it was Kym's idea about the jet."

"Thank you. I really appreciate it," Philip said.

"Another thing, Philip," Mr. Keon said in a discouragingly way. "Better let you know the board review of your proposal. I wouldn't want you to be wondering what's going on here while flying back to the States." Philip looked at Kym as she looked away from him. "Philip, we have decided to accept the proposal. We want to do this. There is a saying in America," he said, as he picked up Charles' proposal, "this is a gold mine. This is a gold mine that we're eager to start as soon as possible."

Then Kym looked at Philip and smiled.

"Congratulations, Mr. Franklin. We're looking forward to working with TELCOM of America," Kym said, as she shook Philip's hand.

Kym went with Philip to pick up his associates and luggage from the hotel then they went to the jet. Philip and Kym stood inside the jet.

"Well, Philip, it was great. I can't wait to meet your family and the impressive people you have working for you at TELCOM. Call us and let us know how many girls and boys you have," Kym said, as she hugged Philip.

"Thank you for arranging this. I'll call you later." Philip said.

"Okay. I better go so you can get going," Kym said as she smiled. She walked down the steps of the jet. Then she got into the limousine and watched the jet take off.

The next day Courtney was begging the doctor to take the babies. Five hours later her doctor decided to go ahead and let her deliver. Ashley went to change and went into the delivering room. Courtney was sweating and using her own breathing techniques. Courtney didn't pay any attention to who was coming into the delivery room. Then she heard a familiar voice and a special touch on her hand. It was Philip.

"You made it, Philip," Courtney said in tears. She was really pleased to see him.

"Yes," Philip said, as he kissed her forehead.

"These pains are so unbearable, but now they aren't so bad since my prince is here with me," Courtney said, as Philip took her hand again.

Courtney gave birth to twin boys. Philip was so proud holding his two sons and becoming a father for the third time. Courtney was thanking God to herself that it was over and the babies were fine. Then she felt more pains.

"Mrs. Franklin, what's wrong?" One of the nurses asked.

"I'm still having contractions," Courtney said, as she grabbed the sides of the rail on the bed. "Oh, it hurts!"

"It's probably the after birth," the nurse said.

"No, it's not the after birth," the doctor said. "Mrs. Franklin, you're about to deliver another baby! I don't know why the tests didn't show a third child before but the monitor here and what you are experiencing Mrs. Franklin, you are about to deliver another baby."

The other nurse came over to get the boys from Philip. Then Philip looked like he was about to faint himself not expecting a third child.

"Are you sure?" Courtney asked. "It really hurts!" she said in agony.

Philip took Courtney's hand and began to talk in her ear.

The doctor requested another physician to come and assistant him. Courtney begged the doctor to tell her what was going on. Courtney and Philip were told the baby wasn't fully ready to be delivered and the umbilical cord seemed to be around the baby's neck so they had to do a C-section. Courtney panicked. She begged the doctors to save her baby in any way they could, even if it meant she had to lose her life. Her doctor assured Philip and her that wouldn't be necessary. When the baby was taken from Courtney's womb they removed the umbilical cord from around baby's neck. The baby wasn't doing anything. Courtney believed the worst.

"It's a girl, Mrs. Franklin," The doctor said, smiling. "Congratulations again to the both of you."

"She's not crying. What's wrong?" Courtney asked puzzled.

"She is fine," the doctor said. "She just wanted to arrive in the world quiet. She is underweight and her heartbeat is irregular. We can work with her. The only thing you need to be concerned about is a name for this beautiful little lady."

As the doctor passed the baby girl to the nurse she began to cry. Then they took the baby away in an incubator, Courtney began to cry as Philip continued to comfort her.

While Courtney was resting, Philip went to the chapel in the hospital and prayed for the babies and his wife. Later, Ashley came into the chapel and sat next to Philip.

"You need to go home and get some rest. The triplets are fine. The girls want to see you. I'll stay here with Courtney," Ashley said.

"I appreciate that Ashley, but I'm going to stay here at the hospital with my wife. I already talked to the girls on the telephone to let them know that I'm staying in here tonight with their mother, brothers and sister," he said so proud, as Ashley smiled.

"Lauren was here earlier and your mother has been calling to check on Courtney. Your mother wants you to call her when you get a chance."

"Thanks. I will," he said.

When Courtney woke up the next day she saw Philip feeding Joseph, while Junior was asleep.

"Hello there, Mrs. Franklin," the nurse said, as she came into the room.

"I wanted to breastfeed my children," Courtney said to the nurse.

"I know," the nurse said. "The babies were hungry and

you needed your rest. The formula we used for the boys is just like breast milk. If you are up for it, you can breast feed them in a couple hours. Someone will be here shortly to show you the proper way to breast feed your babies. The doctor will be in soon. How do you feel?"

"Sore," Courtney said, as she sat up. "How is our daughter?"

"She's doing good. Would you mind thinking of a name for her. Now if you can't think of one, you can name her Sharon. That's my name," the nurse said, smiling as she passed little Philip to her. "I'll check back later to see if you need anything."

Courtney immediately checked the babies' arms, fingers, legs, and toes. The doctor came into the room. He explained to Courtney and Philip about their baby girl before they brought her in. Everything the doctor explained was nothing like they thought as their imaginations went wild. When the nurse brought the baby girl in she had a small monitor that was checking her breathing and a tube in her nose.

Another nurse came in and began talking to Courtney about breastfeeding her daughter. After the nurse left, Philip put the boys down since they were sleeping and then walked over to Courtney and their daughter. He told Courtney how beautiful she was. After Courtney fed her new daughter, she kissed her.

"I'm sorry," Courtney said to her daughter, as tears ran down her face. Then she put her daughter on her shoulder to be burped. Courtney felt it was her fault that her daughter wasn't healthy like her brothers.

"Honey, Jackee' is going to be fine," Philip said. "This is not your fault. The doctor said in the next few weeks she will be 100% perfect."

"You want to name her after my mother?" Courtney asked surprised.

"Yes, if that's okay. I think our mother would be pleased if we name her granddaughter after her," he said, as Courtney smiled.

Later that night Philip came home exhausted. He sat his luggage by the door. Then he walked to the kitchen to get something to drink. Patricia was wiping the island counter top off.

"Philip!" Patricia said smiling. "Congratulations. How are Courtney and the babies doing?"

"Hi, Patricia. They are great!" He said with enthusiasm as they hugged. "How are things going around here?"

"Fine of course. The little women have been waiting for you to come home all evening. I finally got them into bed," she said.

"I'm sorry, I should have called to let you and the girls know I was going to stay a little longer than planned," he said taking the orange juice container out the refrigerator.

"I understand and so do the girls," she said. "You look beat. The orange juice is not going to do you justice. Why don't you give me five minutes and let me fix you some herbal tea to relax you," she said putting the juice back into the refrigerator.

"Thank you, Patricia," Philip said.

Philip went upstairs to the girls' room and saw they weren't there. Then he walked into his bedroom and there they were in bed under the covers asleep. He leaned over and kissed Sabrina's forehead and reached over and kissed Kianna's hand. The girls jumped up.

"Daddy! Daddy!" the girls shouted. Then they hugged him.

"Why aren't you in your own beds?" Philip asked, as he sat on the side of the bed.

"We wanted to see you and we were hoping mommy and the babies were coming home with you," Kianna said.

"I'm sorry but like we told you earlier, they have to stay in the hospital for a few more days," he said, as he put his arms around them. "Mommy sends her love and she can't wait to come home to see you. You will get a chance to talk to her tomorrow."

"Daddy, we really missed you!" Sabrina said, as she put her arms around him.

Then there was a knock on the door.

"Come in," Philip said.

"Here is your tea," Patricia said, as she sat it down on the nightstand. Then she looked at the girls. "Why aren't you in your beds, young ladies?" Patricia asked.

"We wanted to see daddy," Kianna said.

"Okay, you saw him. Your father is tired. Come on, let's go," she said, as she opened the door wider.

"We will talk tomorrow. I promise," Philip said, as he helped them out of bed. The girls looked sad because they wanted to stay up and talk to their dad.

"Goodnight, daddy," the girls said at the same time.

"I will check on you two later," Philip said, as Patricia shut the door.

Philip drank the tea then he walked into the nursery. He smiled more and more as he looked at the babies' furniture and clothes thinking they would have to buy more things since God had blessed them with an additional blessing. When Philip checked on the girls they were sound to sleep.

The next morning Philip had breakfast with Sabrina and Kianna, he went to work for a few hours, and then spent the rest of the day at the hospital with Courtney and the babies. Later on that afternoon, Courtney called home to talk to her daughters who had been waiting anxiously to talk to her about their new brothers and sister.

"Mommy, when are you coming home?" Sabrina asked, as Kianna took the phone from her.

"Mommy, I know how to change a pamper. I have been practicing on my dolls. Patricia, got upset with me because I was using the pampers out of the nursery," Kianna said, as Sabrina got on the other phone.

"Mommy!" Sabrina said.

"Wait, sweethearts," Courtney said, as she smiled looking at the babies sleeping. "I can only talk to one person at a time. Sabrina, I should be home in a couple days and Kianna don't worry about how to change pampers. I will teach you and Sabrina later about that. I miss both of you and I can't wait to come home. I love you."

"We love you too, mommy," Sabrina said, as she and Kianna smiled. "Mommy, Aunt Lauren went to the airport to pick up Grandma and Grandpa."

"Your grandparents just left here and they are on their way to see you two," Courtney said.

"We got their room ready," Kianna said.

"Good. I will call back before bedtime. Bye, my angels," Courtney said. They hung up the telephone.

Kianna went to the other room were Sabrina was.

"Since mommy is going to teach us how to change a pamper, lets practice feeding our dolls food," Kianna said. "We can get food out to the refrigerator and smash it up with a fork like Aunt Ashley and Aunt Lauren do for our little cousins."

"No way, Kianna," Sabrina said. "I don't want to get in trouble with Patricia. We will let mommy teach us everything herself then Patricia can't get on our case. Let's draw some pictures for the nursery then when the babies wake up they will have something to look at."

"Yea! That's a great idea. Lets get started then we will finish up later after our grandparents get in," Kianna said, as they walked out of the room.

A few days later, Courtney and the babies were discharged from the hospital. Kianna and Sabrina were looking out of the windows as Philip pulled up to the house. The girls ran outside to meet their siblings who were asleep. Both sides of the family were at the house to see the new arrivals. Philip's mother knew how important it was for a new mom and the babies to have proper rest. You could say that Mother Beverly was planning on running a tight ship around the house for a few weeks until Courtney was able to adjust to her babies and everyday life.

Later on that night, Philip put his arms around Courtney as they watched the babies sleeping in their room. He asked her what she would like from him, since she had given him his longest heart's desire. She told him she already had it, which was him. A pediatrician would come to the house a couple of days a week to check on Jackee' until Courtney had her six-week check up. Ashley would talk to Courtney twice a day since Philip's mother was around the house, she would visit her sister three times a week to see how everything was going for her.

When Courtney and the babies had their six-week check up they were all in perfect health even Jackee's monitor was removed. Even though Courtney had plenty of help she would feel overwhelmed at times. She didn't even remember having postpartum depression unless she had it in her dreams. She had nightmares that she was in the hospital ready to have the babies and they wouldn't come out. The doctor tried to do a C-section but the instrument that the doctor used wouldn't cut her stomach then she screamed out 'Please take my babies!' She would wake up and thank God it was a dream.

The following Sunday Courtney and the babies went to church for the first time. After Reverend Solomon preached his sermon, he called the family and prospective godparents up for the christening. Then the family, godparents, some friends, and Reverend Solomon and his wife went over to Philip's home for a special dinner. A week later, Philip's mother and stepfather went home.

Once again Philip was working diligently at the office. Once in a while he would look at a recent picture that he and his family took at the church of the babies christening. He was personally working on a few projects unrelentingly getting them prepared for presentations for the first converge between the members of his board and the new clients. When it came to clients Philip was opened-minded, not biased because of the dollar signs. He felt it didn't matter how successful a corporation was, the corporations should treat every business contract as if it was their very own. Not by words of mouth, or advertisements, or assumptions that one may project, but by actions that leads to an overwhelming results for both parties.

Chapter Nineteen

Kym and Philip were dining at a restaurant listening to some music. He stood up from the table and reached for her hand while asking her to dance with him. They danced across the dance floor as if they were ice-skating in slow motion. She closed her eyes envisioning Philip as his muscular arms surrounded her waste line bringing her closer to him. At the end of the song she exhaled as he leaned his head toward hers.

Kym opened her eyes as the flight attendant tapped her on the shoulder.

"Excuse me, Ms. Keon," the flight attendant said in Chinese, "you will need to put on your seatbelt. We'll be landing shortly."

"Oh, thank you," Kym said in Chinese.

"Looks like you were having a wonderful dream," the flight attendant said in Chinese.

"Yes, I was," Kym said in Chinese, smiling as she snapped the seatbelt in place. The flight attendant walked away. Then she said to herself in Chinese, "You have no idea."

Kym got off the jet looking for Philip, but she saw Robert Mason one of the directors of TELCOM Communications.

"Hello, Ms. Keon. How was your flight?" Robert asked, as they walked to the limousine.

"Please call me, Kym. The flight was fine. Thank you."

"Good," Robert said, smiling. "Kym, Philip asked me to meet you here because he is still in a meeting. Would you like for the limousine to take you to the hotel first?"

"No. I'm ready to start work," Kym said with enthusiasm.

As Robert introduced Kym to Philip's secretary Diane, people were leaving out of the boardroom. Kym saw Philip talking to someone about business as they looked through a report. While Kym was chatting with Diane she watched Philip to see when the person left out of the boardroom.

"Excuse me, Diane. I don't mean to cut you off," Kym said. Then she whispered, "I want to surprise Philip."

Philip had is back turned towards the door. Kym winked her eye at Diane and smiled, as she shut the doors quietly.

"I'm here!" Kym said.

Philip turned around to see who it was then he smiled.

"So you are," Philip said smiling, as he put the reports down. "How was your flight?" he asked, as they walked to one another.

"Good," Kym replied, as she hugged him.

Then there was a knock on the door as it opened.

"Excuse me. Hi! Sweetheart, are you ready?" Courtney asked.

"Courtney, please come here," he said. When Courtney got to Philip, he kissed her then he smiled at her. He looked over at Kym, "I want you to met Kym Keon. Kym this is my wife, Courtney."

"Hi. Philip, your wife is breathtaking!" Kym said smiling, as she shook Courtney's hand.

"Thank you," Courtney said. "Nice to finally meet you, Ms. Keon. Philip has told me a lot about you. How are your parents?"

"Please, call me, Kym. My parents are fine," Kym replied. "Thank you for asking. They send their love to you and your family."

"Philip and I are going to lunch would you like to join us?" Courtney asked.

"No thank you. I had lunch on the jet. I'm going to my

office and I'll talk to you later, Philip. I'm sure we will see one another again, Mrs. Franklin."

"Please call me, Courtney."

"Very well," Kym said and then she left the boardroom.

"It's so good to see you," Philip said, as he hugged Courtney.

When Philip got back from lunch, he spent the remaining afternoon with Kym discussing business. Then they went into a meeting for her to meet the members of the board. Hours later she called the limousine driver to pick her up from the office.

"I don't see how you do it, Kym. You came straight here from the airfield without getting any rest before the meeting," Philip said.

"Well let's say when I'm truly dedicated to something, I do whatever I need to do to get it done. To make up for it," Kym said, looking at her watch, "in twenty minutes, I'll be getting an oriental massage at the hotel. I can't wait! I'll see you in the morning."

Later on that evening, Kym was sitting up in bed looking over some papers that were becoming boring. She put the papers down and turned on the radio. She turned to different stations to see whether she could hear something that she could fall asleep to. She heard a song called 'Stormy Weather' playing on a jazz station. Kym picked up the remote that was sitting on the stereo and walked back to the bed. She laid on her right side feeling the pillow that was next to her while closing her eyes counting sheep. Then a melody of a song came on that really got her attention called 'I'm Saving All My Love For You.' At the end of the song she said to herself,

"I'm not even close to anything like that song with Philip. My father would kill me if he knew that I would even want a married man," she said to herself. Then Kym took a deep breath. "This is crazy! I'll not let my feelings get the best of me."

The DJ later stated the name of the song and the artist that sang it. Kym got up and wrote it down. The following evening before Kym returned back to the hotel, she had the chauffeur take her to a record store to purchase the CD.

One afternoon Philip, Steve, the senior executive of Philip's company, and Kym were trying to decide what they wanted for lunch.

"I'll have the secretary call my chauffeur to take us to—" Kym begin to say.

"No, that's okay. I can drive us there," Philip said.

"Why?" Kym asked with a repulsive look on her face.

"We can go in separate cars. I don't care for all that attention. I'm a down to earth man who wants to drive. I'll be back," Philip said.

"Please, Kym," Steve said, smiling, "let him drive. Lots of times it's me," he said jokingly, as Philip walked back into the office.

"Philip, why don't you like to use your drivers?" Kym asked.

"It's not that I don't like using a chauffeur but when we're just going down the street, I don't see the need for it. It's a nice sunny day why not take advantage of it." Philip replied. "I only use them when I'm meeting someone in the heart of downtown and I know I won't be able to find a parking place near by. Believe me, the drivers are being used by the executives. Sometimes when I do get lazy I use them. That's what our company pays the drivers for."

Philip invited Kym to his home for a family cook out. Courtney introduced Kym to their family and friends.

"Courtney, your home is beautiful and your family is as lovely as my father mentioned," Kym said.

"Thank you. That's very kind of you to say," Courtney said, as she held Jackee.'

"Is it all right for me to hold Jackee'?" Kym asked, as Jackee' smiled at her.

"Sure. Can I get you something?" Courtney asked Kym, as she passed Jackee' to her.

"No thank you, I'm fine," Kym said smiling at the baby.

"I see there is something I've to get from the kitchen," Courtney said, as she looked over at the table where the meat was sitting. "I'll be back. If Jackee' gets out of hand give her to Zakeya."

Ashley went behind Courtney inside the house.

"Ashley, can you help me with this?" Courtney asked, as she took the hamburgers out the refrigerator.

"Sure, no problem," Ashley said, as she washed her hands. Philip was coming down the swirl back staircase that led to the kitchen. "A word to the wise. Kym is after Philip," she said putting seasoning on the burger. Then Philip stopped on one of the steps listening to Ashley, "She's a snake that will strike at anytime."

"What are you talking about, Ashley? That's enough salt! Do you want to give everyone high blood pressure. Put some more ground beef into the bowl and make sure you really mix it in," Courtney said, as she got a bowl out of the cupboard.

"Fine," she said, walking to the refrigerator. "Did you see how Kym looks at Philip when they are talking? It's like she could melt."

"I see how she responds to my husband," Courtney said, calmly. "It's just an innocent young woman's crush."

"Just like that movie that came out several years ago called the Woman's Mirror. Remember when the woman thought the young woman's crush was innocent and then before the wife realized it the young girl took over her whole household? In the movie it seemed like an innocent crush too."

"No, not that kind of crush. This is not a movie, Ashley. I trust my husband completely." Courtney said with confidence. "Just like you trust yours. Fear is torment and I won't live my life that way."

"Courtney, I know you trust Philip. Some men can't see what a woman is up to until it's too late," Ashley said.

"Ashley, come on," Courtney said, calmly. "Our cook is

waiting on the hamburgers," she said. Then Ashley gave Courtney a grotty look."Okay, I've been warned. Let's go."

Then Kym walked into the kitchen with Jackee.'

"Excuse me, Courtney," Kym said.

"Yes, Kym. Come on in," Courtney said, as Ashley gave Kym a snide look behind her back.

"Miss. Jackee' spit out her pacifier. It needs to be rinsed off," Kym said, as Philip came down the stairs.

"Thanks. Ashley, would you take the hamburgers out." Courtney said, as she rinsed off the pacifier. "Jackee' is just smiling at you, Kym," She said. Then she took the bowl out of Ashley's hands walking outside with Kym and the baby. "Is Jackee' okay with you, Kym? You seem to be a pro at this."

"I don't know about the pro part, but I'm managing. I have one brother and a sister and they have six children of their own. I don't get to spend time with my family much because I am always traveling. Courtney, your children are lovely. You have a host of nieces, nephews, and cousins," Kym said, as Courtney gave the bowl to one of her family members who were cooking on the grill.

"Thank you. My sister is expecting another child and my sister-in-law is as well," Courtney said, as Jackee' smiled at her mother. "Now the Christmas list of names gets even longer."

"You're lucky to have a family that you can spend time with," she said, as Jackee' whined reaching for her mother.

Some people showed Kym the latest dances. As a slow song began to play, Philip walked over to Courtney and asked her to dance with him.

Kym watched them dance as Ashley watched her thinking the worst of her. When Philip kissed Courtney as they continued to dance, Kym's throat all of a sudden became tight. She couldn't swallow as she felt envy and ashamed of waiting on a man that belonged to someone else. Kym got up and walked to the girls' playhouse fighting back her tears.

"Do you like our playhouse?" Kianna asked, as she walked

up to Kym. "No boys are allowed. My daddy will have a tree house built for my brothers when they turn five or six. That will take forever before that happens."

"I see," Kym said, as she laughed. "This is really nice. Your dad thought of building you and your sister a playhouse?"

"No. It was my mommy's idea. Did you have one of these when you were a little girl?" Sabrina asked.

"No, I'm afraid not," Kym replied.

"Come on in. I'll show you around," Kianna said, as she took Kym by the hand.

After Kianna showed Kym the playhouse, Kym told the chauffeur that she was ready to leave while he was trying to enjoy his piece of watermelon. As soon as she got back to the hotel she threw the CD away saying to herself,

"This is crazy! God forgive me for even thinking something so foolish," she said disgruntled in herself. "My parents would be so disappointed in me if they had any idea how I feel about a married man."

Kym flew home weeks later to take care of some other business feeling confident that TELCOM of America would come through as professed.

It seemed that five months flew by and the babies were growing and getting more active as the days passed by. One day Philip and Courtney were sitting in the living room cuddling and relaxing while the babies were sleeping. They had one of the babies' monitor sitting on the center piece table. The girls came into the living room looking bored. Sabrina got on her mother's lap and Kianna on her father's lap.

"Mommy, I don't feel like your baby anymore," Sabrina said, as she put her feet on the couch and snuggled up to her mother like a baby.

"Me either," Kianna said, as she lay her head back on her father's chest.

"You will always be our babies no matter what," Courtney said, as she reached out for Kianna's hand. Kianna smiled as she took her hand. "You don't want your siblings' feelings to be hurt that you are not happy that they are here because you feel you're not our babies anymore?"

"Oh, no," Kianna said. "We are glad that they are here. We just thought you loved them more then us."

"No, we love you all just the same. Remember when your dad and I talked with the both of you before the babies were born about the changes around here?" Courtney asked as the girls nodded their head. "See Junior, Joseph, and Jackee' can't do things for themselves like you can do. So mommy and daddy have to do it for them therefore, they need our attention more than you do. Our love for you two won't change."

"That's right," Philip said. "God hasn't only blessed your mother and me with your brothers and sister, but he blessed you two as well," he said, as the girls smiled at one another.

"That's true," Courtney said, as she stroked Sabrina's head while hugging her more. "You two have a responsibility now."

"A responsibility?" Kianna asked looking at Courtney thinking they would have to do more chores.

"Yes," Philip replied. "You both are big sisters to your siblings. They will be looking up to you to play with them, talk to them, protect them and when they need it tell them right from wrong."

"We will be the best big sisters ever, right Kianna?" Sabrina asked as Kianna smiling nodding her head. Then they heard one of the babies making sounds on the monitor. "Mommy, one of them is up," she said, as she sat up.

"It's okay. Junior is not crying. He's playing," Courtney said.

"Mommy, how do you know it's Junior," she asked with a puzzling look.

"It's a mother's instinct and feeling about her children. You will see when you become a mother someday," Courtney said rubbing Sabrina's back.

"Well, I'm going to check on him," Sabrina said, as she

got off her mother's lap. Then she walked up stairs. Kianna stretched out more putting her head down on her father's lap and her legs on Courtney. Philip stroked Kianna's head gently while talking to her and Courtney smiled as she rubbed her legs. "Hi, Junior," Sabrina said softly to her brother, as he continued to make sounds while smiling. Philip, Courtney and Kianna could hear her on the monitor. "Jackee,' you are up too sucking on your hand. Here is your pacifier," Sabrina said, putting it in her mouth. "Now, I'm going to show you guys some more pictures I drew for you."

Kianna got up.

"Kianna, where are you going?" Courtney asked.

"I want to show them my pictures too," she said, running out of the living room.

Courtney got up to go upstairs.

"Baby," Philip said to Courtney, "I will go up. Just relax," he said as he stood up. Then he kissed her, "I love you."

"I love you too," Courtney said. Then the doorbell rang. Courtney looked at the old grandfather clock and smiled as she got up from the couch. It was Sabrina's godmother who surprised the girls to take them to the Ice Capades.

Kym flew back to Chicago on business. Courtney met Kym at the office one afternoon for lunch. They went to China Town to a nice elegant restaurant.

"What made you give up the limousine and lease a car? It is leased right?"

"Yes. I'm only here in the States for another four weeks. I thought it would be sort of fun to drive myself around as long as I don't get lost," Kym said, as she laughed. "I know how to get from the hotel to the office then here. Your home is far way from the city. I would get lost."

"It's not too bad," Courtney said, smiling. "If you drove from our home everyday you would get used to the distance."

"True enough. When I came to your family gathering I understood why you and Philip moved out there. It's like you are in your own world. It's peaceful. The beautiful green grass, flowers, and the breeze. It's paradise," Kym said. "If I had my choice, I would rather live in the city. Well, anyway this lunch is my treat. You have been so very kind to me and I want you to know I appreciate it."

"That's very kind of you. You are a very nice young lady," Courtney said, as she smiled.

"Thank you. Next week, I'm going to Washington, D.C. on business and to meet some friends that live there. Then I'll spend a couple days in New York," Kym said, then she took a deep breath. "Then I'll come back here for another week. After that I won't be back here until January of next year."

Kym saw a very nice looking Chinese gentleman with a ponytail walked from around an area of the restaurant. She watched him as he talked to one of the employees. Courtney noticed Kym's attention was diverted somewhere else.

"Kym, what's wrong?" Courtney asked, as Kym noticed him coming her way.

"What Courtney?" Kym asked confused while fiddling with the napkins on the table. "Oh, nothing I was listening to you." Then she looked up smiling at the gentleman as he walked past their table.

"I see who has your attention. His name is Victor Kwan," Courtney said.

"You know him?" Kym asked excited.

"I don't know him personally, but my husband and I only eat here when we want Chinese food. He's a nice young man. Sometimes he comes by the tables and talks to the customers. Maybe he will do it today."

"I don't want to meet him. He smiled at me and I smiled back," she said nonchalantly. "Well, anyway what you were saying earlier, I've been to the Arthur M. Sackler Gallery before in Washington D.C. a couple of years ago. Maybe I'll visit it again. See. I told you I was listening," Kym said, as she smiled.

"I see," Courtney said, in a surprised tone.

After Kym finished eating she went to the ladies room to check her makeup and made sure her hair was in place. As she talked to Courtney, she took out her mirror to check her lipstick. Then a couple of seconds later,

"Ladies," Victor said, as he nodded his head. "Mrs. Franklin, how are you?"

"Fine, Victor and yourself?" Courtney asked smiling.

"Good," Victor replied, as he smiled at Kym.

"Excuse my manners, Victor, this is Kym Keon. Kym meet Victor Kwan," Courtney said.

"Nice to met you, Ms. Keon," He said, as he reached for her hand and kissed it.

Courtney looked surprised as she smiled at them.

"Nice to meet you, Mr. Kwan," Kym said.

"Please call me, Victor," he said.

Then Victor and Kym smiled widen more at one another. Courtney felt like they wanted to say something to one another but were shy because of her.

"Before we leave Kym I must go to the ladies room. Please excuse me," Courtney said, as she gave Kym the eye.

"I'll go with you," Kym said getting nervous.

"I know how to go by myself, Kym," Courtney said humorously. Victor began to laugh. "Anyway, I need you to watch my purse. I'll be back," she said then she walked away. Courtney came back five minutes later. Victor was gone and Kym was looking bored.

"So what happened?" Courtney asked, as she sat down.

"Are you ready?" Kym said in a candid tone while looking into her purse to get the car key. "Look," she said smiling, "he gave me his telephone number but I'm not going to call him."

"Why?" Courtney asked puzzled.

"Why should I? I didn't come to the States to meet someone. Anyway, it would be a waste of my time. Beijing is not around the corner."

Kym talked to Victor a couple of times on the phone then

she asked Philip and Courtney to go with them out to dinner. When Philip and Courtney arrived at the restaurant things seems to be going great. The following afternoon Philip and Kym were sitting at a table in his office analyzing a report. After they were finished the report they began to put the paper work together when Philip stated what a nice time he and his wife had last evening with her and Victor. He also expressed that Victor was a nice man.

"Good. I'm glad you and Courtney enjoyed yourselves," Kym said in a snooty tone.

"What? You didn't have a nice time?"

"Let say, I had better times in my life."

"You didn't like him?" Philip asked.

"He's not my type," Kym said boldly, as she closed her leather organizer.

"What is your type?" He expressed with a nonchalant attitude.

Kym looked at Philip and smiled thinking to herself, he was her type.

"I'm not sure. I haven't met him yet. I should have known it was going to be a disaster when he picked me up in his broken down car," Kym said smug.

"What do you mean?" Philip asked.

Kym felt insulted thinking about last evening as she talked to Philip.

"Victor, picked me up in an old car and the passenger's door handle wasn't operational from the inside. He had to get out and open the door for me."

"I'm sure if the passenger's door was functional, he would still be a gentleman and open the door for you," Philip said, as he looked at Kym.

"I wouldn't have it any other way, but suppose we were in an accident and I had to get out right away. I would have been in trouble. That broken car door is dangerous. It's against safety regulations. You would think since his father owns restaurants in the States he could have driven something a little more decent. I didn't want to hurt the man's pride by offering to take the limousine." Kym said, as she got up and looked out of Philip's window. "Can you believe he owns a tie business," she said in a pity tone, while shaking her head. "How can someone make money from that? Now he has his ties, which are his own designs on the streets such as vendors and some side stores that sell them for $8.00. That's crazy. He's a man with dreams, but it seems to me that's all it will be. I don't think my family could accept an $8.00 per tie dream."

"It's your own business whether or not you want to build a friendship with Victor. Your loss," Philip said, as he looked at his watch. "I'll see you tomorrow. I've a 4:00 p.m. meeting then I'm going home to my family."

"What Philip? Are you surprised at me? Please, your opinion means a lot. What do you honestly think of me? I see you as a good friend. What?" Kym asked, waiting anxiously for an answer.

"I'm surprised at you," Philip replied.

"Please say what you mean by that," she said clueless not understanding his response.

"Who do you think you are? You were born with a silver spoon in your mouth, and the best education a person can achieve. But that doesn't mean everyone else has to come from the same background. You chose to become one of the power brains of your father's forum and there is nothing wrong with that.

Victor didn't want to do what his father did to achieve his own success. He wanted to do his own thing and for that he has to start from the bottom and move up to the top. I remember talking to him one day and his father offered him money to start his business, but Victor refused his father's help. Victor saved his money and got a loan to get his business off the ground. As a matter of fact, I bought a couple of his ties that he designed which I'm presently wearing. It's a one of a kind," he said, as

Kym looked at Philip's impressive silk gray tie that matched perfectly with his suit. "You shouldn't look down on people because their achievements may be in other areas that you can't relate to. You need to reevaluate your standards when it comes to people. Anyway," he said getting up from the table, "you didn't come to the States to meet a man. You're here on business and you met someone that found you interesting. I'm sure you get that a lot."

Kym smiled and nodded her head agreeing with Philip. Kym thought about what Philip told her concerning Victor, but at that time nothing hit home to make her opinion change.

When Victor would call Kym, she would tell him that she was busy or she wouldn't return his calls. She didn't talk to Victor before returning back home. When she arrived back in town a couple months later, she and Philip were in meetings constantly. One late afternoon she decided to go past the restaurant to see Victor. While Kym was eating the waiter came over to see if she needed anything else. Kym told the waiter she would like to see Victor. Victor came out of the kitchen to her table with a white apron on. He looked serious and cold heartened.

"Is the food to your liking ma'am?" Victor asked candidly in Chinese.

"Victor, Hi," Kym said, in Chinese as she smiled. "You're working in the kitchen?"

"I work where I'm needed. What can I do for you?" he asked in Chinese.

"Look, I've been very busy. I'm sorry I didn't respond to you sooner," Kym said in Chinese, as she looked up at him.

"That's okay. I'm no longer interested in you," Victor said boldly in Chinese. "I knew sooner or later the inside resembled the outside."

"What is that supposed to mean?" Kym asked in Chinese, as her smile went down.

"To be frank with you, you are an ugly and horrible person inside," Victor said boldly in Chinese. "When I first met you,

you were captivating. You were the most beautiful woman I had ever seen, but when I look at you now, you are becoming more disfigured. I hope you enjoyed your meal, Ms. Keon," he said in Chinese then he walked away.

Victor and Kym weren't loud and they didn't raise their voices. However, there were customers at another table that couldn't understand Chinese, but they knew whatever Victor and Kym were saying to one another wasn't a pleasant conversation. Kym couldn't believe what Victor said to her as she looked down at her lunch. She all of a sudden lost her appetite. She put the money on the table and left right away.

That is what she gets.

Chapter Twenty

Sabrina and Kianna decided to try out for the cheerleading squad at school. Sabrina made the squad but Kianna didn't. After Kianna finished her homework she went to Sabrina's room.

"Are you still going to be a cheerleader?" Kianna asked, as she picked up one of Sabrina's dolls and held it in her arms as she sat on the bed.

"Yes," Sabrina replied. "I don't think I shouldn't be a cheerleader because you didn't make it. I've always wanted to be a cheerleader."

"If I had made the team and you didn't, I wouldn't do it. I thought we would do things together," Kianna said, looking sad.

"I wouldn't ask you to quit something that you like. I'm sorry Kianna, but I'm going to do it," Sabrina said.

Kianna looked at Sabrina, surprised at her remark. Then she became upset.

"Oh, forget it!" Kianna said, as she flung the doll down on the bed. She got up and slammed the door behind her. Then she went to her room and slammed her door.

Philip and Courtney were downstairs playing with the babies. Philip came upstairs to see what was going on. He went to Sabrina's room first.

"Sabrina, what's going on with slamming of the doors?" Philip asked.

"It wasn't me, daddy," She said looking downhearted. "It was Kianna. She's upset with me because she didn't make the cheerleader squad, but I did."

"Honey, that's terrific!" Philip said, as he hugged her. "Why didn't you tell me when I came home?" he asked, as he saw how sad she looked. "Did you tell your mother?"

"Yes. That was the first thing I told her when we were alone. I couldn't tell mommy in front of Kianna, I didn't want her to feel bad. Kianna wants me to quit the team and I'm thinking about doing it," Sabrina said.

"No, Sabrina. Don't do that. There are going to be a lot of things you are going to do that Kianna will not be part of and things she will do that you won't be part of as well. I'll talk to Kianna. Congratulations honey. I'm proud of you. We will do something to celebrate your accomplishment. Everything is going to be fine. I love you, Sabrina," Philip said, while lending over to kiss her forehead.

"I love you too, daddy," Sabrina said, as she smiled.

Philip went to Kianna's room. She was on her bed with a pillow over her head crying. Philip got on Kianna's bed and lay on his stomach and put a pillow over his head not saying a word. Kianna sat up as she wiped her face. Then she looked at her father strangely then she removed the pillow from over his head.

"What's wrong with you, daddy?" Kianna asked concerned.

Philip sat up.

"What's wrong with you, Kianna?"

"Daddy, I didn't make the cheerleading squad. I practiced really hard. Sabrina is being difficult because she won't quit the team." Kianna said, disappointedly.

"Isn't that being selfish?"

"No," Kianna replied slowly looking at her father unsure of her answer.

"Are you sure about that?" Philip asked concerned.

"You're right daddy, that's being selfish, but we do everything together," Kianna said, as her face frowned.

"Kianna, I want you to listen to me carefully," Philip said. "I'm sorry that you didn't make the team. It's not the end of the world or the end of your relationship with your sister. You don't have the right to ask anyone not to do something for any reason because you can't."

"Daddy, if I would have made it and Sabrina didn't I wouldn't do it."

"That would be your decision. You don't do things in life because you believe someone else would do it the same way as you. So what, you didn't make the cheerleading squad. It doesn't make you less than who you are. You are a beautiful young lady; you're bright, and ambitious in your own right. No one is better than you. You can try out for the cheerleading squad again next year.

There are going to be times in your life that you will achieve things that your sisters, brothers, friends, or even your mother and I won't. We don't have the right to tell you not to achieve things you want to do in life," he said, as he reached for Kianna. She came over to him and he held her in his arms. "How about being a pom-pom girl, or playing soccer, or playing baseball, or being in the school band."

"Daddy, mommy and I already discussed that. I wanted to be a cheerleader," Kianna said.

"Hey, try next year," Philip said in an encouraging tone of voice.

"Perhaps I will," Kianna said, as she hugged her father.

"I don't want you to have hard feelings towards your sister," he said. "Sabrina will need your support. Can you do that for me?"

"Yes, sir," Kianna replied.

"That's my girl," Philip said, as he kissed her cheek. "Now, I've to find out who was slamming doors around here," he said, as he stood up.

"Daddy, it was me," Kianna said feeling ashamed.

"You!" Philip said in a surprise tone. "Why?"

"I was upset with Sabrina being on the cheerleader squad. Now I see I was wrong. I'm sorry, daddy."

"Okay," Philip said. "I want you to have better control over your temper. I don't want that to happen again. Is that understood," he said firmly.

"Yes, sir," Kianna replied.

"Don't you owe someone else an apology?"

Kianna went to Sabrina's room to apologize. Kianna would stay after school with Sabrina for cheerleading practice. When there were basketball games the family would be there watching and rooting for the cheerleading squad. As months rolled by Kianna would go to the cheerleading competitions on Saturdays rooting for her sister. There were also times that Kianna find herself bored playing by herself if her sister was at a Saturday practice or at a game performing. Courtney showed Kianna a lot of attention, but she was missing Sabrina. Courtney talked to Philip because Kianna would go to bed as early as 6:00 p.m. Philip knocked on Kianna's room door.

"Are you sleep?" Philip asked.

"No," Kianna replied. "I'm listening to some music. Are you just getting home from work, daddy?"

"Yes. Since tomorrow is Saturday lets go out for breakfast," Philip said.

"Just you and me, daddy?" Kianna asked excited.

"Yes. You want to watch one of your cartoon videos together?" Philip asked.

"Yes, daddy," Kianna replied.

When Sabrina got home she went into Kianna's room and watched the video with them. As Sabrina sat on the other side of bed she leaned her head on Kianna's shoulder and fell asleep. After the movie was over Kianna told her dad that her sister could sleep in her room. She covered Sabrina up with the cover and kissed her goodnight.

The following morning at breakfast Philip found out Kianna wanted to learn how to play the violin. After breakfast they went to a store that sold instruments. Philip purchased a fine violin. Kianna was excited. Someone would come out to the house three times a week to give Kianna lessons. Two months later everyone was surprised how well Kianna was learning and playing notes.

Months later, Philip and his family moved into a mansion with full-time staff. A live in chef, two housekeepers, a part-time nanny that would come in to watch the children if Courtney needed to run errands or if she went with Philip on his business trips, and they also had full-time drivers.

It was the third Sunday in June when Philip and Courtney's church had a family and friends day. They were glad to see their families and friends enjoying the service. Reverend Solomon brought forth the word of God.

"Remember," Reverend Solomon said to the congregation, "We all need Jesus Christ in our lives. You can never live your life so perfect that you don't need Jesus. You may say, I'm a good person. I don't swear, I don't smoke, I don't drink, and I help my fellow man. Don't get me wrong all those things are wonderful, but you still need the Holy Spirit, which is Jesus in your life. Don't ever think you are the most sinful person in the world and that Jesus can't save you. Jesus loves you! He died on the cross for you so your sins would not be your downfall for you not coming to Him. Let Him save you. Allow Jesus to give you eternal life. While Sister Jeanie Brownson is coming up the microphone to sing a song, I want you to come down the altar to give your life to Jesus or if you want prayer, please come now."

Sister Brownson was an elderly woman who stood at one of the microphones. She looked at the musicians and shook her head at them to let them know she didn't need music. The name of the song was 'I Want Jesus To Walk With Me.' There were hands clapping and foot patting. People were coming up for prayer. After Reverend Solomon finished praying for the last person, he reached out his hands to the congregation to see would anyone else like to come up to the altar.

"Courtney," Philip whispered, as he took her hand, "I want you to go up with me." As they stood up, Courtney looked around at the triplets to see they were okay. Courtney was pleased that Philip wanted them to get prayer together.

"Courtney, God bless you." Reverend Solomon said smiling. "Philip, God bless you." Reverend Solomon shook Philip's hand.

"Reverend Solomon, I want to give my life to Jesus." Philip said. Courtney looked at Philip amazed as he put his arms around her. Tears came down her face.

Reverend Solomon picked up a microphone as the woman end the song.

"We have one soul that wants to give his life to Jesus," Reverend Solomon said, as the congratulation clapped. "Would there be anyone else? This is the most important decision of your life!" he said with conviction. "Once Jesus calls you from this life into eternity, where will you spend it? Would there be anyone else?"

Zakeya passed one of the triplets to someone then she stood up and walked down the aisle. Then Ashley, Preston, Sabrina's godmother, and two of Philip and Courtney's friends as well wanted to give their lives to Jesus. Courtney couldn't believe it as the tears continued to flow as she hugged them.

That was a special day for everyone. Then after service and baptism were over the church had their cook out for everyone to break bread and enjoy one another's company.

Kym arrived back in town for a few days. The day before anyone knew at TELCOM she was in town, she went by the restaurant where Victor worked. The waiter informed her that Victor no longer worked there and the waiter couldn't give her anymore information than that. The next day at TELCOM, Kym was sitting in Philip's office waiting on him to return. Philip's secretary brought her in a cup of coffee. Then he walked into his office and placed reports on his desk. He stood in front of his desk and smiled at her.

"Kym, I really like the new look," Philip said, as he looked at her new hair cut.

"Thanks, Philip," Kym said. "If you like it, then I know I look fine. My family almost had a fit when they saw how short I had my hair cut. My father wanted to know why I wanted to come back here in vain. My father is very pleased with everything, Philip. I understand some people from our company would be pleased to come here for a couple of weeks to get more of your prestigious knowledge in other areas on the field."

"I'm glad your father is pleased. He's already expressing that to me. Why don't you come out with it. My 2:00 p.m. appointment will be here shortly. Why are you really here?" Philip asked.

She smiled, "Have you seen Victor?" she asked.

"Yes," Philip replied smiling, as he walked around his desk and sat down.

"Has he been asking about me?" Kym asked.

"No," Philip replied, picking a report from off his desk.

"I stopped at the restaurant and I was told he doesn't work there any longer," Kym said, as she watched Philip closely.

"That's right." Philip said looking through a report.

"Philip! Help me out here. You are almost as bad as the waiter at the restaurant whom I was trying to get information from. It's like trying to pull teeth, but then you find out it's dentures.

"What?" Philip asked, laughing.

"Where is he? Where is Victor?" she asked anxiously.

"While you were gone for seven months, Victor's luck changed literally over night. Investors started coming out of the woodwork. He has his own clothing store in the heart of downtown called Men's Suits and Ties. He doesn't only design his own ties, but suits as well. As his spokesman, I'm wearing one of his custom designed suits now. Here is the address to his establishment," he said, as he wrote down the address on a note pad.

Kym went to Victor's place of business later that evening. She was surprised with the atmosphere and the employees. The store was very busy. She walked to the security desk. As she waited for Victor's secretary to locate him, Kym looked up and saw each level where the operators where assisting customers on the telephone and the last level was made out of glass where Victor's office was.

Victor's secretary came down to get Kym. Kym was waiting in his glass office. She stood by the glass windows and looked down on the lower level. Victor walked in.

"Hello, Kym. I'm sorry you had to wait. I just got out of a meeting," Victor said in Chinese, as he walked to his desk.

"That's okay. I would have called, but I figured you probably wouldn't call me back. This is great!" Kym said in Chinese, as she looked around in his office.

"I know," he said, in Chinese smiling from ear to ear. "Sometimes I have to pinch myself to make sure I'm not dreaming. Let me show you around."

After Victor showed Kym around they went into one of his conference rooms.

"Can I get you something to drink?" Victor asked.

"Yes," Kym replied in Chinese. "Mineral water, please. Thank you."

Victor had his secretary bring Kym water.

"I really like your hairstyle. It's becoming," he said in Chinese, as she smiled. "So how long are you here in town?"

"I'm not sure. Have you eaten today?" Kym asked in Chinese.

"Why?" Victor asked in Chinese.

"Well, I know you only eat one meal a day and if you haven't eaten then we can go out to dinner. My treat to celebrate your accomplishment," she said in Chinese.

"Oh, you don't look down on me anymore?" he asked sarcastically in Chinese, as his smile gradually faded.

"I don't look down on you, Victor," Kym said in Chinese.

"Don't lie, Kym. You did," Victor said candidly in Chinese. "But it's okay. It gave me the strength to work that much harder. You weren't the only one."

"Victor, please!" Kym said in Chinese getting defensive. "I didn't look down on you. I saw a man with a dream starting from the bottom. I must say I could have been honest with you by telling you that I was truly scared of letting my true feelings get involved."

"Spare me! I haven't eaten, but I don't want to go out with you," Victor said in Chinese, as he looked in her eyes. "If there isn't anything else I hope this is truly good bye. Oh," he said in Chinese, as he stood up, "take one of our catalogs with you just in case you see something you may like to purchase for that special man in your life."

Kym's expression changed on her face.

"Fine," she said, in Chinese getting upset, but she wasn't going to let him hear it in her voice. She gracefully picked up her purse as she stood up. Then she walked to the door.

"Please let me get the door for you," Victor said in Chinese, as he walked swiftly from around his desk.

"No, I'm quiet capable of opening the door myself," Kym said in Chinese, as Victor got in front of her. "You are such a—"

"Gentleman," Victor said, in Chinese interrupting her. Then he pulled her to him and kissed her passionately. He took his finger and ran it slowly down her left cheek as his eyes absorbed her beauty like a Chinese Hibiscus flower that soaks up the sunlight to grow. "I wanted to do that the first time I saw you at my father's restaurant. I lied. I would love to have dinner with you. I'm sorry if I hurt your feelings, but I wanted you to feel how I felt when you treated me with those same actions."

"I know," Kym said softly in Chinese. "I'm sorry," she said, still feeling the print of his soft lips on hers.

"Is it okay if I pick you up in an hour? I've some calls I need to make before I leave. Are you at the usual hotel?"

"Yes. Suite 1101," Kym replied in Chinese.

"Very good. I'll see you there," he said in Chinese, as he opened the door for her.

When Kym got downstairs, she looked up to his office. He was standing by the glass looking down at her while he was on the telephone. He waved at her then she walked out of the store.

Later on that evening Philip and Courtney were at home out on the patio alone grilling steaks, potatoes, preparing a toss salad, and a chilled bottle of apple cider. For dessert they shared a vanilla ice cream cone. The girls were gone with Zakeya to visit Beverly in the islands and the triplets were at Lauren's house until the weekend. After dinner, Philip played his first anniversary gift that Courtney made for him. They began to dance.

"Can we do lunch tomorrow?" Philip asked Courtney then he twirled her around and then held her hand more firmly while pulling her closer to him while still dancing.

"I don't believe we should have lunch tomorrow. I wouldn't want you to think that I like you. A lady doesn't always make herself available," Courtney said, as she danced with Philip smiling.

"I hope this lady knows she's the apple of my eye," Philip said, as he stopped dancing, and looked into her eyes. "I thank God for the happiest days of my life with you."

"Thank you for being an example, the result of waiting patiently for the right person can happen. I know what true love is because I'm truly in love with you, Philip. You are the apple of my eye." Courtney said smiling.

"Courtney, I'm your angel as long as God gives me life."

"And, I'm your angel in every word." They both looked into each other dreamy-eyed and then they kissed.

Yeahy what happen to Victor and Kym.

Finished on 9-21-06

I hope you have enjoyed "I'm Your Angel." I would truly love to know what you thought about it. Please visit me on my website at www.truthinthelight.com. Your comments would be greatly appreciated. And remember—no matter what your dreams are, God can bring them to pass. His plan is perfect, and it will reveal itself like a rainbow after the storm. God Bless.

Contact Veronica A. Grayson
or order more copies of this book at

TATE PUBLISHING, LLC

127 East Trade Center Terrace
Mustang, Oklahoma 73064

(888) 361 - 9473

Tate Publishing, LLC

www.tatepublishing.com